SYNCHRONICITY

MARCUS MCGEE

PEGASUS BOOKS

ISBN 978-0-9673123-3-0

Comments about *SYNCHRONICITY* and requests for additional copies may be addressed to Pegasus Books c/o Ms. McGhee, P.O. Box 235, Neptune, New Jersey, 07754, or you can send them via e-mail to marcus.media@yahoo.com

For

Rinnetta and Jenean

In all you are and in all you've accomplished,
You have taught me to love, respect and, above all, admire women

Thank you for being my sisters!

SYNCHRONICITY

Editor: Susan Steffes

Cover Art: Rinnetta McGhee

THE CLUB

Percival Pettigrew died on the operating table when his heart faultered and stopped. Dr. Assagai had given up all hope even as he requested the final burst of electricity that restored the steady beeping accompanied by the bright green spiked line on the EKG monitor. Percival had rested between life and death for seven minutes, in that *undiscovered country from whose borne no traveler returns.* He was dead for seven minutes before being resurrected by the instruments of modern technology.

Though his heart stopped beating for four hundred twenty seconds, his mind remained active. Oddly, he knew everything that was happening in the operating room. He could hear what the doctors were saying, he could see the instruments and the blood and he could even see his own body convulse with each burst of electricity delivered from the defibrillator.

His eyes were wide open. His outstretched, flailing arms were numb and unresponsive. He felt a tremendous weight bearing down on him. He could feel his mind fighting to survive, his body battling for life, his chest struggling to reanimate its heavy master.

In the moment his heart began beating again, he forced a triumphant smile for a nurse who seemed shocked as she nervously averted her eyes and turned away. In that instant he knew he had conquered death and what little fear he had ever felt in his thirty-three years of life.

He knew he would rise from the table with a new resolve and drive to accomplish his lifelong goals: the accumulation of immense wealth and the complete mastery over his own fate.

There was no one waiting in the recovery room and not a single visitor as he recuperated for seven days. His parents in New Jersey had no idea he had undergone the elective appendectomy. During pre-surgery considerations, he had signed a release, which held the hospital free from liability if he died as a result of the anesthesia, and ironically it was the anesthesia, or the inattention of the anesthesiologist, that caused the sudden cardiac arrest he suffered on the operating table.

Six hours before the surgery, he drove himself to the hospital and checked himself in. On the eighth day of recovery in the fourth floor hospital room from which he would be released, he sat sullen in the uncomfortable bed, saddened, reflecting on the life he had lived.

The reason no one had come to visit was that he had no friends, no one he was close to, no one who cared about him. Why? He admitted to himself that no one cared about him because he had lived his life not caring about anyone else. He had been selfish. He was a driven man who thought only of himself and his intense desire for wealth and freedom.

"When I've achieved all my goals," he always imagined, "then I'll have time to make real friends. I'll be able to take good care of my friends, once I make them."

On the day scheduled for his release, the short, pretty, red-haired nurse, who constantly insisted she was happily married, came into his room and told him he had a visitor. Sitting up, he ran his fingers and palm over his short black hair, trying to appear presentable.

There was something familiar about the man who entered thereafter, though Percival could not discern what it was.

"You were dead for seven minutes, Mr. Pettigrew. How do you feel?"

Percival balked, suspicious of the man bundled in the huge gray overcoat.

"Who are you?"

"Oh, I'm sorry. Allow me to introduce myself. My name is Lucius Crossland Haydes."

Where most people would have extended an arm for a handshake, the shivering old man remained bundled, though Percival had extended his own hand.

"Your experience interests me, Mr. Pettigrew. I went through something very similar when I was young like you."

Percival looked around at all the beeping, blinking computerized instruments and then skeptically toward the old man. After a moment, Lucius Crossland Haydes smiled, understanding.

"Of course, there wasn't all this technology back then, but believe it or not, I was resurrected. I was brought back from the dead, just like you."

Percival shuddered, sensing something eerie in the old man's last three syllables.

"Why? What do you? Why did you come here? What do you want?"

Gray-black beard framing his round face, the old man neared the bed, his voice taking on a somber professional tone.

"I'm a businessman of sorts with an interest in young up-and-comers like you. And this resurrection you experienced—it only confirmed my initial impressions about you. You've definitely got what it takes."

Percival leaned forward, interested. Anything involving "business dealings" was certain to get his attention, but he didn't need the old man to tell him what he already knew. Disguising his interest, he played the game.

"Of *course* I have what it takes. Now, if you've come to offer me a job, you're out of luck. I'm a Stanford Business School graduate. I'm an MBA. I don't need a job."

The old man smiled again, winking an eye.

"Of course you don't. And I don't have any jobs to give away."

Lucius turned toward the rain-splashed, misted window, glancing out at the gray, gloomy October sky, clouds hanging just above the treetops. The pause was intentional.

"No, I didn't come here to offer you a job, and I'm not here with an offer to invest in your little business project."

Percival studied the intense eyes behind the round spectacles.

"So what do you want?"

"From you? I want the answer to a question," replied the old man. "The question, Percival, is this: Now that you've defeated death, what is it that *you* want?"

Percival thought for a moment before responding.

"Nothing's changed," he said to himself, and then to the old man. "The fact that I was dead changes nothing. I want the same things I wanted before."

"You want success?"

"Of course I do. Doesn't everybody?"

The old man nodded.

"Many people do, but not like you. You have an unnatural thirst for it. You've sacrificed for it. You have no friends. You're in deep debt. You have no wife, no children, no warm, comfortable house to go to. Other people value those things, but you've put them off and invested everything you've ever owned into your little computer chip implant business, the one you call GTO."

Percival glanced up at Lucius in amazement. The information about his business was public knowledge, but his personal sacrifices? How did the old man know? Nevertheless, he answered.

"That's the way it's done. Ask any successful person how they did it, and they'll tell you. You have to make certain sacrifices. Isn't that what you did?"

Lucius closed his eyes, smiling, as he nodded.

"Of course. It's just like you said. That's the way it's done. It's the sacrifices we make, for the success we want."

The old man walked over to the door and shut it, wedging a chair under the knob to prevent interference, before returning to the patient's bedside. His voice was almost a whisper.

"But Percival, in spite of all the sacrifices *you've* made in your thirty-three years of life, nothing's paid off for you, right?"

Percival nodded as Lucius paused and continued.

"And it isn't because you're not working hard. In fact, you work much harder than anyone you know. You've been close, you've been damn close, but there's always been something, maybe just one piece of the puzzle, something that has always been missing. Once it was bad timing, and then the next time someone beat you to the punch. Another time, your financing fell through and then there was the lawsuit. It's always been just that one thing that came between you and your success. Isn't that how it's been?"

Percival stared at the old man in bewilderment.

"How do you know so much about me?"

Lucius smiled.

"It's like I told you. It was the same for me until my little accident. I fell to my death and I came back to life. After that, things got better."

"How? What happened?"

Ignoring the questions, the old man pulled a chair close to the bed, sat and leaned toward Percival, whispering.

"What if I were to tell you that if you made one more sacrifice, just one more—you would be successful in anything you ever attempted, successful beyond your wildest imagining. Would you be willing to make one last sacrifice?"

Percival did not answer. Instead he leaned away, his eyes scrutinizing the old man. He wondered to himself if he was dreaming or awake, if the old man was nothing more than a by-product or reaction to the handful of pills he had taken that morning. He caught the flesh between the index finger and thumb of his left hand and pinched hard, wincing as the pain shot to his spine. He was awake all right.

"Well Percival, would you be willing to make one last sacrifice?"

"What, what type of sacrifice are you talking about?"

"Naturally, a substantial one."

In that moment, abrupt and angry banging on the door startled both men from the intensity of the discussion. From without, an angry voice shouted.

"Open this door! This door should never be shut! Open this door right now!"

Lucius winked at Percival.

"We'll talk later. You think about that one last sacrifice. Next time we talk, you let me know."

The bundled old man rose and went to the door, opening it to a barrage of complaints and warnings from the red-faced nurse who didn't seem to see him. When Percival turned and looked toward the hallway, Lucius was gone.

He had the procedure performed on himself to demonstrate how simple and risk-free it was. The benefits, once the population realized them, would far outweigh the minor irritation that accompanied the three-quarter inch incision in the left armpit.

The computer chip, a dime-thin, perfect one-half inch square, was a barely noticeable irregularity under the skin once the tiny sutures were removed, but the advantages it offered were nothing short of phenomenal.

Powered by body heat and an emergency back-up battery, it could be guaranteed for the lifetime of the user. Password protected and activated through a secure server, all its functions would be programmed and directed by the person who subscribed to the service. The cost for the chip: $299. The cost for the implant surgery: $159. The cost for basic service: $24.99 per month/ $275 pre-paid for a year/ $1,299 pre-paid for five years. Subscribers could use the service, which he called GTO (Global Tracking Options), to monitor up to five chips.

Initially, it would be a basic global tracking device, linked to the Internet through satellites in space. Parents with concerns for the safety and well-being of their children could track them to and from school and positively know if they had attended classes.

In abduction cases, children and other victims could be located and rescued. Missing skiers and hikers could be discovered regardless of weather conditions. Victims of boating accidents and airplane disasters could be recovered and positively identified within minutes. To many financiers, his business plan seemed potentially profitable, but even the most enthusiastic bankers balked when considering the provision for government regulation.

Percival would need support from the Federal Communications Commission, the American Medical Association and the Food and Drug Administration. After four years of haggling with the FDA and another five years of testing, the agency had finally signed off on the project, but according to investors, the FDA was much less a concern than the other two.

In fact, the AMA seemed disinclined to endorse and provide required restrictions and guidelines for such implant technology because "it did not serve to save, better or prolong human life." Furthermore, the FCC director opposed the plan, claiming that its implementation would be prohibitively expensive and would unduly tax the commission's already strained time and resources.

Percival faced further challenges from the public, the most notable of them a U.S. Senator from Colorado who called the plan "an engraved invitation and welcome mat for *Big Brother*." There were a few groups who endorsed the technology: these included the national PTA, several state school superintendents and the lobbies for many state prisons. The greater public, however, had been conditioned over the years to view new technologies in the "give it to me for free, and I'll see if I like it" mindset. Thus Percival and a key financial backer were convinced that if the technology did become available to the public, and if the public was given an opportunity to realize the device's advantages and the privacy security measures in place, his company and GTO could quickly grow to Intel and Microsoft proportions.

He had recovered from his near-death experience one week after he returned to his apartment, one week after he had met the strange old man. Absorbed in his work, he hardly gave the episode at the hospital another thought. He had legal documents drawn, he tweaked the business plan and attended meetings with various contacts on a daily basis.

In December, he sat to dinner with two FCC board members in Washington at a meeting that proved to be another frustrating setback. One member asserted that even if the FCC initially approved his plan, it would be eight to ten years before an actual license could be granted.

Eight to ten years in the high-tech industry, an incredulous Percival argued, might as well be ten thousand! Unsympathetic, the impassive members apologized, paid for the dinner, and left the grief-stricken MBA in a pronounced state of catalepsy.

Percival sat motionless at the table for forty-five minutes, ignoring questions by the busser, two servers and, finally, the maitre d'. The first feeling began to return to his body when a warm tear ran from the corner of his left eye and streaked its way down his face. Startled to his senses, he was reminded for a fleeting instant of the moment his pulse returned as he lay on the operating table, a unique moment of clarity.

He glanced around the restaurant at other guests and noticed some were staring. Though he wanted to leave, he realized he really had nowhere to go. His flight back to Sacramento wouldn't leave until 8:20 a.m.

Out of money, he had planned to sleep at Dulles International in one of the uncomfortable black chairs near the Continental terminal, but it was only 6:30 p.m., much too early to head on over there.

Then he remembered. The FCC board members had told the server to bring him whatever else he wanted and to bill it to their house account. He thought to order another dinner, but he didn't feel hungry.

So instead, he ordered a Belvedere vodka martini on a stem and sat at the table, sipping solemnly, frustrated that this enterprise, more than all the others—this plan, which had put him on the verge of the greatest success, was bound to become another vexatious defeat.

"You know, even if smiling wouldn't make you *feel* better, it might make you look a little better."

Percival first noticed her eyes. They were large, expressive and intense.

"Excuse me?"

"Your face," she laughed. "You just got some bad news. Face tells the story."

He smiled, his eyes falling toward an empty seat at the table. She understood the cue, nodded and sat.

"Truth be told, I just got some bad news too. I'm blown away, but I'm laughing."

"Why?"

"Because I was just so stupid! I was so naive! Is that a martini you're drinking?"

A few minutes later, the server had placed two new drinks on the table.

"By the way, my name's Karen. And yours?"

He extended a hand.

"Percival Pettigrew. And you're Karen?"

"Bright. Karen Bright."

She sipped the vodka.

"That's the original name, the one I use now."

"So you're divorced?"

She smiled.

"That's what the court calls it. Truth is I got screwed for seven years. Know what I mean?"

He studied her face. She was such a pretty woman with well-proportioned, delicate features. Yet he could tell that though she feigned toughness, she was on the verge of tears.

"So, what happened to *you* tonight?" he asked.

"Met a girlfriend here for dinner... Or someone I *thought* was a girlfriend."

She stared toward the table where she had sat for dinner, replaying the recent past in her memory as she spoke.

"Without making the story too long, she told me she had been a stripper when she met my husband at his bachelor party, and apparently they had an affair the entire time we were married."

As he discreetly examined Karen's shapely body, he wondered how any man, after having the privilege of enjoying such a treasure at his disposal, could want for anything else.

"Any kids?"

"Thank God, no. And what about you? You married or attached?"

"No."

"You gay?"

"No, do I look gay?"

Sensing he had taken insult from the question, she explained.

"It was a compliment. All the best-looking guys are gay. It's a proven fact. By asking I was kind of indirectly saying I think you're good-looking."

"Thanks, I think."

She flicked the bell of the glass with a polished fingernail. It resounded with a soft ping.

"Can we get me another martini?"

When the drink came, she gulped it down.

"That's it for me. I think I'm getting drunk."

She reached across the table, taking his hand, rubbing his fingers.

"So Percival, enough about me. What's your bad news?"

He started in, stuttering, but he stopped.

"Aw, nevermind. You wouldn't understand."

Suddenly, she sounded sober.

"What do you mean *I wouldn't understand*? You think I'm dumb? You think because I got big tits and a nice ass I'm too dumb to understand your problem?"

"I, I didn't say that."

She continued in an angry tone.

"You know what my job is? You know what I do?"

"No."

"I work for the Senate Majority Leader. Graduated law school at Yale. I write the legislative foundation for the laws that govern you and the rest of this country, and you think I'm too dumb to understand your pathetic little problem!"

She stood, opening her purse.

"You know, I came over here thinking you were a nice guy. I thought we could commiserate. I thought that after I had my teeth kicked in, it'd be nice to just *talk* to someone, but once again, I picked the wrong guy. I have a knack for that, you know."

She threw money on the table and would have turned away if Percival hadn't grabbed her wrist.

"No! Please Karen, don't go! I'm sorry. You're right. I may have made some assumptions about you. That was wrong. Look, I *do* want to commiserate, share with you if you, you wouldn't mind listening."

He spent the next hour telling her about his life, about his struggles and sacrifices, about his ambitions and the unavoidable disappointments that he suffered. Then he told her about GTO and about the news from the FCC board members earlier. She listened, saying little, until finally she volunteered.

"Sounds like you need an angel."

"An angel?"

"Yeah. Could be me, could be someone else who can get you over those last hurdles that always trip you up."

As they conversed, he began to feel drawn to Karen, and it had more to do with her attitude about life and her insights than it did her beckoning figure, more to do with her unique views than her beauty. She was intelligent, spontaneous and spiritual as she exuded an unmistakable positive energy.

"You know, I minored in English Lit. Did you know Percival was the virgin knight?"

He wasn't sure whether he felt embarrassed or amused.

"Yeah," he intoned in saracasm, "and I pride myself on my virginity."

After he admitted that he had run out of money and didn't want to impose by charging the extra cocktails to the FCC, she paid the tab for the drinks and invited him to stay the night at her apartment.

"Just so long as you know that if you're a virgin now, you'll still be a virgin when I drop you off at the airport tomorrow morning."

They talked through the night. They watched the snowflakes twinkle as they spiraled toward the ground at sunrise.

"An angel is someone who can empower you to change your own fate, show you that you have the power to control your own destiny, and somewhere along the line, an angel can lead you in the direction of truth and clarity. In your lowest moments, your angel gives you hope and light to see."

Percival placed his hand on hers, smiling.

"And where do I find this angel?"

Karen examined his expression, not certain whether or not he was being patronizing. She withdrew her hand and heart into her lap.

"Oh, you don't *find* angels. They find you."

They stood together in the terminal until the flight attendant called for final boarding. Percival peered into Karen's large, watering eyes as the two embraced. For the first time since he looked into them, he saw their deep sadness and pain. Blinking back the tears in his own eyes, he felt so much attraction and compassion for her that, for a moment, he found the boldness to sketch the present design of his heart.

"Karen, I know this sounds silly, but I, I feel like changing my destiny right now. I feel like not getting on that plane. I feel like forgetting everything I was doing in California and staying here with you."

She stepped back, holding him at arm's length.

"Think about it. You can stay if you want to. I welcome you, but is that what you *really* want, Percival?"

He looked into her haunting eyes and then toward the loading doors as the last of the passengers boarded. That's when he realized he couldn't stay. He had left so much unfinished business at home. He had responsibilities toward his business associates. And then there was GTO itself. He hadn't poured his entire life into the project only to throw it all away for a girl. He couldn't stay. He bowed his head, answering.

"No, no. You're right. I want to, but I can't."

Disappointment registered on her face. Her gaze fell to the floor.

"That's all right. I knew you wouldn't stay. It's your choice."

Nervous about missing the plane, he grabbed his briefcase.

"I'd like to, but I can't."

She smiled, and lowering her eyes, she sighed.

"Goodbye."

"Let's stay in touch. I can come back, and you could come out and visit me at Tahoe."

She paused and signaled negation.

"I don't think so."

He tried to kiss her lips, but she turned away.

"You better go. They're closing the doors."

Percival turned to see the attendant pulling the first of the two doors shut. Alarmed, he sprinted across the floor and got to the door just in time to plead his way onto the plane. Karen watched from where she stood. He never looked back.

Percival lived on the California side of the lake, near the base of Mount Heavenly, but he did the majority of his business in Sacramento and Los Angeles. He visited Sacramento to handle governmental affairs, while Los Angeles was to serve as his test market.

The day after he arrived home, he sent certified letters to all the FCC board members, begging the board to reconsider the matter and put it to another vote. No answer was returned, and neither were Percival's daily phone calls.

A week passed, then two and then two more. It seemed that with each week that went by, once-enthusiastic investors began to flake off one by one until only two remained. He had hoped to offset his mounting debt with the first wave of sales, so as the months went by and the projected release date was pushed further and further into the future, the creditors, the state Franchise Tax Board and the Internal Revenue Service were on the verge of forcing liquidation of his inventory in order to secure payment.

He considered bankruptcy as an option. While *Chapter 13* offered protection from creditors, it did nothing to address the state and federal tax liens posted against his corporation and against his person.

One morning in March it happened. An agent from the IRS showed up at his apartment with a levy notice against Percival's four hundred thousand GTO microchips, assessed at $130,000 for the combination of the technology and the raw materials, about ten percent of their market value.

Percival owed a little over $110,000 to the federal government in back taxes and penalties. After delivering the levy notice, the agent stationed a guard to sit outside the warehouse containing the microchips to make certain they weren't sold, traded or otherwise removed.

If Percival wasn't able to pay the taxes in full after forty-eight hours, the agent said the chips would be taken away and stored for thirty days, after which time they would be sold at auction. Any balance left over after the taxes were paid would be returned to Percival, unless the Franchise Tax Board, whose lien amount was $30,000, petitioned for payment.

At worst, Percival would lose all his chips, any hope of ever launching GTO and still owe the state $10,000 plus penalties. The $80,000 he owed in unpaid personal and commercial loans was another matter altogether. He had forty-eight hours to produce.

He considered his options. At that stage, any promise he could have secured from the FCC board may have been helpful. If the FCC board made an assurance that an emergency license could be granted within ninety days, Percival could have been able to go to either of the two investors left with a realistic release date and he would have been able to enact his marketing plan, based on an actual start date.

The investors would then be more inclined to pay off his debts. Pre-sales and the big Internet advertising campaign could begin and the impending flood of sales would start as a small, steady, swelling stream. Notwithstanding, the secretary for the FCC called to make it clear that though the board thought his situation was "regrettable, the necessary research and processing could not be rushed for any reason."

Percival also considered cutting some sort of a deal with the IRS or the agent bringing the action. Unfortunately, the agency, after having granted him extension after extension, was unwilling to engage in any further protracted deliberation and the beadle of an agent in his face was above bribery.

He also considered staging his own suicide, having someone pay his debts off with the death benefit, and returning under an alias to launch his program. As the hours went by, he became more and more desperate for an expedient solution, consequences be damned.

The Hyatt concierge had said it was the best Chinese restaurant in Sacramento. It was just down the street, a block and a half from the Capitol. The place seemed a little dark inside, and it didn't seem very busy on that Thursday night. There were a few women at the far end of the bar shaking dice. They seemed familiar with the hulking Caucasian bartender, Tony, who dwarfed the Chinese servers.

Percival had come to town in a last-ditch effort to persuade one of the investors to loan him money for the taxes, but the man balked, indicating he was involved in too many other financial transactions at the moment. He offered $55,000—half the money required, deliverable in seven days, only if Percival could persuade another investor to come up with the balance. The other investor, who lived in San Francisco, informed Percival during a phone call that he was no longer interested in the project. Thus with only 18 hours left, Percival had run out of ideas.

Everything was lost, his credibility gone. He had no life, no one who even cared about him. He thought of Karen then. He had been too busy and caught up in business to ever call her as he had promised.

She was special, but she was probably angry or disappointed with him for not calling. Sifting through credit card slips in his wallet, he found her number and stumbled his first few steps from the bar stool toward the pay phone, glancing sheepishly back at the bartender who had poured the offending martinis.

He dialed the number, waited and listened as he heard the wonderful, comforting, familiar voice on the answering machine.

"Hi, it's Percival. I, I just called to say 'hi.' I think I'm drunk. I need you."

He felt foolish about the message he left. If she hadn't known he was a loser before, the bungled message would have convinced her. He staggered back to the bar and ordered another vodka martini, a double. Tony hesitated.

"Okay man, but this is gonna hafta be your last unless you get yourself somethin ta eat, man."

Percival wasn't thinking of food. Rather, he thought of the hotel design. There was a high second floor veranda overlooking the main lobby and a restaurant downstairs.

Earlier, he had leaned over the railing and cringed as he considered the horror of falling over its edge. Death would be certain and immediate, especially if he went over headfirst. But he would need more than a double martini—maybe two or three more. Hopefully, this bartender could be persuaded to cooperate, so he slid a twenty toward Tony and winked.

"Keep the change."

Even as the room began to blur, he thought he felt someone tap him on the shoulder.

"Mr. Pettigrew?"

The short maitre d' had placed a gentle hand on Percival's back.

"Yes?"

"Mr. Haydes said you'd be here. He's waiting for you in the back. Right this way."

Without thinking, Percival stood and followed, struggling to understand who would know him in *this* restaurant of all places. The dining room he negotiated as he went deeper into the gut of the building seemed askew, slightly off the horizontal plane. Through a haze, he saw a woman who bore an incredible resemblance to Karen Bright at one of the tables. In fact, he stopped briefly, wanting to approach her, but he lost his nerve in the last instant and staggered after the dark maitre d'.

After going through what seemed like a tunnel, he was conducted to a large booth on the right where he saw a face that produced immediate sobriety. It was the first time he had even thought of that conversation in the hospital.

The man who sat at the table, Lucius Crossland Haydes, was the bizarre man who visited him in the hospital, the same who knew so much about him. As Percival hesitated by the table, considering whether or not he even wanted to sit, the old man smiled.

"I suppose I owe you an explanation, Mr. Pettigrew. So why don't you sit down?"

Percival's eyes darted about the secluded area and returned to the table where a flattened, golden brown bird of some kind rested on a silver platter. Next to it was a plate with a brown sauce, some green onions and white, doughy, still-steaming buns.

"I took the liberty of ordering for us. It's Peking Duck, probably the best thing on the menu. Undoubtedly the worst for your health, but the best on the menu. Sit down, please."

Percival took a deep breath, sighed and slid into the booth across from the old man. He watched as Lucius stuffed a piece of duck into one of the buns.

"What is it with you? Have you been following me?"

Lucius swallowed the juicy mouthful of duck, onions, sauce and dough.

"No need. But I have been *watching* you."

Percival was clearly irked.

"Why? Are *you* the one behind the IRS coming down on me?"

The old man shook his head.

"Absolutely not. Mr. Pettigrew, believe me, I come as a friend."

He squinted at the old man.

"Waitaminute..."

For a moment, Percival thought he had put it all together:

Lucius Haydes had come into the hospital because, as an investor, he was interested in the GTO project; he had been "watching" Percival for a sign of weakness; he found out about the tax liens and had somehow manipulated the IRS in order to get the chips and technology seized. When the liens couldn't be satisfied and the chips went on auction, Lucius Haydes would buy them for pennies on the dollar and launch GTO himself under a different name!

"You've wanted my chips all along, haven't you? You didn't want to be an investor because you just wanted to take them outright?"

Lucius laughed.

"Your thinking reflects something diabolical in your *own* nature because that is not the case. I don't want your chips, I don't want the technology, but I will make you the same offer I was prepared to make to you before."

"And what offer is that?"

"After dinner. I think you need to eat something to clear your head."

Percival enjoyed the Peking Duck, he enjoyed the New York steak and onions, he enjoyed the walnut shrimp and he enjoyed the asparagus steamed with ginger, garlic and light soy. In fact, he couldn't remember having a better meal in years. After the table was cleared, Lucius, shivering, ordered hot tea and sat back in the booth, blowing, sipping.

As Percival studied the old man, he wondered again why the man was so bundled up. Inside the hospital, Lucius Crossland Haydes had worn a huge overcoat, thick gloves and a woolen scarf, and here he was, in a warm, cozy, restaurant, bundled up in the same way. He had removed one of the gloves in order to eat, but aside from that, he was wrapped up tightly.

"For some reason, Mr. Haydes, I don't think you ever got around to making any offer when I was at the hospital."

Lucius placed the teacup on the table.

"No, I didn't. I was prefacing the offer by reminding you of the many times you had come close to success and of the spoiling factors that have always seemed to come between you and your goals, like the necessary FCC approval now."

Annoyed, Percival glared at Lucius and stiffened his jaw.

"Go on."

"I asked if you'd be willing to make one last sacrifice, a substantial sacrifice that would make you successful beyond your most ambitious imagining."

Frustrated, Percival lurched forward toward the old man.

"What do you want from me?"

Lucius hadn't recoiled, though Percival's forward motion had toppled his teacup, spilling the scalding tea on the older man's wrist and hand.

"Simply put: an answer. Would you be willing to make one last sacrifice? Are you willing to do what is required to change your destiny?"

Percival paused, considering his hopeless predicament. Finally, he conceded and answered.

"Well, let's not play games here. You obviously know about the situation I'm in. You know about the IRS, about the State of California, the FCC and the AMA. Are you saying you can help me?"

Lucius re-poured the tea.

"Nothing of the sort. I'm simply asking if you'd be willing to make that last sacrifice."

"Yes, yes!" Percival shouted. "Of course I am! I have no choice. Okay, so what sacrifice are you talking about?"

"Those two."

"My fingers? What do you mean?"

Lucius reached over and grabbed the ring finger and smallest finger on Percival's left hand.

"That's the sacrifice—these two fingers. To me, it doesn't matter how you remove them, as long as it's done. And when you've brought them to me, you can finally look forward to getting everything you've wanted."

Percival snatched his fingers out of the old man's gloved grasp.

"You're sick! I don't think so. I mean, why would you want me to cut off my fingers? What do *you* want with them?"

Lucius smiled.

"The act itself is symbolic, representing a commitment much deeper within you."

Percival sighed, still incredulous.

"Why my *fingers*? And why those two?"

"You'll know that in good time."

Still bewildered, the young man continued.

"Well, how do I know it's going to happen like you say?"

He leaned closer to the old man.

"I mean, let me get this straight. Are you saying that if I cut off my fingers, I'll all of a sudden be successful?"

Lucius' face signaled disappointment.

"No. You'll still have to work. In fact, you'll have to work your ass off. Only once you've made the sacrifice, any effort you put forth will pay off. You'll taste the success you've always craved. I can personally guarantee you that."

Lucius patted Percival on the shoulder.

"You don't have to do it if you don't want to. It is entirely your choice."

He signed the slip and rose.

"It's probably best to think about it for a while. I'll leave you to yourself for that."

As Lucius turned toward the exit, Percival called out, his voice shrill as he stared toward his trembling fingers.

"What if I decide to do it? How do I get a hold of you?"

Lucius winked and smirked, self-assured.

"You don't have to worry about that. I'll find *you*."

The ancient Romans believed there was a relatively important vein called the *vena amoris* that ran directly from the fourth finger of the left hand to the heart. For that reason, the finger has long been associated with love, and by affinity, with marriage. Percival rubbed the finger, reflecting that he'd always fancied having a ring on it.

And the finger next to it—he had never given the digit much thought, since that finger had never given him any trouble. It was a finger that just sort of always fell in line like a good, reliable soldier. It never screamed for attention by being slammed in a door or sprained on the basketball court; it never got in the way of a descending hammer or accused anyone of anything or even developed a hangnail. No, it consistently did its job whether it was typing or writing or skiing or whatever he happened to be doing. The finger simply did its job.

Yet after over twelve hours of deliberation and a half-liter of vodka, it had become a foregone conclusion: both fingers would go. The only question involved was "how?"

He had considered paying a doctor to remove them surgically, but he didn't think he'd be able to convince a medical professional to ignore the potential liability for malpractice and amputate two perfectly good fingers.

Then, he thought about buying a table band saw, turning it on and dragging his hand, the two fingers extended, through the whirling blade. It would be quick and painless, but as he worked out the details in his mind, there existed the potential of injury to or loss of his middle finger.

No matter how he held his hand, it seemed the middle finger would not be completely out of the way. If he was really going to sacrifice his fingers, he figured, they would have to be cut at the base, a precision cut that would be difficult with an electrical saw. No, he would have to cut them with a blade.

The best device, he figured, would be something like a guillotine, a blade that would come down fast and sudden, separating the fingers from the hand. Eyes closed, he could just let gravity cause the blade to fall and it would be over. The only problem with the plan involved actually finding a guillotine in the eight hours he had left before the government confiscated his chips.

He called hardware stores, suppliers for magicians and even the gothic and *Dungeons and Dragons* cult stores, but the only place that sold them was the hobby store, and guillotines were out of stock there until Halloween.

As the deafening seconds ticked inexorably by on the dusty, scarred grandfather clock in his living room, he became so anxious that he could scarcely breathe. Panicking, he rushed to the kitchen and snatched a knife from the drawer.

Cupping its hilt in his hand, the blade aimed directly toward his heart, he stood there, shivering, struggling within himself to find the courage or the brash temerity to act. It was a defining instant, one of those moments in life of rare clarity. Thus relaxing his fingers, he let the knife fall to the floor where it clanged, echoing.

Eyes glazed over, he walked to the front door and opened it, going out toward the stairs. Thoughtful, he went down those stairs and made his way to the apartment landscaping where a series of small boulders were used to contain garden soil. He took a clean, hand-sized stone with a flattened bottom upstairs into his apartment, placing it on the kitchen counter.

Reopening the drawer, he sorted through the cutlery and withdrew a large heavy cleaver and placed it next to the boulder. Stoically, he grabbed the vodka bottle and first took another big swig, and then, placing his left hand on the counter, he poured the vodka over his fingers.

Then, taking a loaf of store-bought wheat bread, he cut through the packaging with the cleaver so that the blade rested vertically between two of its dense slices. He placed the last four fingers of his left hand on the edge of the counter, and then he tucked his index and middle fingers down so that they rested against the counter's vertical edge.

This left two fingers, the fourth and fifth, alone on the counter. On those fingers, he placed the loaf of bread containing the cleaver. Through a series of minor adjustments, Percival was able to maneuver the blade of the cleaver so that it was over the place where the fingers joined the hand. Then he took up the heavy stone in his right. He studied the position of the cleaver and closed his eyes. He raised the boulder.

"I choose success!"

It was a direct hit as the conflict of metal and stone rang aloud in the room. It was done. Percival had pulled back slightly in the last second, but he knew where the fingers had been severed—not more than a quarter inch away from the hand.

Curious, he raised the gushing, spurting hand toward his face and studied. Surprisingly, it didn't hurt as much as he thought it would. In fact, it hardly hurt at all. He was worried about the bleeding though. Somehow, he would have to contain it until he could drive to the hospital for medical treatment.

Eyes never leaving the mutilated hand, he reached over and grabbed a white terry cloth towel on the counter with his right. Taking the towel in his teeth, he draped it over the gushing stumps and hand, anchored it between his left wrist and his chest and wrapped it tight with his right hand. He kept it pressed in his right armpit to maintain pressure against the wounds.

Blood had begun to run from underneath the loaf of bread on the counter. It had welled against the edge and had begun to drip to the floor. By this time, his left hand, throbbing, pulsing in the crimson red, soaking towel, began to burn. Panicking, he knocked the loaf of bread aside and stared at the discolored, still-twitching fingers, soaking in blood. He lifted them and transferred them into a sandwich bag, which he wrapped and slipped into his pant pocket.

Becoming dizzy from the blood loss, he located his car keys, hurried out the door, stumbled toward his car and fell in. He smiled as he drove toward the hospital. It was done. He had made the sacrifice. Success was just around the next corner.

"I'm sorry, Mr. Pettigrew, I realize you're in a great deal of pain, but can you explain what happened one more time for the record?"

"I, I was cutting frozen meat in the kitchen, and the knife slipped."

The gray-haired doctor's face registered confusion and reluctance to record the explanation.

"I'm sorry, but I just don't see it. I mean those cuts couldn't have been any cleaner if someone did them on purpose."

The doctor removed his glasses.

"And you say you don't know what happened to the fingers? If we had them, there's a good chance we could reattach them. They just disappeared?"

Percival nodded.

"Yes."

The stubby ends of Percival's abbreviated fingers had been cleaned, trimmed down, drawn together and sutured. Early on, a local anesthetic had been applied to the wounds, and a nurse administered a generous dosage of codeine to diminish the pain.

The doctor gone, he sat on a cot, staring at his left hand, appalled at how ugly it seemed. He thought of all the things he would no longer be able to do with that hand: tinker on a piano, make a fist, count to five.

He felt deformed. Then he remembered some of the mutilated people he had seen in his lifetime and the way their disfigurements repulsed him. Tears in his eyes, he was already beginning to feel like a freak. But the saving grace—*his* deformity was not in vain. It was for something, for success.

When he was a young teenager, a friend of his got lost in a snowstorm. When rescuers found the boy, his feet were badly frostbitten. He lost three toes. During high school, another kid was goofing around in auto shop. His hand got smashed under an engine block and had to be amputated. Those guys got nothing for their losses, but Percival's sacrifice would yield the success he had always craved.

Then all at once, the existence of an unsettling possibility crept into his conscious thought. What if for some reason the old man was not what he seemed? What if he had convinced Percival to chop off his fingers for some other malevolent purpose? What if Percival had mutilated himself for naught? What if he had been abused, only to be damned?

Yet even as he worried there, he sensed a warm presence and turned in its direction to see Lucius Crossland Haydes, sitting across from him, shivering, bundled in the huge overcoat and scarf.

"Congratulations, Percival. You've just become a member of an exclusive club. Your life, as you've known it, will never be the same. From this point on, you'll be successful at *anything* you attempt."

Percival stared at the old man in silence, unable to respond. Lucius reached out with a gloved hand.

"The fingers, Percival. I'll need the fingers."

Eyes never leaving the man across from him, Percival's right hand fumbled about in his right pocket and withdrew the bloody bag containing the cold, stiff, truncated appendages. He placed them in Lucius' open glove, closing his eyes as he let go. Still shivering, Lucius smiled, tucked the bag into the coat pocket, patted Percival's shoulder and stood.

"Welcome to *The Club*."

Percival stared at the empty place where the gloved hand had closed around his lost fingers for a full minute. They were gone. When he looked back up, Lucius Crossland Haydes was also gone.

The call came shortly before five o'clock a.m. Startled up from sleep, Percival had actually forgotten about the injury to his left hand until he banged it against the nightstand while reaching for the phone. After screaming an obscenity, he cringed, shivering from the pain, rolled over and lifted the receiver with his right. Notwithstanding, the voice on the other end said something that changed his disposition. Bolting up, he stood, responding.

"Oh really? No problem. That'll be no problem at all! I'll be there tonight!"

He spent the early part of the next day with lawyers who had been negotiating with the IRS. There were several important faxes sent out at 10:30, conference calls at 11:00 and 11:15 and an eagerly anticipated e-mail from an investor at 11:30. By noon, Percival was in a recklessly driven taxicab racing for the airport.

The restaurant was located just two blocks from the White House, not far from the Kennedy Center and the National Theater. According to the stewardess, it was a favorite hangout for political insiders and celebrities. After tipping the driver, he hurried toward the restaurant facade and slipped in.

His eyes played on the glitter from the brass and beveled glass in the bright dining room as he stood just inside the door, hoping to recognize a familiar face. He wore his best dark suit, the navy Boss, along with a starched burgundy shirt and a maroon and white patterned tie. His hands trembled in new leather gloves as he placed one on the podium where a young and pretty hostess stood.

"Hi, I'm looking for a, a Mr. Marlowe? He said something about a Cabinet Room?"

She smiled.

"Oh yes! And you must be Mr. Pettigrew. They're expecting you. Follow me."

They walked past mahogany and velvet booths, past antique vases and marble slabs, down a hall to a lacquered wooden door, which the hostess opened.

"Mr. Marlowe. This is Mr. Pettigrew."

Marlowe, who was seated at the head of a long table working to separate a live *Crassostrea virginica* from a half shell, didn't look up. He merely nodded. At his flanks sat persons who were familiar: the majority of the FCC board, though perhaps one or two were missing. An empty spot had been reserved on the table's opposite end for Percival.

Clearing his throat, Percival squared his shoulders and walked toward the seat. He could hear his own footsteps in the silent room and the surreal loud screech as he pulled out the chair. Only after he was seated did Marlowe look up. He scrutinized Percival for a moment, his eye pausing on the young man's gloved hands.

"You can take off the gloves, Mr. Pettigrew. It isn't at all cold in here."

At once, all eyes in the room locked and focused on Percival's hands. Sitting straight up in the chair, his armpits were moist and his breathing became shallow as he struggled to manage a response. Compromise seemed appropriate. He answered as he removed the right glove.

"Thank you. I injured my left hand recently, so I'd like to keep it covered if you don't mind."

Marlowe nodded and almost smiled.

"You like oysters?"

John Marlowe was an older man in his seventies. He had chaired the FCC board for the last fifteen years and had a reputation for being both shrewd and lethal. He inspired fear and respect wherever he went in Washington.

His face was narrow and pinched, but the most conspicuous feature about him was the black patch he wore over his right eye. He was a demanding, no-nonsense chairman with old-fashioned values. His word was "platinum" and his handshake was more reliable than a legal contract.

Because he didn't believe in mixing business with pleasure, no one at the table spoke a word except for orders to the server. The room, throughout dinner, was eerily quiet. Marlowe had the calf's liver with bacon and caramelized onions.

All the board members followed suit, but Percival, because he hated liver, opted for the grilled T-bone pork chop instead. After doing so, he was frowned on by several members who were apparently offended that he had broken one of their unspoken rules. Upon Marlowe's cue, fresh fruit was served as dessert. Then came coffee.

After the meal, a middle-aged woman, who had sat at Marlowe's right, rose and worked her way around the table as she placed a pamphlet in front of each person except Percival. Marlowe tapped on the gavel.

"Let this meeting come to order."

He took up his pamphlet, scanned the front page and tossed it aside.

"For those of you who didn't receive my voicemail and email, the gentleman dining with us tonight is Mr. Percival Pettigrew. He wants us to clear the way so he can get his project off the ground. This afternoon, I took the liberty of having a convoluted motion prepared that will allow him to do that. Would someone care to put that motion to the chair?"

The man seated at Percival's left spoke up.

"Mr. Chairman, I move that the proposal we have before us, relating to Global Tracking Options, be adopted as written."

"Is there a second?"

A woman at middle left seconded.

"Very well. All in favor of the motion, signify by saying 'aye?'"

A pasticcio of "ayes."

"All those opposed?"

Silence.

"Then by a unanimous vote, the motion is approved."

Marlowe looked toward Percival.

"Mr. Pettigrew, it is done. Now it is necessary for you to leave us so we can get on with the rest of our meeting. Good luck."

Percival sat there stunned. It happened so fast that he still wasn't sure it had really happened. Was that it? Was it *that* easy? Marlowe spoke again, his voice this time taking on an irritated edge.

"That means you have to *go*, Mr. Pettigrew. Now move along. You're wasting this board's time."

At once concerned that *wasting the board's time* might cause the motion to be rescinded, Percival rose, thanked the board and rushed toward the door. As he glanced back, his eyes met Marlowe's eye. Marlowe winked it and nodded, though he never allowed himself to smile.

The publicity around the event could not have been any better if it had been staged. Holly Sinclair, a waitress from Rancho Cucamonga had been part of the first group to receive the chip implants.

She had recently divorced her husband, a horrible, violent man who had raped her and sent her to the hospital with a broken nose and a fractured ulna. He was in prison for 18 months and got out two weeks before the divorce was final. Angry about the action, he insisted that she drop the divorce and "honor the marriage." Her refusal to do so angered him even more. She lived with her parents and her four-year-old daughter, working her way through college with the restaurant job.

When she heard about GTO, she thought the technology was "innovative," "secure," and "just a good idea."

She had chips implanted in both herself and her young daughter, and she made sure her parents knew how to access the service.

Then one day, the day care providers phoned her parents to tell them no one had come by to pick up the little girl. When Holly couldn't be reached on her cell phone, her parents became worried and called the police who were not helpful at all. According to the desk clerk, a person had to be missing 48 hours before they could be "officially" considered missing.

Holly's father, fearful and frustrated, finally managed to get a sergeant to listen to him. Reluctant at first, the sergeant allowed him to use a computer and watched as her father accessed the service, activated the chip and located his daughter on a street in Montclair. The sergeant contacted Montclair law enforcement and upon confirmation, a SWAT team was dispatched.

Holly's husband was arrested when he went out to his car to get the bag he planned to put her in after he killed her. On seeing the police, he pulled a gun from his jacket and officers responded, riddling him with bullets. If the police team had arrived any later than they did, Holly would have been dead.

It was an international news event, and naturally, news agencies worked every angle imaginable, exploiting the public's interest in the story. Demand for the chips and the service was immediate and mind-boggling: one million, four hundred thousand chips were ordered in California alone. Suddenly, Global Tracking Options was a household word, and its founder, Percival Pettigrew, was bewildered by how suddenly fame and wealth had overtaken him.

It took lawyers a little over a month to prepare for the public offering of Global Tracking Options stock. Because of Percival's business background, the event had been planned in excruciating detail. Two weeks before the release date, he had been featured in a *Wall Street Journal* article, where a financial feature writer touted him as "the next high-tech billionaire."

Then one week before the release, his face appeared on the covers of *People* magazine, *Money* and *US News and World Report*. Trader interest in the stock issue was nothing short of phenomenal. It opened on a Monday at $17 a share and had shot up to $43 by Friday.

Even before the Holly Sinclair story broke, Percival had moved GTO headquarters from his apartment to a business complex on Lakeshore Boulevard, but now even the new offices were too small, so construction was planned for a GTO complex right next to the lake. When he asked his accountant how much money he had earned since the chips and service went on sale, all the overworked man could say was "Lots! When I catch up, I'll let you know."

But his ambition for Global Tracking Options went far beyond the locator chip, which was merely the first phase of his plan. Percival and programmers were working hard to develop other applications for the technology, including a remote interface transmitter/receiver utilizing digital technology.

Because each chip had a unique signal, Percival's marketing team pitched a plan to global business that would provide for added security. A tiny chip, implanted between the thumb and index finger of the right hand, would allow a computerized security system to recognize employees and grant or deny access or information based on company protocol.

There were also plans for chips that could monitor bodily functions, which included temperature, glucose levels, heart rate and blood alcohol percentage. Thus in spite of his remarkable success, Percival worked even harder than before.

As founder of Global Tracking Options, he was an invited guest at a growing number of social functions. Initially, he resented public appearances because they cut into time that could have been better spent working, yet he realized the business importance of being seen and networking.

He was always surprised at how many people knew so much about him. Once at a party in Washington, the amazing Bill Gates himself came by and struck up a conversation about government regulation. Percival was so awestruck that he almost forgot everything he knew. Mr. Gates' confidence and demeanor, however, made dialogue comfortable and efficient even as he hinted at the future possibility of a shared project.

His social success was equally astounding. On a quick trip to England, Percival was invited to Buckingham Palace where he met the Queen and other members of the Royal Family at dinner. He partnered with Tiger Woods at a celebrity golf tournament in Lake Tahoe.

Realizing his growing importance in the state of California, the governor and other public officials were always eager to take his calls and gave him occasional access to government perks, including a trip to Jerusalem. When he supped in chic Los Angeles restaurants, the movie stars and other celebrities knew who he was. He considered his own celebrity status tentatively at first and then he embraced it robustly. After all, he had earned it through hard work and sacrifice.

Nonetheless, it wasn't until after a one-on-one guest appearance on the *Oprah Winfrey Show* that his bachelor status became a minor obsession with the nation's women. In a spontaneous declaration, he had told Oprah he was looking for "that right person who could be a Mrs. Pettigrew."

Two days later, the mail clerk brought him more than one thousand letters from women who wanted to interview for the job. A month later, a *People* magazine article described him as "perhaps the world's most eligible bachelor."

The mail kept coming and the women he met at social events and restaurants grew bold beyond belief. Some women would wait outside the GTO complex in hopes of meeting him, while others got themselves inside under the guise of doing business. A pretty UCLA Law School graduate seemed genuinely offended when he declined to hire her to perform mundane housekeeping duties at his home.

All the attention was flattering, especially since Percival never saw himself as "attractive" before and didn't think women in general did either. Now the most attractive women he had ever seen were begging for any attention he might be willing to give them, even selfish attention. Yet he always declined the offers. The right woman was somewhere out there, he thought, and he believed that for all his sacrifices, he deserved nothing less than the best.

The solo name, Tyler, seemed indefinite, but the woman who possessed it was one of the best-known personalities in the fashion and entertainment world. Her father was a renowned cardiac surgeon from Santa Barbara and her mother was a Broadway actress.

At the age of fourteen, she was discovered by a Revlon executive and given a three-year contract. She was a pretty girl who had become a beautiful woman. Her strict father had always been draconian about academics, and for that reason Tyler, the honors student, was a UCLA Business School graduate, *summa cum laude.*

An international supermodel by the age of nineteen, she adjusted her work schedule to accommodate school. By the age of twenty-three, she was CEO of a company called TYLER INC. She had been lucky—in the right place at the right time, with the right looks and the right background.

At twenty-eight, she was still one of the hardest working models in the business. She dated infrequently, though even her most casual male acquaintance inspired gossip.

They met aboard the private Lear jet belonging to Maxwell Lipp, a lawyer they had in common. Max was entertaining his most valuable clients by treating them to a gambling weekend at the Grand Beach Resort & Casino in Aruba. Percival was placed next to Tyler at dinner Friday night.

Of course, Max dominated the conversation at dinner, but Percival and Tyler did have an opportunity to share a brief exchange. Percival told her he enjoyed her acting in a recent film, and she joked, telling him she wanted to be "implanted" with one of his GTO chips.

Later in the casino, they sat at the same blackjack table for three hands. The next day, she stopped and took a seat next to him at the baccarat table, asking if he'd show her how to play. Percival wasn't sure how to take the attention he was getting from a woman as remarkable as Tyler.

At first he thought she was just being friendly, and then he wondered if his own secret fantasies about her were making him imagine clues that just weren't there. She told him on two separate occasions that she wasn't dating anyone seriously. She point-blank asked why he wasn't married or involved. She smiled and touched a lot.

But when she leaned over and kissed him as the jet descended on John Wayne Airport, he almost leapt from the seat in excitement, finally having it confirmed that Tyler the supermodel/actress was coming onto him.

So struggling to remain calm, he asked her for a phone number and invited her up to Tahoe for dinner and to take a look at his operation. Smiling, she accepted and the two planned their first date for *a week from Friday.*

They went to a great Mexican place on the boulevard in Incline Village and then to a dance club down the street. Tyler loved dancing, and yet while Percival did his best, he felt a little self-conscious and foolish dancing with such a beautiful woman. After a few songs, he retired to a table, leaving Tyler out there content dancing by herself.

It wasn't long before the men in the club began to migrate toward the floor, each stalking forward like lions on the hunt. Finally, one very tall, handsome man gulped down a tequila shot, walked onto the floor and tried to dance with her, but she excused herself and left the floor.

Sighing, she slumped into the seat next to Percival.

"Leave it to men to ruin my fun."

He seemed confused.

"Why'd you stop dancing?"

She turned and pointed a finger, matter-of-factly.

"One thing you should know about Tyler. If she goes out with a guy, he's the only guy she dances with, drinks with or does anything else with. The rest of the losers out there can kiss her ass."

Percival nodded, not sure about how to react.

"Would you care for a cocktail?"

"Tyler does not drink alcohol. It dries the skin. But a glass of juice would be nice."

The tour of the GTO complex had gone well, the conversation over dinner had been wonderful and a little dancing was a perfect way to finish the night. He found Tyler much more down-to-earth than he ever imagined.

She understood business and she understood people. She was intelligent, though she seemed a little maladjusted psychologically, or maybe it bothered him that she referred to herself in the third person. He just wasn't sure about how to address her.

"Would Tyler like to go to my favorite place for coffee and dessert?"

She laughed.

"Sure, I'd love to. I absolutely *love* coffee. But Tyler can't have it—ages the face."

The waitress brought him his regular espresso despite the fact that he'd been loath to order it. Even as they sat down at the table, he had been conscious to sit to her left so that his body would be between her and the deformity of his left hand. Whenever Tyler was around, he tucked the hand in a pocket or otherwise hid it. He could tell she was curious. Her eyes stealthily followed the hand whenever it left the pocket. After they had eaten dessert, he held her left hand with his right, thanking her for making it "such a memorable day." She smiled and turned his face to look into his eyes.

"You know, when you marry Tyler, you are going to have to stop hiding that hand. What happened anyway?"

He never heard the question.

"Marry?"

"Don't act so surprised. I've known it from the start, from the day we met. You want to marry Tyler, and Tyler wants to marry you. The rest is all ritual and detail, that's all."

He laughed to himself.

"When, when is this going to happen?"

She sighed, sitting back, staring straight ahead.

"About a year and a half. Marketing for a wedding of such grand proportions takes time. We'll make it the biggest event of the new millennium. It'll be good for both of us."

He was suddenly nervous, stuttering.

"But do, do you think we're compatible?"

"Of course we are. As compatible as any of the rest of them. All men are cheaters, you *know* that?"

"They are?"

She gave him a look of incredulity.

"Look, Tyler's been hit on by pious little old priests, by preachers, by *every* married man she's ever met, by public officials and even by presidents. You all cheat. Some of you are blatant and crude about it. The rest of you have a neurotic way of rationalizing that you're not hitting on women even when you know you are."

Tyler stopped herself, laughing.

"I guess I sound a little cynical, don't I?"

"A little?"

"It's just the work Tyler does. I get so tired of the way men treat me sometimes. I'm sorry."

Embarrassed, she wiped a tear from the corner of her left eye.

"Are you going to tell me what happened to your hand there?"

He pushed the hand further into his pocket as he struggled to reply.

"It, it was an accident."

"Really? What kind of accident?"

Percival remembered how skeptical the doctor had been about the dubious kitchen knife explanation. Since that time, however, he had labored to fashion a better story. He put the hand on the table.

"Shark fishing in San Francisco Bay. Hooked a five-foot *seven gill*, got it on the deck, thought it was dead. I went to tie it so we could take it off the boat, but it all of a sudden came to life, whipped its head around and got the fingers—lucky it wasn't the whole hand."

She cringed in the seat, appalled and terrified.

"I'm going to have nightmares. Tyler is deathly afraid of sharks."

She looked toward the mangled hand.

"I'm sorry."

He studied her face.

"Does my hand repulse you?"

She couldn't stop staring at it.

"Yes. If that ever happened to Tyler, she'd probably kill herself. I mean, I bet you'd give up all the money you've made your whole life long to have those fingers back, wouldn't you?"

He returned the hand to the hiding place in his pocket. Thoughtfully, he answered.

"No. No, I wouldn't."

By the time the fabrication facility was marginally operational, GTO had over fifteen hundred full-time employees. The new product line, a remote hand-held tracker, was completely fabricated and assembled at the facility.

On the sales front, Percival was under negotiations with General Motors, the Ford Motor company, Nissan and other car manufacturers about a heat-resistant chip, insulated and placed near the engine block, that could be accessed in the event of car theft or in the wake of accidents or disasters. It doubled as a hi-speed microprocessor that ran a powerful on-board personal computer. Within the year, he hoped to launch the first satellite of a Global Tracking Options Satellite System.

True to what Lucius Crossland Haydes promised, Percival was successful at every project he attempted. He was so successful, in fact, that he was forced to select lieutenants who could be trusted to handle entire divisions of the company.

He designated Trace Markus, his second-in-command, to handle the implementation of networks, sales and technical support for tracking systems purchased by the Federal Bureau of Prisons and the local agencies at the recommendation of the American Probation and Parole Association.

The Internet sales division of the company was entrusted to Ronda Antiope, his number three. She was an aggressive marketer who had made the reputation of a ubiquitous on-line retail company. Ronda was chosen because she was one of the shrewdest individuals Percival had ever met.

Akiro Watanabe, a man whose Korean-based fabrication company Percival had bought, along with software genius Bart Scott, were selected to head up research and development. The four were not only his most trusted employees, but the personal relationship he held with Trace was the closest he had ever come to friendship.

Unlike Percival, Trace had come from a privileged, "old money" family. Raised on his father's estate just outside Cambridge, Maryland, he possessed an impressive *curriculum vitae*: high school at the Army and Navy Academy, Carlsbad, CA; undergrad at Annapolis Naval Academy, Annapolis, MD; and MBA at Harvard University. His first job was at the Pentagon, where at twenty-four years old, he worked for the Secretary of the Navy.

Two years later, Trace accepted a production management entry-level position at the General Dynamics Corporation, where he worked on the initial F-16 project, and he moved to Lockheed when that company took over production of the fighter jet. At Lockheed, he became fascinated with "computer-assisted human potentials," or computer-enhanced performance. With much effort, he managed to get himself reassigned to the computer division, where he worked in "pilot controls/pilot interface."

In 1975, he began hearing stories about a peculiar undergrad he remembered meeting while he was doing his MBA. Apparently, this young man had dropped out of school to start up a software company. Inspired by the kid's gumption, Trace almost left Lockheed to launch his own human performance enhancement interface software business, but his wife threatened to divorce him if he ever quit his job, so he never got the nerve to do it.

As a result, he continued with the F-16 and other projects until he met Spenser Caroll, one of Percival's recruiters. Spenser was successful at recruiting Trace where many others had failed because he appealed to Trace's sense of adventure. By joining GTO at its near-inception, Trace was able to experience the wonder and excitement that accompanied the birth and rise of an empire without assuming substantial risk.

Though he was some twelve years older than his boss, Trace actually enjoyed watching the young chairman at the helm, creating realities from "what-ifs" and the strange, eccentric notions he often expounded upon for hours at a time. In the beginning, Trace was a chauvinistically loyal lieutenant, but over the course of the months they worked together, he felt he and Percival had developed a genuine, yet odd, friendship.

Sometimes he accompanied Percival to trade shows, conventions and media events. He even sat beside his boss on the two occasions Percival was asked to testify before Congress. Best of all, he had watched success transform an introverted, apprehensive and unassuming "kid" into a confident visionary with the power of the future at his command.

The friendship, like Percival's moods, had its limitations, however. There were times when Percival seemed resentful and angry at the human race for no apparent reason.

There were rare times when he'd say he was alone against the world, like Timon of Athens. There were times when he'd rail against humanity, declaring he had no friends and would never have any friends, much to the disappointment and confusion of his solo audience.

Days later, he'd apologize to Trace, reaffirming the affection and the limited friendship he felt, though he admitted he and Trace did not possess "kindred souls" and could never be "true friends." Trace tried to understand the distinction, though he sensed that Percival's soul was either profoundly sad or missing something—something that was related to his reclusive left hand and the two fingers it was missing.

"You ever think about just walking off and leaving it all behind?"

"Leaving what?"

Tyler's eyes panned, scanning the posh living room from left to right as she answered.

"This! All this stuff. All this commitment. All this pressure!"

He paused from his eight-fingered typing on the laptop, glancing sidelong at the woman.

"I've sacrificed a lot for this stuff."

"I know. But sometimes, don't you think it's all bullshit?"

She walked to the huge window, yanking open the drapes.

"I mean look at that."

Percival turned toward her.

"At what?"

"That's just it. It's there, but you can't even *see* it."

"See what?"

"The sunset, the most glorious thing that happens every day, and it's free. It's no better for us than it is for anyone else. Only, some people actually get a chance to enjoy it. We don't."

Percival rose, smiling. He walked over to where she stood, gazing out the window of his beach house at Monterey. Standing behind her, he slid his hands around her waist. Then he pulled her close, resting his chin on her shoulder.

Outside the window, the red-orange sun was setting on the Pacific Ocean. There were actually two huge images burning at the horizon: there was a bright red sun glowing at the edge of the twilight sky, and then there was a muted, cooler, almost purplish sun that floated on the water. Yet together they were one sun.

At such a distance from the water, he could barely detect the motion of the gentle, gray-capped waves as they crawled up the white beach. Even more subtle were the gossamer silhouettes of gulls and pelicans playing in the fading summer skies.

He closed his eyes, drew a deep breath and kissed her neck. Over the course of three months, he had grown accustomed to the eccentricity of conversation with his pretty girlfriend, and this was one of her rare moments of vulnerability. This was the woman he adored.

"It would make a great screen saver."

She shrugged to get his chin off her shoulder and pushed him away.

"No, I'm serious. Sometimes I just want to quit. I'm so tired of this! I just want to go somewhere where no one knows Tyler. Maybe to Tahiti like Gauguin. I'd lay in the sun, stop shaving my legs, stop taking laxatives after every meal, stop with the drugs. Just let it all go. Don't you ever feel that way?"

He sighed, withdrawing.

"Sometimes, but do you know how impossible that would be for me?"

"Yes, I do—no more impossible than it would be for me, but I have a way."

Confused, he responded.

"What?"

"I have a way to do it, to leave all this, to get away."

"Really? And how's that?

"I have to get rid of Tyler. I have to kill her. That's the only way."

Not long after he started dating Tyler, he realized that the company of an attractive woman made the man she was with more desirable to other beautiful women. As a result, Percival became a popular target for other supermodels and celebrities who flirted and came on to him, and these were remarkably beautiful women, women he could have only fantasized about less than a year earlier. Tyler didn't seem to mind the blatant coquetry. In fact, she seemed turned on by it.

Public reaction to their sudden wedding engagement announcement was splashed across the covers of all the tabloids, complete with rumors of a Tyler pregnancy. Two of the rags depicted Percival as a rugged, high-tech playboy with a penchant for swinging and multiple partners. But nothing could have been further from the truth.

Percival was practically a virgin. Notwithstanding, it wasn't that there hadn't been opportunities. During his senior year of high school, he had chosen to abstain from women indefinitely, swearing to maintain celibacy until he achieved the success he craved, and thus Tyler was the first person he ever dated.

He wasn't sure if it was the protocols of dating or the fact that he was going out with a supermodel, but the whole ritual was awkward, bordering on the ridiculous. It seemed dating was a big game in which dishonesty was more desirable than truthfulness, a practice in which openness indicated weakness, a struggle in which the threat of infidelity was the ultimate trump card.

Tyler was his teacher of sorts. "Don't marry the person you love," she quoted her mother as saying, "Marry someone who loves *you*." She insisted to Percival that it would be his job to care about her, to make her happy, to make her feel loved.

Inexperienced at such matters, he worked hard to become what she wanted. He lavished her with gifts, he took her on exotic adventures and he let her shine at all the social events they attended together. When she seemed to come on to other men, he understood that "flirtation is a big part of a supermodel's career."

He ridiculed himself for feeling jealous when Tyler left him alone at a table for hours at a time while she discussed business with agents and directors over innuendo, laughter and drinks.

Yet after a while, he began to feel sad and unsatisfied with the relationship. What little intimacy they shared involved him catering to her whims, her moods and her direction. The only saving grace was that other person, the wonderful person he saw in rare glimpses when Tyler was somehow "gone" at times.

During such moments, there was something strangely familiar about her eyes. He felt *connected* to her. It was as if he had known her from before. This other person was sweet, profound and real. Her vulnerability and honesty made her strangely powerful, and those qualities made her threatening to Tyler.

This was the person Percival began to love, but her appearances were beginning to become increasingly rare. The relationship between them was an enigma he would have never tried to explain to anyone, and yet it made sense to him. So even if no one else understood what she meant when she said she wanted to "kill" Tyler in order to be free, Percival certainly did. In fact, he was willing to help her.

Trace hadn't reported to work for two weeks in a row, citing "family problems" as the reason for his absence. He had Ronda cover for him at an important meeting with the "prison people," but he failed to properly brief her about the specifications on the new I-3 hacker-proof/tamper-resistant chip, scheduled for release in the spring. The omission resulted in an embarrassing fiasco of a presentation for the meticulous Ronda and an incensed complaint to Percival.

Fortunately, Percival was able to reschedule the meeting, allay the board's concerns and finalize the order, but not without conceding slightly on wholesale prices and shipping costs. Furthermore, the board reduced the size of the order, electing to spend money to test the stability and reliability of an up-and-coming competitor. In the end, Trace's problems cost GTO millions of dollars in lost revenue and a lesser share of the market.

Both angry and concerned, Percival insisted on an immediate meeting with Trace. They met in a corner of the huge, largely dark boardroom at GTO headquarters at midnight, their voices echoing in its cold vastness.

"She doesn't believe I love her, says I'm never there for her when she needs me. Says she no longer wants to be married to a man who's married to his work."

"Do you realize *that* woman is what's been standing between you and any real success? Did you tell her you're one of the vice presidents of a firm that does over a billion dollars in annual sales?"

Trace nodded.

"She knows that. That's not important to her."

Percival's voice took on a stern tone.

"Look Trace, the company needs you. You know how this business works. We have to be here, *absolutely* ready for our customers when they need us, in every way they need us and for as long as they need us. We have to anticipate their needs, their concerns, the politics and the market. We're creating the future here."

In a daze, Trace's response was listless.

"You're right. I'm not like you."

Percival's eyes snapped over, his inflection signaling confusion.

"Excuse me?"

"I care. You don't."

Percival put a hand on Trace's shoulder.

"No, no. It's not that I don't care. I just know what I have to do, and I do it."

Tears swelled in Trace's eyes.

"Unlike me. I *think* I know what I have to do, but I've always had a hard time doing it. I get confused. I never know if I'm doing the right thing."

Percival's eyes narrowed as he responded.

"You *have* to know. Success is a result of conviction. You have to see every issue for what it is, you have to know your convictions and you have to act on those convictions."

Wiping a tear from his face with the back of his hand, Trace laughed to himself.

"Yeah, right. Did I ever tell you about my experience with the Peace Corps?"

"No."

"There were four of us kids in the family. My old man had this thing about the Peace Corps, ya know. In the 1960 election, he and my mother were real big Jack Kennedy supporters."

The emotion gone, it was evident Trace was retelling a story he had told at least a few times before.

"It turns out they were at the University of Michigan in October when Kennedy came out and proposed this thing. He wanted young Americans to advance the cause of peace by living and working in developing countries."

He poured and swigged another shot of gin before continuing.

"You weren't even born then. I was five—the youngest. Anyway, my father got the notion to go. He knew it was what he wanted to do, so he just left us. My mom—bless her soul— she actually encouraged him. He went to Tanzania and stayed there till I was ten. Came back missin a foot. Lost it to a crocodile on the *Sibiti*."

Trace smiled, amused that Percival seemed interested in the story.

"Said he had no regrets. In fact, he got it in his head that all his kids were supposed to volunteer a minimum of two years after college. Oldest brother was killed by a hippo while trying ta save a native girl on the same river where my father lost his foot. Literally ripped in two and mauled to a pulp. Bloody, gory scene. Took a tusk through the forehead. They sent back pictures and all."

He batted his eyes and continued.

"Sister got malaria in Ghana. Still has problems because of it—chills, fever. Next brother came back in pretty good shape, but he had bowel problems for two years after. He was in Bangladesh for three years."

He shot another gin and slammed the glass on the counter.

"So then it came down to me. I volunteered, but I didn't want to go to Africa for obvious reasons. I kind of figured the Philippines would be an easier assignment for me. I thought I could go over there and help save the mangrove forests, but during the initiation I started hearing the stories about god-

awful parasites and deadly snakes and fungal diseases I never
knew existed. I got all freaked out, so I ran. I never went."

His eyes swelled with tears.

"Old man was pissed! Never talked to me again, never
again till the day he died. Cut me out of his will."

He turned back toward Percival.

"So that's the story of my life. I should have gone, but I
didn't. I can't go back and change that. I've wished I could a
hundred times, but I can't. Things would've turned out
different. Maybe I'd be in control of my life. My wife wouldn't
be holding me over a barrel."

Percival interrupted.

"I'm sorry, but what do you mean when you say she's
'holding you over a barrel'?"

"If I don't start spending more 'quality time' with her
and the family, she's going to take the kids and leave me. God,
I love her! We've been married 18 years. I couldn't imagine life
without her."

He busted out in tears, choking on his words.

"I don't want to lose her, goddammit!"

Percival placed a firm, comforting hand on the broken
man's shoulder.

"The question, Trace, is simple. What do you want? Do
you want to continue to be a part of GTO and the future of the
world?"

Trace straightened his back in the chair, answering in
spite of his sniffling and a stiffly held jaw.

"Yes. Yes I do."

"Then the answer is also simple: you have to choose. It's
no different now than it was with the Peace Corps. If you want
to be here, then *decide* to be here, and that means if your wife
is really choosing to leave you for having the determination
and conviction to follow your dreams, then you have to
prepare yourself for the pain of losing her and you have to let
her go. You have to move on without her. It's a no-brainer."

"Well, well, Mr. Pettigrew. I knew from the first moment I saw you that you'd be enormously successful, and as strange as it may seem, I knew you'd eventually come back to me so we would have the conversation that we'll be having tonight."

He raised the glass, smiling.

"But for now, care to join me in a cognac?"

The ancient, ivy-covered mansion in venerable Arlington, Virginia was enormous, and the scent emanating from the massive cherry wood log aflame in the fireplace lent a spirit of peace to the private room inside. The spacious chamber's walls and ceiling were aged mahogany while the floor was polished oak.

The room, a conglomeration of an eighteenth-century dining table and chairs, nineteenth-century armchairs, throw rugs and oil paintings, a huge twentieth-century overstuffed black leather sofa and a twenty-first-century mainframe computer, possessed a warmth that produced a feeling of ease and euphoria in the young man who stood at the fireplace, enchanted by the dancing of the flames.

John Marlowe handed him a warm snifter of the fragrant spirit and directed him to one of the armchairs that sat directly before the fire at a forty-five degree angle. Marlowe sat in the armchair across from Percival at an opposing though complementary angle. He drew a nose full of essence from the snifter and sighed amorously.

"Fortunately I'm not so old that I can no longer enjoy the pleasures of cognac."

Percival sipped and almost coughed. He smiled, clearing his throat as he spoke.

"So you know why I came?"

"I know *that*, my boy, even better than you."

Silence. Percival studied the old man as he alternately sniffed and sipped the golden-brown liquid.

"I was going to—"

Marlowe interrupted.

"You were going to ask me about my eye, but you really came here to know more."

Percival glanced from his left hand to the black patch on Marlowe's face.

"Yes. So, so what happened to your eye?"

"Cork from a bottle of champagne. That's what I tell people. Makes a good story. I like watching them shudder and cringe as I go into the bloody details. But you and I know that's not what happened."

Marlowe turned toward Percival, setting the snifter on a table.

"Truth is, when I was twenty-one, I was a proud member of the U.S. 1st Infantry."

The old man's eye stared blankly into the fireplace flames.

"Well, on June 6th, 1944—date probably means nothing to you. On that day we were assigned ta storm Omaha Beach at Normandy at 0600. Lotta good men died that day. I was shot three times before I fell into a trench and passed out. When I woke up, I was under a pile of four still-bleedin bodies and I was wounded, so I couldn't move. I could hear gunfire farther up the beach, but I couldn't get up. I was there for two days before the medics found me. Bastards couldn't believe I was still alive. With all the blood loss, I should have died."

"So that's how you lost your eye?"

Marlowe's voice took on an irritated edge.

"You didn't let me finish. Anyway, I was in the hospital recuperating when I met an old man who congratulated me for defeating death. He asked me what I wanted and I told him. I said I wanted power, the power ta punish my enemies and ta help my friends."

"So he asked for your eye in exchange?"

Marlowe flipped the patch up, exposing the fleshy, empty socket. It blinked.

"Gave it to him on the spot. Took a small knife, stabbed it, squished the jelly out and cut the rest of it off right there."

"And you got the power you wanted?"

"My very life is the sequel. I've punished alotta enemies and helped alotta friends over the years. I've known every President since '45 personally, and every last one of them owed me a few favors by the time they were sworn in. Power—I got it, just like the old man promised. He said I would see him again, and when I did, I'd know."

Percival was both intrigued and uneasy.

"Has it ever frightened you? I mean, do you think you'll have hell to pay eventually?"

Marlowe laughed.

"My life *is* hell. My life has always been hell. I'd be right at home in hell."

He took up the cognac again and sipped. Looking at Percival, he laughed.

"You're much too young to be concerned with the end of it all. Now's the time for you to enjoy what you've earned."

No answer. The young man's thoughts were lost in the flames.

"You know, Percival, you and I are members of a very exclusive club, but we're not the *only* members. Check your history: Abraham at Jehovah-jireh, Jacob at Peniel, Alexander at Cilicia, Julius Caesar at the Rubicon, Brutus at Philippi, Napoleon at Elba, me at Omaha Beach, Martin Luther King at a New York City hospital in April 1958. Look to the people the world admires most. They've all had moments where choices had to be made, and they chose to join. Except for Brutus—he chose not to join."

Marlowe cleared his throat, sipping the cognac and swallowing his fate.

"Me? I'm at the end of my time. I've played the game from start to finish. I made my choices and I've lived with them. Now, I've got no choices, really."

Percival peered over as the old man readjusted the eye patch.

"Okay, so what's the end of it all? What's the overall benefit to being in?"

Marlowe laughed, sarcasm reeking more than the cognac.

"That's just it. There *is* no benefit. When it's over, we die like the rest of them die, but at least some of us, if we're lucky, realize that we have lived."

"Please explain."

Marlowe finished the final remnant from the snifter, sighing sensually.

"Tell me, Percival—you ever have a moment of complete clarity?"

"I don't know what you mean."

"A moment of complete clarity—a fleeting instant in which the three elements of universe, time and reality come into one sharp focus. In that moment, you understand what it's all about, and you, you accept it. It's a rare instant that redefines your past, present and future. It gives them sense and purpose."

Percival thought immediately back to that memorable night in his kitchen, to the brief minute or two before he severed his fingers. He remembered the fleeting sense of calm, purpose and unity he felt in that instant. It wasn't a moment of *complete* clarity, but it made him realize such a state of being was possible. He innately knew Marlowe was yearning for a more profound sense of the feeling he experienced right before stabbing himself in the eye and squishing out its contents.

"How do you get there?"

"You keep living and you wait for the moment to come around again. You recognize it and you take it."

Marlowe slumped in the chair, a sense of sadness overwhelming him, his glassy eye lost in the flickering flames.

"You'll know what you have to do."

He caught himself staring more often than he wanted to admit, and he couldn't understand why. His eyes would follow the hand and lock in on the fingers, the ring and fifth fingers of the left hand. Then he would gaze on his own hand, so mutilated and deformed.

He could vividly remember the first time he became conscious of the peculiar obsession. His secretary, Anisette, had wonderful hands, which she had an unconscious habit of modeling whenever she talked. Her hands were perfect, her fingers slender and delicate. All while she spoke, his eyes followed that left hand.

He would hold his breath, hoping the hand would rest in one place long enough for him to get a glimpse of the fingers. He would remember their exact juxtaposition on such occasions, even hours after she had left the room. He yearned to touch those fingers, to caress them, so he struggled to suppress his urges when she was present. In fact, she intimidated him because her fingers were so beautiful—so much so that he began avoiding any interaction with her.

In his mind, even Tyler, for all her fame and beauty, was no match for a woman with such wonderful fingers. Yet realizing such sentiments were a potential liability, he transferred Anisette to an assignment far away, with no possibility of a return.

Then he realized it wasn't just Anisette's fingers. Once at a party he was hosting, he began to look around and notice everyone's hands. He was the only person at the party missing fingers.

They were *all* laughing, swilling expensive champagne and enjoying an event he was paying for, an event that would have never been possible without the immolation he had endured. They had sacrificed nothing, and yet they were benefiting from his self-mutilation.

He noticed how several of them reacted at seeing his hand, how one couple had cringed and backed away, afraid that the deformity might be contagious. He saw others whispering and pointing, apparently repulsed by the sight of the disfigurement. It was enough to make him angry.

These dullards were supposedly the best society and the world had to offer. They were the premiere socialites, the up-and-comers, the jet setters, the names that would redefine corporate America.

But in truth they were shallow persons who had sacrificed *nothing!* Would never sacrifice anything! Who did not understand the significance and importance of sacrifice! It was why they had fingers and he did not. Disgusted with their ilk, he shut the party down and ceased to host or be present at other such events.

Further, he cut back on the regular fêtes he attended with Tyler. Yet with each day that passed, his obsession with the ring and smallest finger of the left hand grew more pronounced and his resentment grew more profound.

Fortunately, the demands of business provided an escape from the realization of the growing obsession and the sense of bitterness that accompanied it. Owing to Percival's knack for organization, GTO operated smoothly, profits were better than projected, and the company continued to grow.

In the spring, GTO launched its own Internet Service Provider division with more options and greater access for customers subscribing to tracking services. The company ran so smoothly in fact that Percival's presence was unnecessary for most day-to-day operations. His vice presidents and managers handled all but the most sensitive negotiations and decision-making, leaving Percival to operate in the capacity he had fashioned for himself: the leader, the visionary in whose hand rested the future of the technical world.

He further escaped the ghost of his lost fingers by traveling the world in search of greater knowledge. He visited

India and wandered down the paths that Sidhartha once walked. He visited Israel and traveled the roads the son of Mary traversed. He considered the footsteps of the Prophet on a pilgrimage from Medina to Mecca.

Yet when he returned, all the knowledge he had gained was vanity. The minute he walked into GTO corporate offices, all he saw was hands, perfect hands with no missing fingers. He could not escape the obsession.

He was angry and irrational, so he determined to affix his anger on a single person rather than on all of humanity. He chose the person carefully and for cause. This person became for him the embodiment of all the human cowardice, incertitude and selfishness he resented with such an implacable passion. This person became the *bête noire*, the anathema. Thus by directing his hate, anger and resentment toward one man, Percival was able to contain his utter contempt for the world at large.

He sat at his desk many nights, murdering the man over and over. He imagined the knife, the hot gushing blood, the expression on his enemy's face, the guttural groan, the eyes set in their sockets as the spirit of life flew from the quivering body.

"Take that, evil old fiend, for what you've done to me!"

He laughed as he imagined cutting off all the man's fingers and tossing them wildly into the air. Then he wept. He wept for the loss of his ignorant innocence, for his abused fingers, for his self-proscribed damnation.

When morning came, he recovered his composure by immersing himself in a new software project. He almost felt content, until one morning he came face to face with the object of his scorn.

"Trace, I need to talk to you."

Trace hesitated, his eyes attempting to peel back the impenetrable shroud from his boss' face. There was something troubling in the tone of Percival's voice, something Trace had heard on perhaps one occasion before, except it had never been so grave.

Yet the resonance of the silence that followed was unnerving and familiar. Obedient, he headed toward his office with Percival following. Once inside, Trace turned on his antagonist, angry.

"What?"

"What the hell are you doing?"

Trace looked into the hallway where, in a reception area on the left, his secretary was no doubt eavesdropping. He walked over and slammed the door.

"I'm working. What the hell does it *look* like I'm doing, asshole!"

His office was the second largest in the complex, some five hundred square feet less than Percival's.

Trace's obsession with Picasso was recognizable to most people who entered the room. It looked more like a gallery than an office. A large, oil on canvas copy of *Guernica* was centered on the long wall just across from his immaculate, dust-free ebony wood desk.

An oversized framed, matted print of *Les Desmoiselles d'Avignon* was displayed next to the large window. On the desk and about the room, there were small-framed duplicates of various drawings and paintings and there were miniatures of several three-dimensional works by the artist.

Yet the largest of all the Picasso copies in his office was a photograph of a mural from a Paris building. Trace even included the title on a lacquered wooden plaque next to the piece. It was called *La chute d'Icare* or *The Fall of Icarus*.

"On your own you've decided to work four days a week instead of five, is that it?"

"They're fourteen to sixteen hour days! I'm giving you better than full time."

Percival turned toward the window to control his overwhelming sense of hostility. He took a deep breath and answered, never looking at Trace.

"You know how many straight employees give me 14-hour days and more? You're a vice president—you've got percentages—you've got a great package here. Yeah you earned it, but I ought to be able to expect more from you."

Trace flinched in anger on hearing his father's final barb.

"Maybe you expect too much of us! You got hurt. You lost, and now you want all of *us* to lose too!"

"No success comes without sacrifice."

"Success? Is that what you call it? It's mutilation. It's not sacrifice—it's self-mutilation."

Bold, Trace stared toward Percival's hand.

"There was no crocodile."

He sighed aloud.

"Benefiting mankind? You know, I think you're miserable about what you lost and you want the rest of us to be just as miserable. You go out and think you're really doing somethin special, you're helping humanity an all, but you know what it all boils down to? You're the real losers! Sometimes we admire you for bein able to put it on the line when we can't. Sometimes we even envy your success and the deliberate way you go through life. But most of the time we pity you. You're distorted individuals. You're freaks! You condemn me as weak, but what kind of husband were you?"

Trace shivered, closing his eyes a moment before continuing.

"What kind of father were you? You threw away your family to help humanity! Something I *can't* do! And that somehow makes you better than me?"

Percival interrupted, answering.

"You don't have a clue, evil old man. You think you've got me. You think I'm so far in that I can't get out of it! But you're wrong. I'm going to beat you! You came to me and you took. You put the choices before me. You made me go through with it. Now it's your turn."

Trace was confused.

"What are you talking about?"

"I had to choose between success and losing something very dear to me. For all of us, that's what it comes down to. Only most people don't recognize the moment when it's right there. Most people don't even understand they're making choices even when they are. You chose not to go, remember?"

"I wanted to go. I couldn't go. I knew I'd suffer like the rest."

"You suffered anyway. Only, they benefited and you lost. *Your* choice."

Though he batted his eyes to control the emotion, a tear streaked down Trace's face as he exploded.

"I know! Don't you think I know that! Do you know how many times I've gone back to that? It's ruined my life. I wish I could go back to that moment. I would have gone if I had it to do again!"

"But you can't. So now we have a new moment."

He placed his right hand on Trace's shoulder.

"You and your wife have separate destinies. You know that deep inside. You know you'll never be successful as long as you stay with her. If you continue with her, you forfeit your future. If you cut her out of your life, you'll have all the success you've ever craved. We're at that point, old man. Few people get second opportunities to make that choice, but here we are. You made me chose. Now it's your turn."

Trace then recognized Percival's actual motivation for the meeting.

"No. You can't. You want to make me chose between my job and my wife? I can't do that."

Percival approached Trace, peering into two troubled eyes.

"You already have. You have forty-eight hours to vacate the premises. Ronda will be taking over for you beginning on Friday."

"There's just no easy way to put this, Percy, but your value to Tyler has exceeded its usefulness. When we first announced the engagement, it was big news. That lasted all of about six months, and then they went back to doing the stories about the was-beens and the wanna-bees. Tyler got a movie out of it, though."

She outlined her lips in plum pencil, adjusting a small circular mirror to maintain perfection.

"Then the pregnancy rumor got us an extra six weeks, but I really don't see much of a future for us. I mean, you're not the kind of guy who's going to go out and get arrested once or twice a year. You don't go out for wild nights at strip bars. You don't slap Tyler around, ever. Then you don't go before the press and insult Bill Gates or your other competition even after Tyler begged you to. When Tyler met you, she was just expecting a little more."

He watched as she applied the wine-colored lipstick and closed the compact. Taking her hand, he pleaded.

"I love you. Do you know that? I love *you*—not Tyler. You can't let her do this to us!"

"Tyler's a star, you're a dweeb with missing fingers. Your heads are in completely different airspace. Tyler just doesn't believe you're the right guy."

"Of *course* I'm not the right person for her! But I am for you! We love each other."

She returned the compact to the small purse on the table without looking at him.

"Tyler regrets that you're being so immature about all this."

Frustrated, he sighed aloud, wagging his head.

"So the engagement is off? Tyler doesn't want to marry me anymore?"

She blotted her lips with the linen napkin, sighing.

"It's just that, the wedding would be big. Outrageous, actually. But what happens after that?"

She patted the back of his hand.

"You're just too nice a guy, Percy. Tyler needs a bad boy—someone who can keep it exciting, make it interesting, stay on the front pages. You need to find someone a little less high-profile, a little more boring... like you."

He peered into her eyes.

"I thought I did. I thought I found the person for me."

"That's the whole problem with you. You're boring because you always know what you want. You take risks, but you don't take chances. Taking a chance means *having it all*, and being willing to throw it all away for a not-so-sure thing—like love."

The server cleared the table, removing everything but Percival's coffee cup. He attempted to make eye contact with Tyler, though without success.

"Percy, what if I were to ask you to get up right now and run away with me—to leave it all behind and start all over again, together. What would you say?"

"I'd, I'd say you can't be serious. Knowing you and knowing me? Our schedules?"

She interrupted.

"Wrong answer. You just don't get it, and that's why Tyler has decided to extend the courtesy of letting you break things off with her. This weekend, she will go into a New York nightclub, have a little to drink, and get involved in a steamy affair with a certain pop star. You'll naturally get mad, call her an insipid little tramp publicly and break off the engagement."

He stared at her in disbelief.

"No, I won't do that. I'm not going to do that."

"Then Tyler will dump you for being the insufferable little bore that you are. Either way, it'll be big news."

There were hundreds at the graveside service, despite the fury of the worst storm of the season. At the church on 10th, the head usher estimated that over two thousand had attended the funeral.

Among the crowd of mourners were two former U.S. presidents, a vice president, a dozen senators, various congressional representatives, an envoy from the British Parliament, along with the prime minister, and other heads of state. The District of Columbia in its entirety seemed to pause for a moment to pay tribute to a man who had been a luminary, a figure of mythical proportions.

Arguably, decorated WWII veteran John Marlowe had been one of the most powerful Washington insiders ever. During his career he had chaired the National Security Council for fifteen years, the Federal Communications Commission for eleven years, and he had been director for the Central Intelligence Agency for seven years.

He sat on the Federal Reserve Board, was an advisor to the chairman of the Joint Chiefs of Staff, and he had been appointed to special committees by eight U.S. presidents. To the end, he was a fiercely patriotic guardian of the nation's most valuable secrets. His obituary read like a Hollywood movie story line. Percival sat silent in the audience, listening to all the comments, the anecdotes and the legends surrounding John Marlowe.

He mused that of all the long-time friends and close acquaintances crowded in Kennedy Center for the nighttime memorial, perhaps no one knew Mr. Marlowe quite the way he did. No one else knew what it felt like to be a part of the club. No one knew the kinship Marlowe felt for Alexander, Caesar and Napoleon. He wondered about Marlowe's last moment, wondered if he had reached that point of complete clarity.

The circumstances surrounding his death were irregular for a man of his age. According to stories from the newspapers, he was in a fistfight with a "bundled-up" old man in a tavern over a debt he owed the man. They wrestled on the floor and they exchanged blows, but then suddenly Marlowe froze and turned ghastly white, leaning against the bar rail, his one eye wide open. Marlowe's antagonist then clutched him, his face against Marlowe's, as the spirit left his body.

The owner called for an ambulance and for the police, but in all the commotion, the bundled-up old man somehow disappeared. Marlowe was rushed to an emergency room where the attending physician pronounced him dead on arrival.

The announcement and story of Marlowe's death shocked Percival, who had imagined his ancient colleague perishing in the armchair before the fire, cognac in his hand as he savored that last moment of complete clarity.

Percival felt the loss perhaps more than anyone in the room. Marlowe had never married and had no children, so there was no family, except for Percival, in a way. Percival was a fellow member of the club, and Marlowe, by virtue of guiding him and educating him on its history and the opportunities and dangers it offered, seemed like a father.

Yet Percival wondered if he had any brothers or sisters in attendance, any other fellow club members. If they were out there, he wanted to meet them. He looked for other mutilated individuals in the crowd, but he found none.

Then as he was exiting the building, he realized a mistake he had made on a subconscious level: He had slipped his hand into his coat pocket the way he had always done in public. If any other member had looked, seeking to identify him by his distinguishing mutilation, the hand was hidden. It was a missed opportunity and he didn't know when or if he'd ever get another chance to meet another member of the club.

The phone call came at 3:30 a.m., startling him awake. His personal secretary was weeping pitifully as she spoke. She had received an angry and hysterical phone call from Grace Markus, Trace's wife. Two days after being "let go" by Percival, Trace had locked himself in his room at home, placed a shotgun in his mouth and pulled the trigger, spattering skull fragments, bones and bits of brain all over the bedroom wall and ceiling. Grace was threatening to sue Percival for "murdering" her husband. When he called Grace to apologize, he wasn't prepared for all the anger, hate and blame she would direct toward him. She cursed his name, declaring he'd "burn in hell" for what he did to Trace.

And then, if the news about Trace wasn't distressing enough, the morning newspaper headline made Percival sink to his knees in grief even as he took the paper from the sympathetic bellman's hand. In a banner across the top, the copy read, *SUPERMODEL TYLER, DEAD AT AGE THIRTY.*

It had been three months since the official break-up, so he hadn't spoken with her for at least seven weeks. His stomach churned as he read the story. According to the rags, Tyler became a party-girl after the break-up. She even began drinking real cocktails and getting drunk in public.

She was on a yacht with a group of other models and their dates off the Florida Keys two nights before. One of the girls said she had just "done some Ecstasy," a drug that enhanced sensory perception in pleasurable ways. The friend said everyone heard a splash about three o'clock a.m., but they had all drunk so much that no one got up to investigate. When Tyler was missing the next morning, the Coast Guard was alerted and a full-scale search was conducted.

Volunteers found her ripped, bloody shirt and one of her shoes that afternoon. Her body was never recovered and the possibility of finding it grew more and more remote as the hours passed, especially since the area was home to thousands of hungry crocodilians, several species of sharks and other carnivorous fishes.

Though her parents wanted to prolong the search, authorities assured the public, reciting the details from previous incidents, that if the body hadn't been recovered in twenty-four hours, it had been completely consumed by the denizens of the keys.

Thus it was that within the course of three days, Percival had lost the three most significant people in his life. Sitting alone in a Washington, D.C. hotel room, he realized that earlier in his life, while he was pursuing success, he had been sad, disappointed and lonely. It was only then, after attaining "success," that he learned the meaning of misery.

Misery made success irrelevant, it made freedom irrelevant and it even made choice irrelevant. Misery made life itself irrelevant. He reflected on that night many months before, when he had considered getting drunk and falling to his death over the railing at the Hyatt in Sacramento.

He had chosen success instead. Now more than ever he wanted to end it all, to leave it all behind. He alternately drank brandy and slept for two days, neglecting to eat, shower and shave.

On the second night, he threw on a wrinkled shirt, zipped the pants he had slept in and stumbled into the hotel hallway. He never bothered to tie his shoes or button the shirt. The maitre d' at the hotel restaurant would have never allowed such a slovenly dressed person to take a table, but he recognized Percival and seated him in a dark remote corner of the room.

There, Percival determined, he was going to have his last meal. Then he was going to head over to Columbia Heights, pick a fight with the biggest, meanest gang member he could find, call him a few choice names, maybe insult his mother and gladly suffer the consequences.

He ordered a double vodka martini, gulped it down, and then he ordered a porterhouse steak. He never ate the steak, because he passed out on the table. When he awoke, his vision was hazy. There was someone sitting across from him, nudging him, calling his name. When the image sharpened, he drew a deep breath and sat up, blinking his eyes, feeling sober.

"You? I dreamed about you! And now you're here!"

She smiled, squeezing his hand.

"Of *course* I'm here. You called me. Is that a martini you're drinking?"

Percival ordered her a drink and re-ordered dinner for two. Without a prompt, he began to tell her about his life since that poignant moment they shared at the airport. He told her about the problems with the IRS, about the call from Marlowe's secretary, about GTO's incredible success, about Tyler, about Trace and about his misery. He told her about everything but the fact that he had taken a cleaver and chopped off the ring and fifth finger of his left hand. In fact, he kept the hand hidden.

She listened all while he spoke, rubbing his right hand at moments where he fell apart and wept. Finally, after he had emptied his soul into her heart, she reached into his lap, took the mangled hand and kissed the nubs that had been his fingers.

"Everything will be all right if you want it to be."

"What do you mean?"

"It seems now or very soon, you'll have to answer a very important question."

Strangely, he didn't feel uncomfortable with her touching the abbreviations. Her touch brought him comfort.

"What question?"

"Now that you've achieved the success you thought you wanted before, what do you *really* want?"

Bowing his head, he looked toward his hand, and then he looked into her large, expressive wonderful eyes.

"Two things. I want my fingers back. I'd give up everything just to have my fingers back."

"But you can never have those back. They're gone. Unfortunately, some things done in life cannot be undone."

He caressed her hand.

"And you. I want you. There have been so many times when I've been sad or lonely, and I've thought about you. I always think back to that last moment at the airport when I was ready to change my destiny and stay with you. You don't know how many times I've wished I had done that."

She smiled.

"I know."

"I made the wrong choice. I should have stayed. I want to stay right now. I want to stay with you and never leave."

She paused and signaled negation.

"I don't think so. That moment is passed and gone. You made a choice. For better or for worse, we can't undo the choices we make."

She clenched his hand before releasing it and sitting back.

"Now if you don't mind, I'd like to tell you a few things you might *not* know."

"Like what?"

"The day you left me at the airport—I went to one of the men I worked for, the Senate Majority Leader, and I told him about you and your project. He really liked the idea. A few weeks later, at a private dinner with John Marlowe, he urged John to give your tracking chips a fair chance. That's why Marlowe's secretary called you."

Percival was stunned. Thus recalling the experience with great severity, he told her about Lucius Crossland Haydes and the three times he appeared. She was the only person he had ever told about the strange old man and the peculiar bargain he offered. Oddly, she didn't seem fazed by the bizarre story.

"Either way you chose, you would have been making a substantial sacrifice. If you had chosen me, I would have never gone to my boss, and Global Tracking Options would have never happened. Choices are funny that way—a sacrifice at either side."

He stared at her in silence before speaking.

"How do you know so much about sacrifices?"

"The rules aren't very difficult to understand. Whether you see it or not, any success, whether it's money or power or happiness or a long life, comes at its owner's expense. You all try to hide it, but you're all victims of self-mutilation. You're all maimed, disfigured."

She watched him tuck his hand away, and she continued.

"John Marlowe was missing an eye. He lacked the balance to see how much good he could have accomplished with the power he possessed. He used it selfishly and died without ever understanding that. Your friend Trace took self-mutilation to the ultimate level. In every suicide there is a martyr. In the end, he out-sacrificed his father. Who can argue with that?"

She leaned forward, almost whispering.

"And then there's Tyler, the one you loved. She was probably the most mutilated of all, though she was as close as anyone could come to physical perfection. There's always a price to pay for success. She put the choice before you, and you chose."

"When? What choice?"

"Didn't you tell me that on the last night you saw her, she asked you to 'leave it all behind' and start over again with her?"

His eyes widened as he remembered.

"Yeah, but—"

"And you chose. You chose *not* to. Don't you see? It's not very different than it was with me at the airport. There's a certain consistency to the choices you have made in your past, so if you're miserable, you really need to consider the choices you'll have to make from this moment on. Existence is about choice, otherwise that tree would have never existed in the garden. You can't have both."

As he took and squeezed her hand, he felt a sudden flash of clarity.

"I know."

"So we're back at the beginning. The question, Percival, still is: What is it that you *want*?"

A flash, and then a complete, wonderful moment that transcended time, space and reality.

"You! You're—"

She stood, looking to the door.

"I'm sorry, but I have to go. I'm late."

He stood and reached toward her, clutching her shoulders.

"Wait! Will I see you again?"

She smiled and kissed him on the lips, amused before becoming serious.

"You'll see *one* of us. That will all depends on the choices you make."

❖❖❖❖❖❖❖❖❖❖

Only after two months did he realize how difficult a thing it was for a billionaire to divest himself of all wealth. He'd give away millions at a time to various charities, but the money would always return in the form of tax breaks, incentives and in other uncanny ways.

He would have sold the Internet division of GTO to a competitor, but profit on the transaction would have been prohibitively high. More than anything, he wanted to get *rid* of the money.

Thus he donated to the Peace Corps, to the Heart Foundation, to the Cancer Institute and a long list of other such organizations. After consulting an expert private accountant on the matter, he prepared to sell his outstanding GTO shares to other shareholders and use the money to benefit humanity.

He would create a Trace Markus foundation, dedicated to the prevention of suicide, an organization that provided regular medical care for poor children and a dozen more charitable trusts.

Every penny from the sale of GTO shares, from his houses, from his other property and investments, from his stock portfolios, from his art collection, from his cars, his yacht and his savings—every penny would go to one benevolent foundation or another.

He would reserve the right to intervene if any foundation or trust failed to follow the directives of its charter. In the end, all the wealth he had worked so hard to acquire, the very success that he sacrificed two fingers to achieve, would be gone, save $783.41.

His retirement announcement resulted in losses on traded shares, as investors grew concerned and uneasy about who would take over the helm at Global Tracking Options. However, once it became clear that Percival's successor would be Ronda, his second-in-command, prices stabilized and most of the initial losses were recovered.

Investors had great faith in Ronda's leadership and in her abilities, though there was some concern about her physical condition. Weeks earlier, she had taken time off for medical reasons. She told her staff she would be undergoing a procedure to have a lump removed from her right breast.

When she returned, she confirmed that doctors had actually performed a radical mastectomy, but she asserted they had given her "a clean bill of health."

Over the course of two months, Percival sold everything he owned and donated the money to organizations dedicated to benefit humanity. Thus he was no longer in debt.

The streets outside the airport in Sacramento were quiet on that heated Saturday morning. The skies were hazy and gray, though there was not a cloud in them. Ronda's silver Lexus slinked around the gradual curve of the main road, followed the signs leading to the terminals and came to a gentle stop.

"Well, here you are."

He smiled.

"Yes. Yes, thank you so much for the ride."

She placed her right palm against his cheek.

"Not even a suitcase. Are you sure you know what you're doing? I mean, where the hell are you going?"

He nodded.

"Yes, and I'm not saying."

He opened the door, got out, closed it and walked around the car to her side. She rolled down the window and leaned out to kiss his lips.

"You know Ronda, before I go—I just want you to do something for me."

"What's that?"

"Ask yourself a question. You don't have to answer it now, maybe not for a couple of years, but you have to keep asking it."

She squinted in confusion.

"What's the question?"

He leaned close, speaking into her ear.

"What is it that you really want?"

Inside, the terminal bustled with activity, though no one seemed to be in much of a hurry. Re-examining his notes as he walked, Percival looked up occasionally to scan the names of airlines as he passed customer service counters. Finally, he found the name of the small carrier.

Because there was no line at all, he wasn't sure if the young woman seated at the counter was taking reservations. Unfolding a sheet of paper, he handed it to her. She read the sheet, put on a pair of glasses and began typing on the computer. She stopped a few times and read the screen, only to begin the typing again. At last she stopped and waited for the printer to finish.

"Okay, that's the 10:35 shuttle into Oakland, out on flight CRL940, departing Oakland at 12:28 and arriving at Tahiti-Faaa International at 3:35 p.m. One-way. Anything else I can assist you with at this time?"

He sighed.

"No, that'll be all."

"Can I help you with any luggage."

"No."

She presented the chit.

"Okay, that'll be seven hundred eighty-three dollars and forty-one cents."

He sat on the soft, powdery, white-sand beach, his green pareos shirt flapping in the warm breeze as he watched the sun set on the edge of a cerulean horizon. It had been a week of incredible sunsets, a week of peace, a week of solitude.

For seven days, the only sounds he heard were the roar of the ocean as it broke onto the beach, the cacophony of a million birds on the shore and in the skies and the random thuds from coconuts as they dropped thirty feet from their treetop nests.

He had hiked over three miles from the village in order to reach the secluded strip of sand on the western side of the island. For provisions, he had swept and mopped a local merchant's floor in exchange for a sleeping bag, a large pouch of dates, a loaf of bread, a shovel, a used pot, a knife and several books of matches.

He ate fish and crabs mostly, supplemented by fruits and nuts he foraged from the forest. For seven days, he hadn't heard the sound of a human voice, not even his own. He set up camp in a small clearing, not far from the lagoon, where he spent the nights in the sleeping bag next to a fire. He realized that he'd eventually have to go back to the village, back to the world and back to reality.

He knew he'd have to apply himself to some employment as he fashioned a new life for himself, but for the time being, he was content to sit on the beach and watch the birds squabble overhead, he was content to sit at the water's edge twice a day and watch the tiny creatures patiently adjust to the tide's ebbs and flows at the lagoon, he was content to marvel at rainstorms and sunsets and rainbows and fish eyes. All these things were free.

For the first time in his life he had the freedom to enjoy them. He never thought once about his hand, never once about his missing fingers. He felt complete. Though the clarity he felt during that moment in the restaurant became less and less distinct with each day that passed, he knew he had made the right choice.

He fancied he saw a figure walking along the beach the next morning, headed toward him as he sat on a rocky perch watching the sun outline the mountains along the eastern edge of the island. As it drew nearer, he realized the human form in the distance was no phantom at all.

It was a woman in baggy jeans, an oversized coat and a large straw hat. Apprehensive, he stood, anxious about encountering the first person he had seen in more than a week.

Then, when she came within the outer reaches of detailed eyesight, he began to recognize the familiar idiosyncrasies: the way she had been trained to walk, the proud way she held her chin, the exaggerated way she swayed her hips. But it couldn't be! Hesitant, he descended the rocky lookout, stumbling onto the beach.

He walked toward her even as she walked toward him. Then just as they came eye-to-eye, noses almost touching, both stopped. It seemed like her. Only this woman was perhaps 12 pounds heavier, there was more color and life to her skin and she wore no make-up.

He remembered the eyes. Her eyebrows were fuller, her butt was a bit bigger and her nails weren't done. Yet she was still pretty. Her hair was pulled back under the hat, but a few unruly curls had escaped to dangle at her forehead.

He closed his eyes, struggling to reconcile the image of the woman before him with the woman he remembered. He did not understand.

"Tyler?"

"Tyler's dead."

"You—"

Her voice was insistent.

"Yes. Tyler's dead. She fell off a boat and drowned. She was eaten by sharks. I'm just a woman who lives and works on this island."

He smiled.

"Really? Well, what kind of work do you do?"

"For now? I paint beautiful sunsets."

"Are you any good at it?"

She laughed, shrugging one shoulder.

"Not really, but who cares? I get better with each day that passes."

She took his hand.

"The villagers told me a man had come, and when they described him, I knew it was you. I'm glad you decided to take a chance."

"It wasn't a chance. It was a choice."

"All the better."

They sat on the beach and watched the sunrise in awe and wonderment, hardly speaking a word to each other for an hour.

"I have a small place on the southern side of the island not far from the water. Isn't much, but it's big enough for two. We can hike out on the isthmus every day and watch the sun set."

They had walked a mile down the beach, shoes off, jeans rolled up, breakers rushing over their feet, when he stopped.

"Okay, Tyler's dead. So who are you? I mean, what do I call you?"

"You can call me by my real name. It's Karen. Does it suit me?"

He laughed to himself. Then he put his arm around her waist as they continued strolling down the beach. He smiled, glancing toward the glistening blue and white horizon.

"It's fine. The name suits you just fine."

ESTÉBAN

"¿*Quieres un cochinito, Carlito?*"

Grinning with wide-spaced, uneven teeth, the wiry little ten-year-old, his eyes never averting from the spectacle of eleven greedy three-week-old piglets fighting over ten grossly swollen teats, pleaded to his father.

"Can I please have one, Papa—I *promise* I'll take care of it."

Juan Pedro Villa Gonzales, picking his tobacco and coffee-stained teeth with a straw, sneered for the fetid odors emanating from the alfalfa hay-lined pen as he looked at the nasty little animals, a few of them smeared with green and brown colored portions of still-wet feces. One of the pinkish babies with characteristic black markings, the runt, a piglet who hadn't managed to get a nipple, had crawled around to the other side of its mother and had slumped to the floor, whining, until the young boy picked it up. Carlos held it out toward his father, who seeming threatened, backed away.

"*Papa, por favor!* Can I please have him?"

"I donno Carlos. He's dirty and he stinks, and when that thing grows up he'll be bigger than even me. Then you think you can still take care of him?"

"*Sí, Papa!* I *know* I can!"

It was four o'clock. The afternoon sun burned the still air all around the makeshift little barn, trapping the stench in the immediate area of the dim enclosure. Outside the door, the sky through the heat-distorted atmosphere was hazy and cerulean. Most of the valley was unpleasant, hot and dry, but the intense heat signaled an end to the season.

The heat was good for the grapes. It ripened the fruit. Soon would come the harvest—first the *chardonnay* and *sauvignon blanc* in mid to late September, but there were other white grapes. Señor Mahler, the winemaker, or *el jefe* as the workers called him, had planted almost five acres of *semillion* four years earlier, and there would also be limited production from the little *chenin blanc* and *gewërtzraminer* plots along the northern parts of the property. A few weeks after the whites came in, Juan Pedro and his crew would set on *cabernet sauvignon, pinot noir, merlot, sangiovesse, pinot muenier, petit verdot* and the other reds.

Juan Pedro was a serious, old-fashioned and conservative man who, in his mid-forties, took on many of the labor-related concerns for the two hundered or so harvest workers on the huge Mondial Vineyards estate. The workers trusted Juan Pedro, who spoke better English than most, to negotiate for annual pay increases, for overtime consideration, for improvements in working conditions and for better family housing.

Señor Mahler would sometimes put up with Juan Pedro coming in to voice workers' concerns, but he never listened to a passionate word the foreman spoke, even when Juan Pedro threatened a strike. As a result, the winery got by doing as little as it could for the workers.

Juan Pedro described the winery's treatment of workers as "harsh and inhuman." The majority, those who did piecework, averaged less than minimum wage working 16-hour days, while the permanent workers, who lived in the squalid housing provided by the winery, earned perhaps $18 a day more.

Many of the laborers had come up from Juan Pedro's small home village of Encinal, near Tecate on the California-Mexico border. In a few younger families, husbands, wives and children of working age came up, leaving infants with grandparents at home. Yet the labor force for the wine grape harvest was largely male, as many of the wives and children found better conditions harvesting other agricultural crops north, south and east of the valley.

The estate had some housing for workers who stayed all year to maintain the vineyards, but for those transient laborers who came from August through October for the critical fruit harvest, there was little to nothing. Many brought tents or constructed dwellings from discarded pallets or cardboard, erecting them at a common camp on the property. Thus the camp at night, families huddled around a big fire and pitched housing in the background, resembled the transitory settlements of the ancient *Patwins* and *Miwoks*, the Native American tribes who lived in the valley long before the Spaniards came.

Juan Pedro and Carlos stayed for eleven months out of the year in estate housing. They simply had a room with two beds, and they shared a common kitchen and common bathroom with other full-time workers and their families. Juan Pedro's wife had died three years earlier in that room during the birth of a second child, a daughter who died with her.

Carlos had been born in that room, and because his birth was registered in California by the county welfare agency, he was an American citizen. As such, he was entitled to attend the local elementary school, where as a fourth grader, he was considered "a bright little boy with a promising future."

Carlos, like his father, was handsome and dark with thick, wavy jet-black hair. He admired his lean and often sullen father, though he always fretted when Juan Pedro complained about problems in America and expressed intentions of taking Carlos back down to Encinal for good so he could be raised in "the traditional Mexican way."

Outside the little barn for the animals, its construction was obvious. The floor was made of broken and worn wooden pallets. The walls were irregular-sized plywood panels, nailed and hinged together at unsealed corners and bracketed at the bottom. The flat roof was a quilt-like hodgepodge construction of odd-sized wooden planks, panels and 2x4s, all wired or nailed together, unworthy of keeping out streaks of sunlight, let alone any possible rain.

Yet it hadn't rained since April, so the unrelenting heat had baked a hard crust onto the loamy soil outside the structure. The little shack seemed to sit in the middle of nowhere. Rows of trellis-supported deep green vines, laden with dark fruit, seemed to stretch on forever on three sides while a dusty road on the fourth led back to the camp where the laborers lived.

Señor Orlando Gomez, the old man who offered Carlos the pig, had erected a chicken wire reinforced wooden fence around his "barn" to keep the pigs in. In an adjacent enclosure, he had seven hens and a turkey. Señor Gomez had lived on the property before even Señor Mahler, *el jefe*, came to Mondial, since even before wine grapes became so popular in the valley. In fact, he had helped replace the last of the prune orchards with grapes in the 60s. Sensing that Juan Pedro could be won over with a little nudging, stout, sturdy and gray-haired Señor Gomez intervened on Carlos' behalf.

"Let him have the pig, Juan Pedro. You'll have all the *carnitas* and bacon you could want by Easter."

Juan Pedro struggled and managed to direct a brief though uncomfortable smile in the older man's direction before turning sternly toward his son.

"I'm going to let you have it, Carlos, so you can understand what 'responsibility' means. If you wanna take it home, it'll be your pig. That means *you* have to take care of it."

Never looking up, Carlos answered, his fingers rubbing the nose of the whining baby in search of a nipple.

"*No problemo*, Papa. I promise I'll take care of it."

A year later, five women stood along the wide conveyor belt, picking out leaves, branches, dead animals, dirt clods and muted clusters which didn't seem quite ripe. It was 10 a.m. and the sun was just beginning to heat the still air on the valley floor. For four hours the women had been there, standing at the belt, eyes trained on the tons of translucent yellow-green clumps of grapes passing by. During the harvest, the women typically got a thirty minute lunch break at noon and got to go home at seven or eight o'clock, a thirteen or fourteen-hour day for most. Yet the women had the easy job.

The day started just as early for Juan Pedro and his men, six o'clock a.m., but the seemingly endless job of harvesting ton after ton of *el gringo's* precious winegrapes was both exhausting and body wrenching. At 5:30, even before the sun's glory began to trace the edges along the mountain line in the East, Señor Mahler told Juan Pedro which sections of grapes had ripened sufficiently during the previous day and identified which portions of which lots had to be harvested. The two would detail a plan and Juan Pedro would have his crew out in the field by six o'clock.

Señor Gomez, *el viejo*, drove the tractor along the path that ran perpendicular to the rows while the men and boys did the actual gathering. As the men moved along the rows, it was amazing to see how swiftly and efficiently they worked, their hands often becoming blurs in the process.

In one seeming action, the leaves would be stripped and held back with hooks, exposing the clusters along "the fruit zone," and bunches of grapes would be clipped and placed in baskets, or lugs, below. In a split second some clusters would be taken while others would wait for tomorrow's pass through the same lot.

The boys helped dump the full baskets into the large bin behind the tractor. Then Carlos and the others would go with Señor Gomez to take the bin to the dark green hopper where it would be emptied and hurried back to the field.

One day during lunch, as Carlos and Juan Pedro sat under a huge black oak tree watching the women watching the grapes pass by, the boy was struck with the strangest notion.

"*Papa*, who *eats* all these grapes?"

Juan Pedro was surprised his son didn't know better.

"No one. No one eats em. They make *wine* outavem."

"*Allavem?*"

"*Sí.*"

Carlos finished the last of his cold leftover Spanish rice.

"Must be alotta wine."

"*Sí.*"

He looked toward the grapes, still incredulous.

"Who *drinks* all that wine?"

His face serious, Juan Pedro spoke sternly to his son.

"People who don't care about workers like us. People who don't care we work sometimes 20 hours a day, who don't care we're the hardest workers in America who make less than their teenagers get at McDonald's."

He stood, stretching, as his aching back cracked.

"No, they're bastards! All of em! They drink the wine, but they don't care, cuz if they paid us like they should, a bottle of wine would cost maybe two dollars more! Two extra dollars and they don't want that."

Jerking his head, he signaled to his son that the break was over.

"No, they don't wanna pay two dollars more, so they turn their heads and try ta pretend we don't exist. They don't think about us when they're sipping on that wine at their big houses or in those fancy restaurants. No, they don't wanna feel guilty, so they pretend we don't exist, that we aren't human beins. It's easier that way."

Carlos at once remembered a comment he had heard in the general store on the main highway just the day before. A woman, looking out at the vines, had asked the manager if "all those grapes" were harvested by machine. When the man told her that many were harvested by people, she insisted he had to be mistaken. She said she had visited the valley over one hundred times in the last eleven years and she had never seen any "*people* working out there." It was the first time Carlos ever felt a distinct sense of insignificance. He had felt sad that day, though he didn't understand why.

Juan Pedro, already out in the hot sun, sighed as he waited for his son to rise. But Carlos had something else on his mind that afternoon, something that was all at once wondrous and frightening, something remarkable and natural. Thus he stood tentatively, determined to reveal the secret to his serious father.

"No, wait Papa! I need to tell you something!"

Squinting his eyes as he watched the other workers heading back out to the field, Juan Pedro answered, annoyed.

"What?"

Nervous, Carlos began.

"It's, it's Estéban. I've taught him how to talk."

Juan Pedro said nothing. He only turned and walked toward the field, his exasperated manner indicating that his son should follow. Carlos was almost running to keep up.

"It's true, Papa. Estéban is like no other pig. Estéban can *talk*!"

Juan Pedro stopped, the strained lines in his face and his voice conveying all the anger and regret he felt.

"That pig has been nothin but trouble since I let you have him. I'm gonna get *ridda* that pig!"

Terror-stricken, Carlos fell silent. Surely his father didn't mean it. How could he get rid of Estéban? Estéban was like family. And it was true! Estéban *could* talk.

Carlos had first recognized his pig's propensity for speech when Estéban was only five months old. Often when he was playing with the pig, Carlos spoke aloud to the animal, as if in a make-believe conversation. Sometimes he would give the pig detailed instructions, which his grunting friend followed without flaw. Señor Gomez credited Carlos as a very good animal trainer, but Carlos sensed there was something extra special about his pig.

It followed that one day in April, on a day when Carlos was late coming home to feed his pet, he arrived at the pen to find Estéban bucking and bounding about the space, excited to see him.

"Hi!" the pig shouted, "Hi, hi!"

The little voice was porcine in nature, in the upper reaches of the baritone register, and the quality was largely nasal. Despite the fact that Carlos heard the well-articulated words coming from the mouth of a farm animal, he seemed hardly surprised.

Parrots had bird brains and they could talk, he thought, so why not pigs? But parrots and other talking birds were only mimicking human sounds and had no idea what they were saying.

Early on, Carlos believed his pig was doing the same thing, and yet as weeks went by, it became obvious Estéban was beginning to master the essentials of human speech. Far beyond merely repeating sounds, he identified words with objects, names with people and inflection with meaning. His early sentences were unintelligible, yet little by little some of the words came into focus.

"This what?" he would grunt toward Carlos, who would say the name of the object, which Estéban would repeat again and again until he got it right. Thus by July, Estéban's nominal vocabulary was extensive, though he still struggled with the mechanics of human language, and more with English syntax. Notwithstanding, he was capable of simple conversation in the present tense.

"Man mad why?" Estéban snorted after Carlos and Juan Pedro had come home late that evening. The boy had showered, changed his clothes, and being exhausted, had slouched against the building wall, sitting next to the pig.

"I dunno," Carlos sighed. "My father's always upset about something. If he isn't mad about the growers, then he's angry with the workers. If it isn't me, then it's you. It's always something."

"Man me no like why?"

The boy ran lithe fingers across the coarse hairs along the animal's head.

"No, it ain't that he don't like you. He just don't believe you can talk."

"I him talk *can*."

Carlos smiled, glancing as the light went out in the bedroom where his father slept.

"I think you need just a little more practice and then I'll let you do it. Not only will you surprise my father, you'll surprise the whole world!"

By early October, many of the workers had gone home, leaving Juan Pedro with a tiny crew that patiently waited for the late-harvest *gewërtzraminer* to reach forty brix, a nearly 40% sugar level. It was a tricky process that Señor Mahler oversaw. The white man even went out and helped pick the precious half-rotten grapes.

When that lot was finished, all the workers would go home, and Juan Pedro would go to work inside the winery. Carlos, since mid-September, had left the field to focus his energies on his schoolwork and his very intelligent pig.

"Man me cut why?"

Carlos examined the scars and the missing pouch at the base of Estéban's corpulent body.

"Oh yeah, they cut off your balls."

"Balls cut why off?"

Carlos thought a moment, remembering the very day Señor Gomez used the sharp knife to slice open each side of his pig's scrotum and extract the large testicles from the sac. Señor Gomez ate them for dinner that night. He had laughed, calling the unusual delicacy "mountain oysters." Carlos struggled to explain.

"Well I, they—Señor Gomez, he said they hadta cut cha, cuz if they don't, you'll get all mean and won't be tame anymore. He said you'd stink, that you'd turn on me if he didn't do it."

Yet he didn't tell Estéban the other reason the old man gave for cutting him.

"Any animal with balls, Carlito, is a dangerous animal. Ya gotta cut em out ta kill *el machismo, el virilidad.* Besides, you leave the balls in, you'll never be able ta eat the meat. It'll be too tough and it'll taste bad."

The idea of anyone eating his pig! It was just a scary, horrible, sick thought, but Carlos had a plan. Once the world knew how truly amazing and intelligent Estéban was, the pig would be famous and would never be slaughtered, boiled and butchered like the others he'd seen. Carlos had stopped eating pork all together. He preferred going to bed without dinner rather than eating one of Estéban's relatives.

In irony however, Estéban ate pork regularly, bolting down the fat and the sundry remains of pigs, which had been scraped into the slopjar from the dinner table. Carlos could distinctly recall watching Estéban unwittingly gobble down portions of two porker siblings.

Smart though he was, the animal was so concerned with his own sustenance that he never made the connection that he was cannibalizing his own brothers. Nonetheless, Carlos' mind was set. No one was going to eat Estéban, so he intensified the teaching sessions, determined to educate Estéban in the finest manner.

Over the weeks, as the pig's language skills improved, Carlos explored the notion of teaching the remarkable animal to understand written language.

To his utter surprise, Carlos discovered that because he had become a teacher of sorts, his own understanding of English language mechanics improved dramatically. At school, Mrs. Walker, his fifth grade teacher, was amazed at his development. Where months earlier he lagged behind all but one other classmate in language skills, over the course of nine weeks he became the premiere language arts student at the school.

Naturally, Mrs. Walker took credit for her "little Carlito's" remarkable turnaround, touting a controversial "novel approach to teaching ESL (English as a Second Language) students" which she called "the Walker technique."

Many colleagues ridiculed her methods until Carlos qualified for the respective state and national spelling bees. Even though Carlos lost in a tough, hard-fought final round, several commercial publishers engaged in a bidding war, which resulted in a book deal for his teacher.

Yet more remarkable than Carlos' improvement was Estéban's, proof that, given the opportunity, pigs could demonstrate great intelligence and ability. Estéban learned to read in three weeks, and by nine weeks he had already read a few of the classics, Plato's *Republic* his favorite among them. With the reading came a better understanding of English grammar, syntax, mechanics and vocabulary. His speech and diction, though still heavily accented with involuntary snorts and an uncomfortable porky nasalness, was flawless.

Because Carlos was away at school so much of the time, Estéban read voraciously. He read Aristotle's *Nicomachean Ethics*, his *Politics* and *Rhetoric*. He read Descartes' *Discourse* and Machaivelli's *The Prince* and *The Art of War*, and he read Kant's *Critique of Pure Reason*. Then one day, after discussing the plight of the winery and vineyard workers with Carlos, Estéban asked for a pamphlet by Marx and Engels called *The Communist Manifesto*. It took Carlos a week to find it and Estéban four hours to read and re-read it.

A day later, the pig told Carlos he could help Juan Pedro and all the workers on the property if he could only speak before them as an assembled body. Carlos balked, convinced that he'd never be able to get the workers to listen to an inspirational speech uttered by a pig. Even if he had been able to get the workers together, very few would have been able to understand Estéban's words because few spoke English. To most of them, his speech would have sounded like pig gibberish.

Despite all his education, Estéban was still very much a hog. At no time was his nature more evident than when he ate. He smacked, he snorted, he grunted, he farted and he belched. He was revolting.

Carlos wasn't sure if it was greed or a trance-like feeding frenzy that transformed his friend at dinnertime, but Estéban always overate at the trough, loosed his bowels publicly in a disgusting, foul manner and collapsed onto the hay for a nap, tail twitching until he fell asleep. His unhealthy eating and lack of exercise led to obesity. He grew fat, weighing in at more than two hundred fifty pounds on Señor Gomez's old scale.

Though he tried to disguise it, Juan Pedro eventually began to fear Estéban's size and avoided proximity and any possible encounter with the huge pig. Thus seeking to rid himself of the threat, he began suggesting to Carlos that Estéban would better fulfill his purpose in life by serving as Easter dinner and as necessary sustenance throughout the summer.

Carlos objected angrily and vociferously, threatening to hate his father forever if he ever hurt Estéban. Proud, Juan Pedro refused to yield to his son's desperate blackmail attempt,

"Estéban is a pig who has given you nothing. I am your father who has given you everything. I've taught you better'n that. I am your father. We will eat that pig."

By January, Estéban weighed over three hundred pounds and had begun to grow huge tusks, which jutted from both sides of his mouth, giving him a fearsome appearance. Still, he read every day, thanks to Carlos raiding *el jefe's* trashcan. Estéban read the *Wall Street Journal* and the *Los Angeles Times* each morning in addition to the books he read at night.

Because he had no fingers, turning the pages of books and newspapers presented a problem early on, but he had perfected his snorts in a way so that with proper aim and the right intensity, he was able to adeptly move from page to page.

It was in January, as he read a novel by George Orwell, that he began to feel a great sadness for the plight of all the disadvantaged pigs in the world. With that sadness came the realization that thousands of pigs were being slaughtered in America and all over the world on a daily basis.

The thought that pigs were food like half-witted cows and bird-brained chickens and turkeys was distressing to Estéban. The wholesale slaughter of pigs for meat, silk purses and footballs would have to end. Despondent, Estéban went to his best friend.

"We *must* do something, Carlos. You must let me talk to your father. Soon."

Carlos nodded, thinking of Juan Pedro's gruesome plans for the pig.

"You're right. What will you say?"

"I'll, I'll," Estéban snorted, "reason with him. Your father is a reasonable man."

Carlos' expression wasn't hopeful.

"Okay. We'll try it. *Bueno.* What do we got to lose?"

Over the next two weeks, Juan Pedro flatly refused Carlos' request for a meeting with Estéban. He also refused to believe Carlos' repeated assertion that his pig could speak and read.

"I'm forty-five years old, and I seen alotta pigs. Pigs are to eat, not to talk with. They're not *meant* ta talk. That's why they only grunt."

Carlos sighed.

"Why don't you just test it out, Papa? Let me bring him in. You'll hear him. You'll see, come on! I'll go get him."

Juan Pedro shot a menacing look toward his son before warning,

"He's dirty. He's nasty! The only way he'll come in my house'll be after they've wrapped im up in butcher paper!"

Concerned for his friend, Carlos answered, ignoring the implied threat.

"Then come out with me and talk with him! I don't understand why you won't do that!"

And then,

"What is it, Papa? Are you *afraid* of him?"

Without warning Juan Pedro snatched his son up by the collar in anger, pulling his face close, sneering.

"Look *Hijo*, he's a nasty animal, and you're a boy. You're eleven years old now. I don't wantcha spendin any more time with that stupid pig, ya understan?"

Carlos only looked toward his father, unable to disguise the defiance that consumed his very being. Juan Pedro could see it. It was unmistakable. It was almost frightening. Frustrated, he shoved his son against the wall, letting him go.

"*¡Te importa mas el cochino que tu propio padre!*"

Carlos' nose had begun bleeding. He could feel the warm mucus-like blood from his left nostril welling at the top of his lip. He wiped, smearing a crimson trail across the right side of his face.

"You really *are* afraid, aren't you, Papa?"

Juan Pedro looked at the blood on his son's face and then he looked away, regretting.

"Yes. Yes, I'm afraid. I don't know if your pig can talk, but there's somethin about him I don't trust, somethin I don't like. He's dangerous. Besides, if your pig or any pig really could talk, I don't think the world's ready ta hear what he might have ta say. I'm sorry Carlos, but I gotta get rid of im."

Estéban crouched next to the wall, awaiting an opportunity to block the man inside. Señor Gomez's hens were laying an egg a day, and Juan Pedro typically went in at six o'clock to get a few for breakfast. Señor Gomez had moved the chickens and turkeys into the makeshift barn during the cooler months and had built perches and nests inside.

The old sow had been sent to the slaughterhouse in December, and Señor Gomez shared the meat with all the permanent workers who lived on the estate. The older turkey had been cooked at Thanksgiving.

Estéban, squatting there, could actually remember watching the turkey's execution, could remember watching her ignoble end, her headless body running about in circles, flapping, convulsing, blood squirting from her once-graceful neck, her hacked-off head on the ground, eyes still blinking. Yet he didn't realize he had eaten her boiled entrails in his trough that night and other portions of her after Thanksgiving dinner.

"How many pigs today," he thought, "would be slaughtered so that humans could enjoy flesh with hen's eggs?"

A door slammed and footsteps became louder as someone approached the barn. The voice, singing to himself in Spanish, was instantly recognizable. It was Juan Pedro, who barefoot, swung around the corner and, ducking to clear the low doorway, slipped into the little rickety barn. Only when he knew the man was inside did Estéban round the corner, his enormous body blocking the door.

"Juan Pedro!" he pronounced, his huge head, ferocious tusks jutting out, sticking through the barn door, "I must speak with you."

Juan Pedro stopped, turning toward the sound of the nasal voice. He looked at the pig, saying nothing.

"Juan Pedro, I want to help you and your workers, but first you have to understand that the world does not revolve or exist for vineyard workers only. There are many others who also feel the same oppression and worse. While you complain about the vineyard workers' plight, all over the world, others are sacrificed for *your* own comfort and convenience. What we the oppressed must do, Juan Pedro, is unite for the benefit of all."

Juan Pedro just stood there, dumbfounded, wagging his head and batting his eyes as the pig spoke.

"Those blue jeans you wear, Juan Pedro—have you ever considered the conditions of the workers who sew them in East Asia? Do you know of their long days and low pay in sweatshops? Have you ever, as you pulled those jeans on, considered the lifestyle your cooperation with their oppressors condemns *them* to?"

"Estéban?" Carlos called. His father missing from bed, Carlos had gone out to the barn to find him. "Estéban? Who are you talking to? Papa? Are you in the barn?"

"Your pig's got me trapped!" answered Juan Pedro's nervous voice. "Hurry! Go get me my gun!"

Carlos had approached the rickety little structure. Through the irregular spacing between slats, he could see his father's back as he stood facing the huge hog's head.

"Estéban doesn't want to hurt you, Papa. I heard him talking to you."

Juan Pedro answered, never turning.

"I, I heard nothing. Pigs can't talk."

Estéban snorted, startling the uneasy man.

"Of *course* we can talk, but you humans do not want to believe it. It is easier for you to think we are dumb animals as you settle down to eat your side of bacon in the morning. Chickens and cows really *are* dumb, but you lump us in with them to justify your inhumanity toward pigs. We are at least as smart as dolphins, but we do not see humans eating porpoise pot roast for Sunday dinner. We are much smarter than dogs and cats, and you do not eat them. Have you ever for once thought about how pigs feel?"

Juan Pedro shivered there, barely twitching. Glancing back over his shoulder, he called to his son.

"Carlos, tell him to move. Tell him to let me out."

The boy, who had approached the pig, patted his rump.

"Come on, Estéban. I told you he wouldn't listen."

Yet the animal refused to budge.

"Do you realize, Juan Pedro, that we are feeling, thinking beings too?"

He snorted again, continuing.

"As I said before, I am willing to speak out on your behalf, on behalf of all the workers in the world, on behalf of all pigs as well."

Juan Pedro laughed.

"And the world will listen to a pig?"

He ducked slightly and squinted, trying to identify his son's position based on the soft whispering he could hear coming from outside the barn.

"Carlito, tell im to let me out. Now!"

Slowly, Estéban backed out the door, his eyes fixed on the obdurate man.

"We'll talk again."

Later that day, Carlos walked with his father along one of the rows, watching as Juan Pedro broke off newly-formed buds that were just beginning to sprout from the yellow green, awakening vines.

He had seen his father do it last year, and he could never tell why his father left some and broke off others. There was certainly a pattern to it, and even though his father tried to explain why, it was one Carlos still struggled to understand.

Juan Pedro wore jeans and a red and black plaid shirt. In the dusty worn cowboy boots and the hat he wore, he looked like a character from an old western. Carlos wore black corduroy slacks, a white polo shirt and tennis shoes, his school uniform.

Not a word was spoken as father and son took the first break of the morning. Neither wanted to broach the uncomfortable topic at lunch either, and yet by the time they began walking back toward worker housing, the silence became too ponderous for Carlos to bear.

"At least you know he can talk now."

Still walking, Juan Pedro stared straight ahead.

"I heard nothing. Pigs do not talk."

Both were quiet during dinner. Too tired to cook, Juan Pedro had driven to the nearest fast food location and purchased two complete meals as Carlos did homework. As they ate, Juan Pedro looked over at his son and sighed.

"That burger you're eating. It's a cow."

Carlos swallowed, nodding.

"I know."

"Cows, pigs, what's the difference? They're here for us to eat."

The boy did his best to be respectful even as he disagreed.

"No, Papa. We were never supposed to eat pigs. It's in the Bible. Estéban showed me—*Leviticus 11:8*. It says, '*And the swine, of their flesh shall ye not eat, and their carcase shall ye not touch.*'"

Juan Pedro studied his son for a moment.

"That ain't in the Bible."

"Yes it is, Papa. I can show you."

"No, you *can't* show me cuz it's not there. Besides, the Pope eats pork, so that's good enough for me."

Unable to think up a good response, the boy fell silent before changing direction.

"But you *did* hear him talk?"

Juan Pedro chewed the last of his burger and took a sip of orange soda before answering.

"He didn't talk. I heard nothing. Just grunting, just snorting."

"No Papa. He talked, and we *both* heard him."

After about five minutes of silence, Juan Pedro sighed, speaking aloud.

"So what do you expect me to do, Carlito? Let him go into the wild? He wouldn't last a week out there. He'd get shot or die of starvation."

"We could *keep* him."

"Then we'd hafta feed im, and you know how much he eats. But what good is it to feed a pig you can't eat! He'd just *take* from us and give nothin back. What would we *do* with im?"

Carlos thought a moment.

"Protect him."

"Why? What good would that do? It won't change anything."

"Maybe not, but if it wasn't for us eating pigs, we wouldn't have this problem in the first place. He'd be livin in the wild the way he was supposed to be."

Juan Pedro was beginning to grow impatient with his son.

"In the wild, pigs get eaten, Carlos. God made pigs for us to eat."

Carlos stood to make a point.

"No he didn't. He said it in the Bible. Otherwise he wouldn't have made em so smart."

Juan Pedro stood, sighing, studying his son.

"So what if Estéban *can* talk and read? What does he want? What is he gonna do? Teach other pigs to talk and read too?"

"That's what he said he wants to do."

"So then what would we have? A world full of pigs who read and talk?"

"Yeah. What's wrong with that?"

"So then what do we do? If we don't kill em an eat em, whadda we do?"

Carlos thought a moment and answered.

"We try ta understand each other. We all try ta get along."

"So when we're all gettin along, what are we all gonna eat?"

The boy answered.

"Vegetables."

"No meat?"

Carlos thought.

"Well, maybe chicken, maybe chicken and beef, but no pigs."

"But what if chickens and cows learn to talk and read? Then what do we do?"

The answer, low-pitched and profoundly nasal, came from the open window. Estéban had forced his head in, ruining the screen.

"Birds and cows will never learn to read or talk. They are dumb animals. When will man stop lumping pigs in with dumb animals?"

Juan Pedro, startled, had fallen backward in his chair. He struggled to his feet, terror-struck by the huge, tusk-endowed, speaking hog's head jutting through the open window. Standing, he held the chair out horizontally, defensively to protect himself.

"Carlos! Your pig!"

Carlos went to his friend, grabbing a tusk and whispering into the hog's ear.

"Estéban, you shouldn't have interrupted. We were talking. He was finally listening."

Juan Pedro interrupted.

"I wasn't listening. I was disagreeing, Carlito. What makes you think that if your pig can talk and read, he's somehow *better* than cows and chickens?"

"Cuz he's smart, Papa."

"Well, I thought we were talkin about *feeling*. You gotta be smart ta feel when someone cuts your throat? Huh? Chops off your head?"

In the absence of an answer, he continued.

"I don't think it's wrong ta kill pigs or cows or chickens. We raise em to eat. Pigs are no better than any other animals cuz you say your pig can talk."

Estéban interrupted.

"I *can* talk! You can hear me."

Juan Pedro only stared straight ahead, not reacting in any way to the words. Carlos looked at his father and then back to Estéban. Finally, he approached, trying to make eye contact. He tugged his father's muscular red and black plaid-covered arm.

"You can *hear* him, can't you Papa?"

Juan Pedro's eyes flicked over to gauge the pig's position.

"No. Just grunting."

Saddened, Carlos sighed, walking away.

"You know, Papa, we could be famous. We could be rich! We'd be the only ones in the world to have a talking pig! We could buy us a house and never have to work again."

It was obvious Juan Pedro was intrigued by the idea of wealth and fame, but he was careful.

"I dunno, Carlito. If your pig could talk and be famous, what would he say?"

"I don't know. I thought the talking would be enough. What would you want him to say?"

"Well, not that dangerous talk. None of that talk that all pigs could learn ta speak and read. None of that stuff about people not eating pigs, changin everything."

Carlos seemed confused.

"Well, if he couldn't say that, what, what *would* he say?"

Juan Pedro imitated the pig's voice in a silly, animated way.

"He could say, 'Hi, my name is Estéban, and I'm the crazy talking pig! I'm fat, I'm silly. I'm a big, dumb pig!' and maybe he could tell jokes or dance or somethin, but none of that 'changin things' stuff. It wouldn't be good."

The boar snorted.

"No. I would *never* agree to that! Pigs finally have a voice, and I have something important to say!"

Juan Pedro, though never acknowledging Estéban's statement, sneered toward the huge beast and turned back toward his son.

"On second thought, Carlito, I don't think the world *needs* a talking pig. Get that animal out my house!"

Owing to an olfactory superiority over humans, he knew where Juan Pedro was at all times. *Knowing* was the most crucial element of his plan. He also had to make sure Carlos and Señor Gomez were not within earshot of the place he had chosen for the final confrontation.

Though his balls were gone, and with them much of his bestial inclination, he instinctively sensed the mortal power of his tusks and how they might best be employed in battle. He resented the fact that he had been castrated in his youth and had never been allowed to develop to his true boar form with all its spirit and potency, and he resented all humans, even Carlos, for that loss.

Yet he did not realize the testosterone he lacked had been key in his mental development and that, had those balls remained, it was doubtful if he would have ever learned to talk, let alone ruminate, read and reason.

While he loved Carlos for his idealistic world view and his conviction to fairness and equality, Estéban believed man's educational system and pressure from a society built on oppressing less literate and less organized forms would eventually win the boy over. Carlos could not be a boy forever. He'd eventually marry and have children, and his priorities would change.

So rather than championing the cause of pigs, his primary duty would involve providing for his family, which included feeding them flesh. Thus he would perpetuate the cruel cycle of oppression. As much as he tried and professed otherwise, Carlos could never understand the plight of pigs in the world.

Estéban had come to accept that he would begin to fight the war alone. All the other pigs he had encountered, though intelligent, were simply too consumed by the events of their daily lives to think on the necessity of a global revolution. The other pigs were isolated by greed, selfishness, sloth and man's calculated methods for keeping them dull, weak and unorganized.

Through research of farming methods, Estéban discovered that men learned their oppressive techniques specific to pigs at colleges and universities and from think tanks around the world.

He understood that intentional overfeeding made pigs slow and dull-witted, that selective castration and breeding for meat production rather than for intelligence weakened the gene pool, and that the silent assassination of any potential leader among pigs kept them from organizing.

Surely in the world there were others like him, Estéban thought. Where they were and how many, no one could tell. The only sure way to reach those comrades would be to send up a flare of sorts, and Estéban thought to do this by murdering his oppressor, Juan Pedro, in a bloodbath.

During the television and newspaper publicity ensuing from the murder, Estéban would break his silence by taking full responsibility on behalf of the world's persecuted pigs, calling them all to arms, proclaiming *Sic Semper Tyrannis!* And thus the revolution would begin.

For two weeks he waited, crouching low, listening to whispered conversations, biding his time. He often imagined the moment. He could see, could hear one of his tusks ripping open Juan Pedro's abdomen.

In his mind, he watched the pale flesh lying open in that moment just before the blood began to flow. He imagined the integrity of that cavity failing, quivering, the newly opened fault inevitably yielding to gravity and Juan Pedro's entrails exploding outward, spilling to the earth. Juan Pedro's eyes would be open wide and his hand would be flailing, futilely reaching, clutching at the precious, steamy, bloody mass escaping his body. Weakened, he would fall to his knees. He would try to call out, to scream for help, to beg for mercy, but lacking the use of his stomach muscles, he would only manage a throaty groan.

Only then would Estéban close in for the kill. But first, he would peer into Juan Pedro's eyes, establishing his own superiority, and he would say, "Ever so to tyrants!" before piercing the man's jugular with a tusk and ripping open his neck. Then after getting a good taste of his enemy's flowing blood, Estéban would establish the revolution's first tradition: He would eat Juan Pedro's spilled intestines.

Estéban made up his mind to commit the murder only after he overheard a conversation between Juan Pedro and Señor Gomez weeks earlier. The two men were planning a large barbecue for the end of May. They had invited the families who owned Mondial Vineyards, they had invited Señor Mahler and other staff members, and they had invited their families up from Encinal and elsewhere.

There was to be a feast. There were to be games for the children (the piñatas had already been purchased) and there would be a fine mariachi group and dancing for everyone. Señor Gomez' grandson would bring up the *Mezcal* from Monte Alban. Juan Pedro would get three or four kegs of Dos Equis and then there would be wine.

Of course, there would be wine—merlots, pinots, cabs, chards, sau blancs, flowing by the gallons, and there would no doubt be a few remarkable "library wines" at the owners' table. Chafing dishes would be lined on a long table containing Spanish rice, tamales, frijoles, nopales, squash, fried corn and fresh sliced tomatoes. There would be salsas, cheeses, hand-made tortillas and flautas; it would be a real feast. The main event however, would be the whole barbecued hog, the one Juan Pedro promised to provide for the day, the ferocious-looking, casterated boar his son called Estéban.

The brutal murder of Juan Pedro would attract publicity, and Carlos would no doubt tell the story of Estéban and his cause. Estéban was convinced that there were certainly other pigs like him, pigs who could read, pigs who realized that the only solution to their oppression was a bloody revolution, pigs who could be leaders in *la revolución*! The news story, when printed, would attract their attention. The greatest difficulty would be getting them to understand his plan.

After the murder, he would run away. He would escape and take up a life in the woods. Then, after a few days, he would visit Carlos in the night, promising to turn himself in on the condition that he could speak with the press. During the media interview, the human public would be so amazed at the spectacle of a talking pig that they wouldn't recognize his insidious call for a pig revolution until it was too late. He'd call all thinking pigs to attack their human oppressors in like manner and flee into the country's woods, forests, mountains and other hard-to-navigate places.

There they would organize themselves, take unwitting humans as prisoners to breed for labor and consumption, set up a defense, develop weapons, create a pig army, begin educating lesser pigs, incorporate various desirable traits of wild pigs into the gene pool, claim territories and set up boundaries.

Only then would humans understand they were dealing with an equal, if not superior, species. Eventually, pigs and man would either learn to live with each other or decide the question in a final all-out war.

The day finally arrived. It happened on *Cinco de Mayo*. Carlos was away on a rare Saturday school field trip to the Six Flags amusement park. *El viejo*, the old man, had been away visiting his daughter in Mexicali and wasn't expected back until late evening. Juan Pedro, locked in his room, coughed constantly blew his nose. Still in his pajamas, he went out occasionally to the kitchen to make himself hot tea.

While his body had already been weakened by the *rhinovirus*, the generic allergy medication he took every four hours made him woozy and disoriented, almost delusional. The fever and chills came every other hour, causing Juan Pedro to throw off the blankets, panting, only to bundle them around his shivering body minutes later. His skin ached as it switched back and forth from producing sweat to producing goose bumps.

Estéban waited outside the door, squatting along the wall, his tusks sharpened for the occasion. Eventually, the man would get hungry and would head for Señor Gomez' chicken shed for eggs. It was a daily ritual for Juan Pedro. When the screen door creaked open at 4:38 that afternoon, the time had come for the revolution to begin.

"Juan Pedro!"

The man stopped, at once sensing the hog's intentions. Estéban had cornered him in the courtyard. Escape was unlikely, as the stucco-covered, five-foot-tall walls of the Spanish-style enclosure were topped with a pointed iron railing. Beyond that, Juan Pedro felt woozy and light-headed from the medication he was taking. His arms and legs were slow to respond as he backed away.

The confident hog closed on the trembling, vulnerable man.

"I am going to kill you, but first I am going to make you talk to me."

Juan Pedro's pupils bounced as they darted from left to right and left again. Through the haze, he thought, *not a weapon in sight.*

"You can hear me, Juan Pedro. Why can you not accept what is before you? Does my speaking *threaten* you?"

Juan Pedro almost fell over as he motioned with his arm.

"Get, get back, pig! Shoo!"

"Is it because the only thing that has made you humans superior for all this time is your ability to communicate and organize?"

Juan Pedro, eyes never leaving his adversary, reached down and grabbed a piece of brick that had broken loose from the planter around the courtyard tree and raised it, threateningly.

"Get away! Ha! Shoo!"

The man shook his head, trying to clear it after almost falling over. Estéban studied his clumsy reaction before continuing.

"After I teach other pigs what I know, what will you humans have over us then? Who will be the superior species then?"

The brick his only defense, Juan Pedro wavered, reluctant to use it.

"Who is the superior species now? It is just you and me, Juan Pedro, man against pig. Who is the superior species now?"

Juan Pedro stomped his bare foot.

"Get away! You nasty, stinkin pig!"

Estéban only began to ease closer.

"Before I rip your guts out and eat your liver, Juan Pedro, I will give you one chance to save your life."

Reluctant, the man listened, and yet he still refused to endorse the fact that Estéban was speaking.

"Your only chance for survival lies in accepting me, listening to my words, acknowledging that I am a person too. You might not believe pigs are your equals, but if I have something important to say, if I have an important work to do, you do not have to help me, but you must not interfere."

Juan Pedro breathed deeply, fearing, but he remained resolved.

"I can't hear you! Pigs cannot talk!"

"For this reason I am innocent of your blood and I have not betrayed your son, Carlos, who is my friend. You have left me no choice. *Alea iacta est!* You must die!"

Snorting aloud, Estéban lowered his head, grunted and rushed toward Juan Pedro, who sidestepped in the last moment as he threw the piece of brick. The brick hit Estéban in the forehead, causing him to turn his head slightly to the left. Thus, instead of overwhelming the man with his great mass, the hog only managed to clip the outside of Juan Pedro's right knee with a sharp tusk, ripping it open.

"*¡Ai-yi-yi-yi-yi! Cochino malvado! Cochino maldito!*"

The knee no long functional, Juan Pedro, limping, lunged for the tree in the planter and clung to it as Estéban turned to renew the attack. However, Juan Pedro's desperate tree defense, though unplanned, proved somewhat effective.

First, the red-leafed plum tree laden with tiny red fruit, its trunk about fifteen inches in diameter, limited the pig's ability to charge the man behind it. Then the seven-inch-high planter around the tree further hindered the pig's maneuverability. Unable to charge, Estéban worried that Juan Pedro would climb the tree to escape him until Señor Gomez returned.

Thus his strategy changed even as he approached the injured man. Rather than lunging directly, he decided to attack Juan Pedro's flanks, eventually wounding him to the point that he'd fall to his knees or lose his balance and fall back. In either case, he could then be slaughtered and ripped open.

Nearly all Juan Pedro's weight was on his trembling left leg as he stood there, so Estéban surged toward it, but he tripped over the planter and slammed headfirst into the tree as the frightened man scooted left. Stumbling to his feet, the hog jerked his head leftwise, hoping to catch the man's leg, but he only gored the tree trunk.

Backing to gauge the man, he started forward left and suddenly veered right, throwing his head back in the last moment. A scratch! A deep scratch to the left thigh, but Juan Pedro remained mobile.

During the next pass, Estéban was poked in the face, nearly in the eye, by a sharp branch Juan Pedro had managed to tear from the tree. Rather than rushing forth the next time, Estéban walked around the tree, pursuing the man, and he would have struck a direct hit if Juan Pedro hadn't punched him atop the head.

Unable to escape the pig as he resumed the pursuit, Juan Pedro, clinging to the tree, threw out his hand to push the beast away. He heard the crunching sound even before he felt what had happened. By accident, the ring and pinkie fingers of his right hand had slipped from the pig's snout into its mouth where they were crushed and severed immediately. The tip of his middle finger was also shredded beyond repair in the process.

Estéban sucked the blood from the still twitching appendages, crushed them with his back teeth and swallowed them with a grunt. As Juan Pedro stared at his mangled hand, finger stumps pulsing blood that ran down his arm, panic set in.

Eventually, he concluded, the pig would kill him unless he could make it back to the house and shut the door behind him. He eyed another loose brick in the planter, reached down and raised it.

"Get back, pig! I will kill you with this!"

In the moment Estéban stopped his advance, Juan Pedro hurled the brick toward the pig's face with all his might, turned and stumbled toward the house as fast as he could. Estéban's squeal let him know that the brick hit the mark. It bought very little time, but Juan Pedro was only twenty feet from the door when he heard the grunt as the angry pig began charging.

Grimacing, Juan Pedro ignored the instability of his right knee as he lurched toward the doorway, and he might have made it inside if he hadn't tripped on a raised and exposed tree root next to the concrete pathway leading to the door.

Lowering his head, Estéban rushed toward his victim, snapping his head back in the moment his snout began to lift the body. The action sent Juan Pedro crashing into the side of the building before falling in a heap where he remained motionless.

Victory at hand, Estéban grunted twice and snorted as he prepared one last attack, this one purposed to rip open his adversary's viscera. Thus lowering his head, he began the mortal charge.

"Estéban! Estéban, please!"

Lacking balls, the pig, hearing, hesitated. He knew the voice. He knew what hearing the voice meant. It was Carlos who was no doubt pleading for the life of Juan Pedro. How regrettable that Carlos would have to see the murder of his father! Estéban never wanted it to happen that way, never wanted to hurt his friend, but the die was cast. His hesitation was brief, hardly noticeable, but it was enough.

Estéban had glanced toward Carlos before lowering his head and charging, but it gave Señor Gomez just enough time for a backswing before sweeping the 2x4 in a path that landed squarely on the pig's forehead.

Estéban stopped in place, swaying left and then right before dropping to the knees of his forelegs. Eyes glazed, he seemed to look again toward Carlos before he fell over sideways, twitched his tail three times, and did not move again.

The 4'x8'x4' cage was constructed of the same 2x4 and three others, with 4x4s composing the main framework. It had been placed under a huge black oak tree about two miles from the barn. The floor was a solid 4x8, inch-thick piece of plywood, covered with straw.

"Free me," Estéban urged, "and I will run into the woods and never come back. I will not be a threat to your father or anyone else."

Carlos, in a daze, watched the cool morning breeze animating the tender new leaves on the grapevines. Many were so bright and green in the springtime, almost yellow-green in color. In contrast, by summer's end the hardy leaves would be a much deeper shade of blue-green with purplish hues.

There were vines in every direction he looked. To the east they extended right to the mountain line, while many of the western mountains had trellised vines extending up near-vertical slopes. Rolling hills dominated the south, a vast green sea with swells breaking out to the horizon.

Mondial Vineyards, situated in the flat, bench-like northern part of the valley, was composed of solid lots, or individual vineyards from the mountains on the west to the river in the east.

Sitting next to the wooden cage, Carlos sighed. He took the last of the wild turnips from his lap and placed them in the cage. Estéban had taught him how to tell the difference between wild mustards and wild turnips.

Before flowering, it was only necessary to break one of the shoots and draw in a deep breath. The entire wild turnip plant smelled exactly like turnips. During the spring blossom, the mustards had bright yellow flowers, while the turnips had white or sometimes pink to purple flowers. Estéban always liked turnips best.

"The key to this lock must be in the house somewhere. Find it and let me out!"

Despondent, Carlos wagged his head.

"I don't know, Estéban. I don't know what to do. He's my father."

The pig snorted.

"Let me go. Set me free."

Carlos could not look into his friend's eyes. Instead, he looked to the south, toward the rolling hills.

"If I let you go, I betray my father."

"If you do not, you betray yourself and everything you believe."

The boy silent, Estéban continued.

"Carlos, do you believe pigs and men are equals?"

Carlos looked toward his imprisoned friend, stuttering through his careful reply.

"Estéban, I believe *you* are equal, but other pigs aren't like you. They're animals. They're nasty. They're not equal to people, they're not equal to you."

"Why am I any better than they are?"

"Because you can talk, because you read, because you're educated."

Estéban grunted, sighing.

"People like your father would not agree with that. He is afraid to admit he can even *hear* me."

"He's afraid of you, period. You tried to kill him."

The pig's tone was angry, resentful.

"Should anyone fault your father for fighting to protect himself when he realized I wanted to kill him?"

"No."

"Then how can anyone blame me for trying to protect myself when I knew your father was planning on killing me? They all want to cook me and eat me. You *know* it."

Carlos thought to protest, but he shook his head, conceding.

"Yes. They're planning a big barbecue."

Estéban rolled to his side so he could reach his arm outside the cage. He touched the boy's shoulder.

"Carlos. I'm your friend. If I knew someone had plans to kill you, I would do everything in my power to save you. Are you telling me you would not do the same for me?"

"But my father—"

Estéban interrupted.

"He will be angry. He will be very angry, but you are his son. He will get over it. He will respect you for being true to yourself."

In the absence of a response, Estéban continued.

"Is it because I'm a pig? Is it because you see me as something less than humans?"

"No! No, that's not true!"

"Is it not though, Carlos? If I were a human and your father and Señor Gomez locked me up like this, if they were planning on murdering me, what would you do? If I was your friend, would you let me go if you could?"

Carlos closed his eyes for a moment and answered, sighing, nodding.

"Yes, I guess I would if I could."

"Then if I am truly your friend, if you truly believe that I am a person too, how can you have any hesitation about setting me free and saving my life?"

Carlos looked into Estéban's eyes as if to measure his reaction to the next question.

"If I let you go, will you attack my father again?"

Estéban sat up, withdrawn.

"I promise you, Carlos. If you let me go, I will never threaten your father's life again."

"And other people, will you attack other people?"

The pig answered, turning away.

"Maybe, but only if they threaten me."

Estéban sighed.

"Carlos, I *know* there are other pigs out there just like me, pigs with enormous potential. I just want to *reach* them. I need to find other pigs like myself. If we can all get together and organize, maybe we can change things. We—"

"I'll do it," Carlos interrupted.

"What?"

"I'll find the key and I'll let you out. I promise."

"*Everything's* goin up, Juan Pedro—the price of sugar, the price of gas, the price of toilet paper! The *gringos* are chargin more for the wine. I saw it in the supermarket. So why aren't our wages goin up?"

Juan Pedro sighed, dragging his fingers through his hair. The first of the year's workers had just begun to arrive, and the thirty-five or so men who sat around the long picnic tables were angry and disappointed.

"*Lo siento, amigos*, it's gonna stay seventy-five cents a lug for the harvest, six dollars an hour otherwise. I'm sorry. Mahler said the winery *lost* money last year, but he said this year would be better. He said there would be more money next year."

El viejo hissed.

"That asshole Mahler's a liar. He said the same thing *last* year."

Frustrated, Juan Pedro became defensive.

"Look you guys, I've done everything, and I've said everything I can say to him. I told him we had families ta feed, that we're gonna walk out on strike if things don't get better! He won't *listen* to me! We're not gettin any more money. Seventy-five cents a lug, that's it."

A churlish, pudgy-faced man in the front row didn't bother to stand before speaking.

"Well, what about the plumbing? The shower hasn't worked in over six months now. Do they think we're some kinda lousy animals? We don't need to wash off?"

"And the toilet!" said another, "most of the time it don't even flush."

Juan Pedro almost felt too ashamed to respond to the question and comments.

"He said the maintenance guy who does the plumbing is out till June. The shower's the first thing on the list ta be fixed, and then he'll do the toilet."

A thin man standing in the back, eyes glowering, shot in his own resentful remark.

"So in the meantime we hafta take our baths in the river or just stink, right?"

Juan Pedro's face was still bruised from his near-mortal encounter with the pig. His right arm was broken and kept pressed close to his body in a sling. The abbreviated tips of the severed fingers on his right hand had been sewn together by the surgeon and were healing nicely. He walked with a noticeable limp, one he would have for the rest of his life. As he looked from table to table into the workers' eyes, he saw the despair, desperation and hopelessness of a group of defeated men.

"And I guess there'll be no more housing," a middle-aged man intoned, "so me and my boys'll be sleepin in cardboard boxes this year, too?"

"Ain't so bad," an older man interjected, "we're just vineyard workers. We don't mean nothing. Nobody gives a damn about us."

"Yeah," agreed another through the widespread mumbling, "we're workers, not people. Once the grapes are in, they'd just as soon throw us away. They don't give a damn."

Struggling, Juan Pedro made his way onto a bench and then to a picnic tabletop. He held his left hand up to quiet the crowd as he shouted.

"No! *No, Amigos!* We *will* be heard! We cannot accept things the way they are!"

The mumbling dissipated, Juan Pedro held the group's attention and interest.

"That's why I say we have to strike. There is no other way. We have to tell Mahler and the owners that until they meet our demands, we will do no work—no weeding, no trellis work, no maintenance, no thinning, no nothing!"

Apprehension about "striking" unsettled many of the faces in the crowd. Noting it, Juan Pedro pressed on.

"Don't you see? The only way they'll ever take us serious is if we take the aggressive, if we confront them directly! We hafta hurt em where it counts!"

"And in the meantime, Juan Pedro," a voice asked, "what are we supposed ta do for *money*?"

"We move ta other wineries," he answered, "and if they're the same, we encourage other workers to join us in our movement. Sooner or later, we'll have all the workers in the valley with us, and then we'll be able to make things better for everybody."

It seemed like a good plan, and Juan Pedro articulated it so convincingly that he won over the group. In fact, before the afternoon was over, many of the drunken men were singing *Nosotros Venceremos* and making speeches.

True to his word, Juan Pedro went to Mahler and the owners threatening a general strike. Mahler told him any strike would be inconvenient for the winery and suggested he reconsider the idea.

Mahler said the owners were aware of the workers concerns but were too involved in the daily business of the winery to take up individual issues. Mahler promised to do whatever he could, though he stopped far short of considering solutions to the questions of equitable pay, decent housing and adequate plumbing.

When he offered Juan Pedro the title of vineyard manager, a position with much higher pay and a private little home on the property, it was obvious the job was offered in exchange for cooperation, influence over the workers and silence on the idea of striking. Acutely aware of Mahler's intent, Juan Pedro refused the bribe.

Two weeks later, Mahler stopped by the place Juan Pedro and Carlos had called home for eleven years to tell them that the space was required for "the new foreman-in-training," a second-year worker from El Mayor by the name of Ricardo Rivera.

Within two weeks, Juan Pedro and his son were living in the rickety roach and mice-infested trailers on the property's edge with the other transitory workers.

As intended, Juan Pedro's punishment quashed any ideas of a strike by the other workers. In fact, the majority stood with Ricardo when he denounced Juan Pedro and his "vineyard workers' movement." Señor Gomez alone of all the workers remained loyal to Juan Pedro, condemning the others as cowards who completely deserved whatever abuses they would suffer in the future.

"Cowards do not count in battle," he said. "They are there, but not in it."

"I've looked everywhere I could look, but I haven't been able to find it."

Carlos peered through the wooden beams at his friend Estéban, who because of the forced inactivity, was fattening up nicely. The boy still visited the cage every day, though the move to the trailer meant he had to travel two miles to the spot under the black oak tree where the pig sat jailed.

Carlos hated the trailers. He missed the humble little place he had called home all his life. He often couldn't help crying at night as he tried to sleep amid the noise, smells and discomfort of the cramped metal enclosure, its true owners scurrying about the counter and floors when the lights went out, leaving little disgusting proprietary reminders in their wake.

Yet Carlos' repugnance and displeasure was small compared to Juan Pedro's. Estéban's jail had a solid frame, sturdy wooden bars supported by a sound crossbeam and a heavy-duty lock, but Juan Pedro's degraded living quarters were more a prison, more a punishment for the brash impertinence the man and pig shared.

While Estéban grew fatter with time in his cage, Juan Pedro withered away in his. When Carlos and his father moved into the trailer on May 13, Juan Pedro was a stout and healthy one hundred eighty pounds, but he had wilted to a gaunt one hundred fifty-five by May 28, a wrinkled, withered husk of the man he had been.

"I was sure I'd be able to find it after the move. I've checked his pants pockets, his wallet—everywhere! I don't know *where* he could've hidden that key!"

Estéban had been quiet and unresponsive all afternoon. He seemed to be far away, drifting in some unreachable realm. He always wanted to know where Carlos had looked for the key, but on that afternoon, the key seemed irrelevant.

"I had a visitor last night."

Carlos turned toward his friend.

"Really? Who?"

"A young pig. His name is Juárez and he can talk just like me."

"Really? Where does he come from?"

Estéban snorted and sighed.

"I'm sorry, Carlos, I cannot tell you that. We cannot afford to let humans know how many of us there are. Not yet."

Carlos seemed confused.

"Well, can he read too?"

The pig wagged his head.

"No, not well, but he's smart. I'll teach him, and he will teach the others."

"Well, is he a farm pig? Is he a wild pig? How did he know about you? Where'd he come from?"

Estéban looked toward the naive boy.

"I cannot tell you those things, Carlos. As much as I like you, you are a human, and we cannot let humans know about us. Not yet."

An hour later, as Carlos readied himself to leave, Estéban was more himself, more like the pig the boy had come to love.

"Carlos, I just want you to know that I appreciate everything you have done for me. I thank you for all the loyalty you've shown me. I owe you everything."

Carlos was uneasy about the pig's tone.

"Why are you saying that, Estéban? Nothing's gonna happen to you."

"We do not know that."

He turned his body toward the boy.

"Just in case you *do not* find the key and something happens to me, I just wanted to thank you for trying."

"I will find that key. I promise."

Estéban spoke gently.

"Even if you do not, I'm content finally knowing there are others out there like me, pigs who will make a difference in the future."

When Carlos got back to the trailer, he sifted through all his father's possessions again, intent on finding the key so he could free his friend. His father had little, so it took only thirty minutes to go through everything. As he put the last of Juan Pedro's things back in place, Carlos was struck with the most profound thought: what if his father had left the key in their old room at the permanent housing on the property! That was it! He must have hidden it there and forgotten to retrieve it!

But Ricardo Rivera was living there now, and Ricardo was a man who hated both Juan Pedro and his son. Getting inside to search would be a major hurdle to overcome, yet the housing had many common areas from which there was access to the room, and once inside, Carlos knew that space better than anyone.

He rode his bike on over, parked it near the barn and slipped into the building through Señor Gomez' back door. Sliding through the space, he ducked into the hallway that led to the shared bathroom, turned left and headed toward Ricardo's room. His sinuses detected the overwhelming presence of the man's cheap, reeking cologne even before he reached the door. The combination of that stench mixed with persisting pollution from the unfiltered generic cigarettes Ricardo smoked made Carlos sick to the stomach.

Still, he ventured inside the gloomy room. It was already 4:30, but the workers didn't usually return until after five o'clock. He moved about the room in the dark, his hands slipping along flat surfaces into cracks in the corners and along crevices between the baseboards and walls. No key. No key anywhere. Careful not to disturb Ricardo's belongings, he checked the closet floor and shelves. Nothing! Out of ideas, he sighed, giving up. There was no other place left on earth he could think to search.

He was just about to leave the room when he heard Big José's truck die sputtering and the prattle from the men returning from the fields. More alarming for him was the distinctive timbre of Ricardo's low voice and sound of his brand new cowboy boots as he came down the hallway toward the room.

Carlos thought to flee via the window, but Ricardo had set up his new stereo in front of it. Hiding was the only alternative, but the room was so small that the closet was the only place he could go.

Sitting back in the corner of the closet, he covered himself with Ricardo's musty, tobacco smoke and cologne-infused clothes and held his breath. Through the pair of rank boxer shorts on his face, he saw the light come on, and then he heard Ricardo's voice.

"Goddammit! *Who's* been in my room?"

Carlos cringed as he heard the man knock an ashtray to the floor in anger while searching between the bed and the wall. Ricardo stomped over to the door, yanking it open and calling out.

"Hey! Which one of you good-for-nothings has been in my room?"

A voice from outside the door called back.

"Oh, get over yourself, Ricardo. No one wants ta go in your room."

The new foreman's voice trembled with anger.

"No, I'm serious. One of you sonna bitches has been in my room, and I wanna know who it is!"

A second voice returned the anger.

"Aw, shut up Ricardo! No one cares about your stinkin room!"

"So it musta been *you*, José, you bastard. What the hell were you doin in my room?"

It was obvious from the tenor and volume of the answer that José, the largest and most muscular of all the workers, had come into the hallway.

"I wasn't in your room before, Ricardo, but you say one more thing to me like that and I'll come in there and kick your sorry ass, *Mamon!*"

Carlos heard the unique metal twang of a compressed blade snapping open and locking in place.

"You come in my room again, José, and I'll kill you. I swear!"

The hallway was suddenly full of the sound of men tussling. There was the sound of a blow followed by the thud of a body hitting the wall. Apparently, José had gotten the better of Ricardo before the other men pulled them apart, because Carlos could hear Ricardo's groans.

"My nose. You bastard, José! You broke my nose! I'm gonna get you for that, I swear!"

At once Carlos imagined himself alone in the room with a wounded Ricardo, an angry, disgraced man with a knife. He imagined Ricardo finding him in the closet with no one around.

If there was ever a time to get out, he had to do it when all the men were still in the hallway. So throwing off the dirty clothing, he scrambled to his feet and stumbled toward the door, clutching the doorjamb as he looked out.

"Carlos! You little bastard! What were you doin in my room?"

Ricardo's face was bloody as he came at the boy. He grabbed Carlos by the shirt and slammed him into the wall, holding the blade to the boy's throat.

"Tell me now! Goddamit! What were you doin in my room?"

The sound of an explosion shook the hallway. It was so loud that the space seemed surreally quiet and slowed as white powder snowed down on the men's heads and shoulders. All eyes snapped toward the source of the noise where Señor Gomez stood with a shotgun, leveled at Ricardo's face.

"Come on, you piece of shit! Give me half a reason! Make one move on that boy with that knife. Sell-outs like you don't even deserve ta live!"

Señor Gomez pumped the rifle, his finger twitching.

"Come on! Give me a reason, you lousy piece of shit!"

Fear in his eyes, Ricardo slowly raised his hands into the air, loosening his fingers and letting the knife tumble to the floor.

"I wasn't really gonna hurt im. I swear."

"Carlos, venga aquí!"

Responding, Carlos, straightening his shirt, brushed past Ricardo and hurried to a place behind the old man. Eyes widening, Ricardo was certain *el viejo* was going to pull the trigger.

"Señor Gomez! Compasión! Por favor!"

"I could kill you right now. I could tell the police I shot ya ta save the boy's life. Ya think anyone here'll say anything different?"

Ricardo glanced at the other faces in the hall, faces that urged the old man to squeeze the trigger. Big José was the first to vocalize the ambient sentiment.

"Kill im, *Viejo*. He's no good. We'll all say he attacked the boy with that knife."

As the other men nodded in agreement, Ricardo began to shake as sweat ran down his face.

"No! No, Señor Gomez. ¡Compasión! ¡Compasión por favor!"

Orlando Gomez approached the shaking man, touching his wet forehead with the barrel of the shotgun. The sound of Ricardo's irregular, labored breathing filled the hallway.

"I'll do anything you want, *Señor*! I'll *quit* if you want me to!"

Señor Gomez stood there motionless for a half minute, harked and spat on the floor beside Ricardo.

"Move out."

"What?"

"Get your stuff and move out. Let Juan Pedro and Carlos have their room back."

Ricardo protested, albeit carefully.

"But that's not up to me! That's up to Mahler. Even if I move out, that don't mean Juan Pedro can get the room back!"

Señor Gomez was insistent.

"And what if you're dead?"

The protest stopped.

"I'll move out tonight. I swear, I *swear*!"

Señor Gomez never asked Carlos why he had broken into Ricardo's room. Perhaps he already knew. Nonetheless, as Carlos waited for his father in the old man's chamber during the hour after the incident in the hallway, he was struck with a thought that gave him a new hope for freeing Estéban. What if the key for the lock on the cage was in the room of *el viejo*?

Fortunately for Carlos, Señor Gomez was intent on speaking with Señor Mahler about restoring the room down the hall to his father, so after giving the boy instructions to remain inside, the old man was gone. Carlos went to the window and watched as Big José swung the old truck up to the building and helped Señor Gomez get inside.

When the dust from the truck cleared, the boy could see Ricardo loading stereo speakers into his old station wagon in the background. Ricardo stopped a moment, squinting, glaring baleful in the direction of *el viejo's* window, causing Carlos to duck out of sight behind the tattered, dry-rotted curtains. He tiptoed over to make sure the door was locked before he began searching for the key.

Señor Gomez' room was piled high with old chests, boxes filled with souvenirs, crates stuffed with papers and books. All along one wall were shelves full of photo albums. There was little moving space between the furniture, a huge dark brown leather couch and overstuffed orange loveseat.

Before the couch was a metal-framed, glass-topped coffee table, its surface obscured by books, family photos, a tool set, a shot-glass collection, a large Bible, two shoe boxes with descriptions written in Spanish on the outside, heavy dust and three red candles.

The space under the table was filled by three translucent plastic containers, packed with items wrapped in yellowed newspaper. Abutting the couch was the circular table in the cramped corner where the old man ate.

Every inch of the wall space was covered, either with shelving, paintings, bookcases or chests of drawers. A painting of the Virgin of Guadalupe, in a royal green robe, surrounded by a bright halo of light, looked down at Carlos over praying hands.

A microwave oven, attached to the one outlet in the room by a long orange extension cord, sat on the table next to the plates, silverware, a jar of pickled jalapeños, a sack of corn flour, condiments and the seasonings Señor Gomez used for cooking. Señor Gomez was a great cook. He made the most wonderful *menudo* in that microwave! As Carlos looked around the room, there didn't seem to be an inch of empty space anywhere.

Old people, he thought, have way too many things! Finding a key in that over-packed space would be like finding a single flea on a bull. Desperation, however, made Carlos clever.

He knew the lock on the cage had been purchased for the specific purpose of confining Estéban, and that meant wherever it was, it had been put there in the last few days. He knew the old man wouldn't have buried it in a big chest or box out of the way because it would need to be in a convenient location in case of trouble.

As he began to search, he skipped over the dusty items, which probably hadn't been touched in months, and he ignored places that seemed undisturbed. Instead, he concentrated on the areas around the places Señor Gomez either sat or slept: under the couch pillows, on the coffee table, on the dinner table, on the shelving nearby.

Though he worried the old man would be home soon, he continued to search until he actually got lucky. There it was! In a little box in front of an old black-and-white photo of an elderly couple and a little girl! The smooth, black-lacquered box had orange and green flowers painted on top of a lid that flipped open horizontally.

Inside were a gold ring, a few Mexican tarnished silver coins, a locket and various keys. The shiniest key caught Carlos' attention—it was the newest. Even better, there was a tag attached to it.

Trembling with excitement, the boy squinted as he tried to make sense of the word sloppily scribbled in bright blue ink. Then finally, his face blossomed with joy and relief as he understood—"*Cochino.*"

He slipped the key into his pocket and headed for the door. Then he walked toward his bicycle in the dark, hoping Ricardo wasn't still lurking around, got on and started pedaling as fast as he could. Tires bumping along the dirt trail leading to the paved road, he laughed to himself, feeling proud.

How surprised Estéban would be! Estéban, who had once said all humans would prove to be "enemies to my cause." Now a boy would save his life. There would be no "cause" for him without the heroics of the boy who set him free!

The tires screeched horribly and the truck, front brakes engaged, swung 180 degrees before stopping. Carlos, trapped in the headlights, also came to a dead stop. He coughed as the sharp smell of burnt rubber wafted into his lungs.

"Carlito! What the hell are you doin out here?"

The voice was his father's. Juan Pedro was leaning out the passenger window of Big José's truck.

"What are you doin way out here this late?"

At first, Carlos didn't know how to respond. He couldn't tell his father he was going out to see Estéban, but there was almost no other way to explain being so far from the housing, riding in a direction opposite the property's trailer site. Still out of breath, he stuttered through the reply.

"Papa, I, I got scared. I, I thought Ricardo would come back. I was gonna hide out here until Señor Gomez got home."

Juan Pedro opened the truck door, got out and limped toward his son, embracing him.

"When Señor Gomez told me Ricardo pulled a knife on you, I got so mad I was gonna go right over there and kill him on the spot, but he showed up over at the trailer beggin ta talk to me."

He tilted his son's head back, looking into the boy's eyes.

"He begged me to forgive him and said he would have never hurt you."

"Did you forgive him?"

"No—some things you cannot forgive. I told him if he ever came around you again or even talked to you, I'd kill im."

He rubbed his son's head.

"You okay?"

Carlos nodded, smiling. Juan Pedro grabbed his bike, lifting it.

"Get in the back of the truck."

"Why?"

"Señor Gomez talked to Mahler. We're goin' home. I got all our stuff in the back of the truck already."

Carlos balked.

"I, I can ride my bike home."

"No, you won't. You're comin with us and we're gonna get moved back in, and then you and me and Señor Gomez're goin out ta dinner ta celebrate."

"But I—"

Juan Pedro interrupted.

"*No, Chico,* you're comin with us, and that's that."

He thought to sneak out in the middle of the night, but his father was a light sleeper. Then he thought to go early in the morning before school, but he would have never made it back in time to catch the bus. Key in his pocket, he decided to do it after school at three o'clock. His father and the rest of the men would be out in the fields working then. He would hurry home from the bus stop, get on his bike, ride out to the hill where Estéban was being held, unlock the lock and set his friend free. Yes, seven hours and Estéban would finally be free!

The school day seemed unusually long. Carlos watched the clock all afternoon, wondering where Estéban would go, what he would eat, how many other pigs would join him out there. He wondered if he'd ever see Estéban again, if Estéban would remember him, if he would remember all the things they talked about, if his friend would ever turn against him out there. It was a bittersweet day. While Carlos was happy that Estéban would go free, he was sad that he might not ever see his best friend again. Two-thirty finally came.

Scurrying off the bus, Carlos, clutching the key in his sweaty hand, ran to his house, dropped off his books and hopped on his bicycle.

Never stopping once to rest, he pedaled all the way out to the hill only to find that the cage and Estéban were gone! Nothing remained except the bin of dried wild turnips next to the tree and a mound of pig manure in the distance.

Spring had established itself in the valley. Life refashioned itself. Memorial Day that year came right in the middle of the grape flowering period. All around, the vines erupted in bursts of tiny flowers, some white, some too fine to be noticed.

The ground was warming, the sun dallied in the sky a little longer each evening and the skies were ever blue with gentle swells of soothing, temperate air. There were new vines, new wildflowers, new saplings, new chicks, new puppies and new pigs. Yet there was great sadness.

The Mondial owners had set aside a special terraced area for the event. In the elevated section under the trees were seven tables, covered with white tablecloths, lined with water glasses and wineglasses, fine silverware, expensive place settings and dozens of unopened wine bottles. There were other tables further down in the full sun: these had no tablecloths, no glasses, no plates—nothing.

The workers and their families were first to arrive. Without considering otherwise, they went to the bare tables and began situating themselves. Soon there was music: *salsa*, *tejano*, *mexicana* and a mixture of various styles. Several of the workers who had brought guitars sang some of the traditional songs quite well.

As the crowd began to grow, the beer kegs were opened and a huge fire was started in an oversized pit. Several men were carrying a large pig on a thick metal pole with lighter crossbars. It had been splayed open so that his forelegs were extended in each direction. His hind legs were similarly extended.

The men raised him vertical when they reached the pit, and then they lowered the pole and crossbars into slots in a framework, which positioned the pig directly over the glowing coals and fire.

Within minutes the smell of roasting pig flesh filled the air. To many it was a delicious aroma, but it sickened Carlos to the point of nausea. He wanted to go home, but his father made him stay against his will. He wept, unashamed, for an hour, glancing over occasionally as the men began to turn the browning pig.

After an hour and a half, the winery owners and others began to fill the elevated, elaborately set group of tables under the trees. Carlos didn't recognize any of them, but he noticed that Ricardo Rivera and a very pretty girl had been allowed to sit at a table near them along one of the outside fringes. Ricardo seemed out of place up there. No one sat next to him, no one talked to him and he never even got any of the expensive wine they were pouring.

Still, he looked down on the workers from where he sat, an air of contempt contorting his face. His "girlfriend" eventually left his side to help the other women serve food and never returned, so he sat up there alone, ignored and irrelevant. He was a sad, pitiful man, this Ricardo Rivera.

Once the pig was fully roasted, Señor Gomez cut him into pieces, which were distributed about the area. Every table got a healthy portion. Carlos sat there listless as he watched and listened to the people at his table devour his friend. To him, it was a macabre funeral in which the guests were greedily gobbling up the deceased.

He watched as people savagely ripped the flesh from Estéban's bones, often swallowing it without chewing. He thought of all the times he and Estéban had spent together, of all the conversations, of the first day he saw the cute little pig. They had been through so much together, had shared so much. To watch such an end to such a great person was almost too much for Carlos to bear.

Thus, ignoring his father's directive, he stood, thinking to run home and cry in his bed. Señor Gomez, however, was a little too sated and too inebriated to let him go without a little gentle ribbing. He gnawed the meat from one of the pig's bones as he spoke.

"Carlos! Your pig was such a good pig! He was delicious!"

Tears in his eyes, Carlos tried to push past the old man.

"Time for you to grow up, Carlos. Ya gotta realize people are people an pigs are pigs. It's okay ta *like* a pig, ta have a pig for a pet even, but pigs were put here for us ta eat."

Carlos did not look at Señor Gomez. Instead he looked toward the elevated tables where the vineyard owners and their guests sat, enjoying not only Estéban's flesh, but dozens of bottles of wine as well, never realizing for a moment the sacrifices suffered in order for them to enjoy these immoral and unnecessary indulgences.

His father rescued him from the drunken old man, stealing him from the grasp of Señor Gomez. It wasn't often that Juan Pedro showed sensitivity to his son's deep feelings, but this time Carlos believed his father understood. They walked away from the tables, father and son, and stood apart from the activity, watching as they spoke.

Juan Pedro relaxed his arm onto Carlos' slumped shoulders.

"You're sad about Estéban, aren't you?"

The boy cried.

"How *could* you, Papa? How could you kill Estéban? You *knew* how I felt."

Juan Pedro was quick to answer.

"I did not kill Estéban, *chico*. The slaughterhouse picked him up. Whatever they do, they did it over there. I didn't kill im."

The excuse wasn't selling, so Juan Pedro made a different appeal.

"Look, he couldn't have stayed in that cage for all his life. *That* would've been cruel. Is that what you wanted?"

Carlos answered without emotion.

"No, I was gonna let him go."

Juan Pedro turned the boy to look into his eyes.

"How can you *say* that, *Chico*? Estéban—I mean that animal—he tried to kill me!"

"You wouldn't listen to him, Papa. Why wouldn't you just *listen* to him?"

The unguarded answer was a result of Juan Pedro's frustration.

"Because I didn't like what he was sayin! It made me *feel* bad! Okay? It made me feel guilty. I didn't wanna hear it."

Carlos stiffened, looking up.

"So you *did* hear him, didn't you? You heard every word he was sayin?"

Juan Pedro sighed, giving up.

"Yes. Yes, I did. I heard everything he said ta me. But ya gotta understand. The world is not ready for thinkin, talkin pigs. The world'll *never* be ready for thinkin, talkin pigs."

He clutched his son's chin in his right hand, peering into the boy's eyes.

"Look, you can't expect the whole world to allovva sudden give up eatin pork, ta change their habits. And equality for pigs and pigs' rights? That would be crazy! You'd be askin for more trouble than you know."

Cloyed by the scene at the tables, Carlos pulled away from his father, speaking to himself, almost thinking out loud.

"Estéban was right. He was right about all of you. He said you'd never be successful in your own struggle until you learned to recognize the struggle of others."

Juan Pedro seemed confused.

"I dunno about that. All I know is, if all pigs could talk and read and think and were treated like persons, if all pigs were smart like Estéban, what would the world do for bacon?"

Carlos sighed, glancing toward Ricardo, toward the Mondial Vineyards owners and at their guests as they ate his best friend, did their grand toasting and swilled the wine his father, Señor Gomez, Big José and many others labored so hard to produce.

"You're right, Papa, and if all vineyard workers were paid better and had decent housing and plumbing and a little respect, what would the world do for wine?"

Mister Peacock

March 31st ended much like all other days in the life of Mister Thelonious A. Peacock, but it was undoubtedly the last as the man they all knew. It wasn't important that no one, his wife included, called him Thelonious or that he had never in his life been referred to as "Theo."

He had truly earned his title: Mister Peacock. Though he had yet to gain the respect of the world at large, the thriving township of Saratoga, at the heart of the San Francisco Bay Area's opulence, knew every detail of his person, or his image so to say. It was on April 1st, ironically, that Mister Peacock found himself prone on his bed staring insouciantly into a hand mirror.

He had had, from his infancy, an extreme fascination for mirrors. His resourceful grandmother, Martha, had even used them as devices for keeping their little Mister Peacock quiet. As he grew older, however, this "cute" fascination was transformed into an all-consuming obsession.

He needed mirrors, claiming that it was important to know what he looked like, lest he forgot. Confidentially, his only crime against society ever was the theft of a small, circular mirror from a Woolworth's department store, and he, only five years old, was clever enough to escape with the item unnoticed.

Later, though his teenage zeal rivaled the money-making efforts of his peers, he sacrificed the fruit of his labor to his secret obsession. While they bought bright, fast cars, he preferred a vast assortment of mirrors in all shapes and sizes.

The young Mister Peacock never invited friends into his silver-bedecked bedroom for fear they might smudge or damage his precious collection. The family often worried that their bizarre young man would eventually "snap" and be committed to the asylum three blocks away. They secretly believed he'd never amount to anything, but he surprised them all and fared far better than his brothers.

To those who did not know the degree of his edacious obsession, though, he was quite a remarkable young man. While his deeply set eyes always carried a detached expression, his face was handsome and well proportioned. He was the object of many high school girls' affections, but his focus was on his studies and an image that was impeccable.

If ever he was viewed outside the glass walls of his atypical abode, his appearance was impressive. He always wore dark tailored suits with crisp white shirts and colorful imported silken ties. His skin, even without the benefit of cologne, effused a warm, pleasant essence and his hair, teeth, fingernails, and toenails were given meticulous daily attention.

Equally impressive was his scholastic ability, as his instructors often remarked they had never encountered such discipline in youth, and his report cards were unmarked by the unsightly appearance of those letters which were not A's.

It was strange and unexpected, however, that during his high school's commencement ceremonies, Thelonious A. Peacock decided he would thenceforth be called simply "Mister Peacock" by the world around him, which included immediate family and friends.

It was eight o'clock, but Mister Peacock remained in bed on this April 1st morning much later than usual (he was always up by five-thirty). He put the oval hand mirror on the nightstand and rolled over to see himself in a large, red-tinted, wooden, floral-bordered mirror.

This was his favorite by far. He thought about that poignant high school graduation. Back then, he was still far from being the man they all knew.

During his college years at the University of California at Los Angeles, Mister Peacock met a striking young lady who, unwittingly, deepened the degree of his obsession. Although her family lived in Watts, a depressed indigent quarter of the great city, she was a splendid flower nurtured by a loving and proud family.

It was agreed: She would call him Mister Peacock, and he would call her Natalie. He thought Natalie was his perfect match. She was brown-skinned like himself, her face was pleasant and unflawed, and she dressed smartly.

Though she was a woman, he could detect traces of a musculature beneath her mocha toned skin that he thought would prove beneficial during child-bearing years. She was not lacking in intellectual or emotional abilities, as she even understood his exigency for mirrors, admitting she was afflicted with an equal love for music boxes.

But what Mister Peacock liked most about Natalie were her eyes, her large brown eyes. He liked them because they seemed like mirrors, and he could always see himself in them.

Nevertheless, their brief encounter with love ended when Natalie's family learned of Mister Peacock's obsession. Her parents and brothers forbade her to see or speak with him.

Resisting at first, she argued that she loved Mister Peacock and understood his preoccupation with mirrors, but being the dutiful daughter and sister she was, she finally succumbed.

This was indeed a sad time for Mister Peacock. He sulked about it for three complete years. In fact, it was then that he began losing much of his humanity.

Still in his bed, he stared into the huge, red-tinted mirror without expression. He remembered then the real pain of losing his unforgettable Natalie. It was, in fact, during that dark period of his life that their Mister Peacock stepped upon the path to becoming the man they all knew.

It was quite a difficult task for Mister Peacock to move all his mirrors the entire length of the country to New Haven, Connecticut, where he attended law school at Yale University. Intricate precautions were taken to minimize breakage. He had acquired so many mirrors by this time that three moving vans were needed for the mirrors alone.

In Meriden, outside New Haven, he rented a cozy five-bedroom cottage so that he could display them all. It was insignificant to Mister Peacock that he was the only black student in his classes at Yale, but he seldom needed to attend classes.

Because his perspicacity did not go unnoticed by his mentors at the school, he was allowed to work in the fortress of his glass asylum, bring his assignments to private conferences, and attend only for midterms and finals. The arrangement worked well and their Mister Peacock graduated first in his class.

He did not go unnoticed, either, by Caroline Bouvier, who finished second to him. Caroline was attracted to a Mister Peacock very different from the man Natalie had loved. He was now literally "the glass of fashion and the mold of form" since his sessions before his ubiquitous mirrors had increased so inordinately.

Caroline initially had wished to find some flaw in Mister Peacock, but he appeared to be perfect in every way. She subsequently learned of his preoccupation for mirrors and bought a large, red-tinted pier glass, as well as a way to his heart.

On visiting her Mister Peacock at his home, Caroline was frightened by his massive collection and feared he was touched by some strange mental affliction. She convinced herself later, however, that the mirrors merely served to confirm the image he wanted to project, and she openly admired his inexorable dedication to that projection.

He considered Caroline very good for that image, and the two were married (in spite of the protests of Caroline's parents) in an elaborate ceremony four months later.

Caroline rolled over in the bed, clutched the pillow, and muttered some garbled phrase. The motion of the mattress shifted Mister Peacock's focus to the heart-shaped mirror at his feet.

Did he ever really *love* his wife? Or was she an accessory to his countless collection of mirrors? He hoped not. Until this moment, he had never even considered such a thought before. Something had changed just that morning for the man they all knew.

It was simple enough for both Mister Peacock and Caroline to pass California's State Bar examination. They then founded a small firm, which would later be known as the prestigious law firm of Peacock and Peacock *that became a favorite for big business in the state.*

The Peacocks invested their monies in the state's agriculture, acquiring large lots in the Napa Valley, even before viticulture became en vogue for wealthy Californians. A shrewd businessperson, Caroline bought a television station.

Finally, the Peacocks settled in Saratoga, a twentieth century Sybarsis in the San Francisco Bay Area. The construction of the couple's twenty-four bedroom, ten bathroom, four fireplace home stretched six years to completion, and it was indeed magnificent to look upon. It sat on a seventeen-acre estate with two large lakes fed by natural springs.

Unfortunately, the twins came only a few weeks after the Peacocks were situated in their new home, and Mister Peacock was unable to visit his wife and newly-born children during their hospital convalescent period.

He had been hard at work finding mirrors to fill all those rooms. This would have been an impossible task for any one person other than Mister Peacock, whose private collection was ample enough to fill the bottom three levels.

He had previously located seventy percent of the quantity of mirrors the undertaking required. It was simply a matter of showing the home's sixteen servants where and how to hang them. The four careless young men who accidentally broke mirrors were fired with no opportunity for appeal. When all the work was done, Mister Peacock was finally content, or was he?

It was eight-thirty. Mister Peacock slowly looked around his brilliant, glistening, shining room, remembering how he had carefully arranged and hung each mirror. What a splendid job! But he did not smile today. Upon reflection, he realized he never really wanted a home like this. Today, he would have preferred a smaller, cozy place like his father's. Was this dazzling mansion merely an accessory to his great collection of mirrors? He hoped not.

Lying back, he saw himself in the huge concave mirror above the bed. The twins chattered in another room; they were teenagers now and had come to depend on mirrors just like their father. Though the morning sun danced brightly on the glass in their rooms, they were in the dark concerning the man they all knew.

It was on a Thursday afternoon that the twins arrived from the hospital, and Mister Peacock was as proud as he had ever been. To him, his twins were a sign of unmatched prosperity.

The elder, who would be required to carry on the legacy of the family name, was logically called Mister Peacock, Jr., and the younger, a girl with large, soft brown eyes, was called Natalie.

Their Mister Peacock took great care to make them as perfect as he was. He had the young boy's hair cut four times each week and only dressed him in tailor-designed garb. For his daughter, he hired an English noblewoman who kept the little girl always pretty, unsoiled, and mannerable. Unsurprisingly enough, the infants grew beyond their darling crib stage and did the inevitable—they broke mirrors.

The twins, fascinated by their reflections, hurled objects toward the hapless mirrors and pounded them unmercifully with hard objects and heavy hands. It was only in the backrooms and kitchens that servants could secretly laugh at their Mister Peacock as he cringed in abject horror on seeing and hearing his precious mirrors broken one by one. Caroline was surprised her husband and the marriage survived the ordeal since she had spent countless nights comforting and re-gluing her broken Mister Peacock.

After a few long, grief-filled years, the children discovered the beauty in the mirrors and ended their consummate tirades. Mister Peacock could finally take serious steps toward replacing his collection that had been all too quickly depleted.

He had lost some mirrors of great sentimental value in the battle. In fact, the mirror he had secretly stolen as a young boy was among the first to go.

In time, unexpectedly enough, the children demonstrated a great zeal in restoring their home to all its silver magnificence. They openly rued and bereaved the loss of that tiny mirror that had meant so much to their father as a boy.

With the terrible years behind them, the children had taken to the mirror-obsessed ways of their father. They, like him, had become nearly perfect, with hardly a flaw. By this time the family had gained the respect of many people in their California and had the Governor over for dinner twice each month.

The state's chief magistrate had an extreme fondness for the duck's liver soup which Babette, the tiniest French cook, prepared. Naturally, it was at the Governor's suggestion and insistence that Mister Peacock decided to take his first steps into the political arena.

Mister Peacock heard his son out in the hallway scolding a servant for neglecting to wash the inside mirrors of the Ferrari. He was so proud of his son. He wondered then why he had decided not to have additional children.

Were his very children merely an added accessory to his great collection? He hoped not. Were they conceived for the projection of his image? The disturbing questions kept coming!

It was nine-thirty and Caroline still slept. How could any human sleep so late? Gazing across the room toward an eagle-shaped vanity, he remembered that he was now a United States' senator.

The people of California had voted him into office by a landslide margin. Disappointingly enough, many of them probably still slept too, and they had no idea what was happening to the man they all knew.

The election produced one of the most bitter, bloodthirsty and mudslinging rivalries the state of California had ever seen. Mister Peacock's opponent, Darryl Averies, did his best to smear the man they all knew in every conceivable way. He constantly made racist remarks regarding black intellect, while claiming that the work of a one-time associate, Mr. Shockley, would corroborate his assertions.

Averies scrutinized Mister Peacock's past, but finding nothing, he became even more suspicious. Since he found no place to attack Mister Peacock's flawless public image, he decided to assault the person.

He ridiculed their man for being "plastic," "lifeless" and seemingly free of human imperfection, hinting that any man with so perfect an image was hiding some dark, evil secret that would surface to injure the public in the worst way.

In the end, he even challenged their Mister Peacock before his home, disparaging him for an apparent lack of humanity. His bitter remarks, however, would prove to be a poison that would take effect almost five months later. Even so, Mister Peacock had become a U.S. senator.

The stiff mattress began to take its toll on Mister Peacock's back. He had been lying for too long. He looked across his sore left shoulder into what he secretly called "the mirror of mirrors," an ancient accident of ingenuity he had purchased from a private collector who provided proof that the mirror once belonged to *the* Lorenzo de' Medici himself.

According to the legend that accompanied this mirror, it reflected only flaws and imperfection and was thus hated and feared by previous owners. Mister Peacock, though, clung to what little flaw the mirror revealed in him. In fact, the little imperfection he saw was alone what made him feel alive, human.

But this morning, for the first time, the mirror was blank, like a sheet of glass. It revealed no fault. Horrified, he leapt from the bed and thrust his face close to the mirror, but even as he squinted and strained to find the remotest fraction of fault, the remotest fraction of flaw, there was nothing.

At first, he didn't know what to make of it, but the questions kept coming. What was happening to him? Wasn't he human any longer? And what about the job he had to do that day? Was his position as a U.S. senator even an accessory for his image in his incredible collection of mirrors? It couldn't be. What manner of creature was Mister Peacock? Was he the image or was he the man?

The questions stopped. In that instant, Mister Peacock ceased his searching and his questioning, for he innately knew the important answers. The ancient mirror revealed no fault in him because he had lost something—something he believed he had always been losing.

In reality, he had begun losing his humanity from the first day he ever stared into a mirror. The loss of the painfully human Natalie had quickened the process. Now he had become an image of his image, and nothing more.

Desperate, he reached and groped for the final shreds of his fleeting humanity, but it was all too late. In this ancient "mirror of mirrors" below the large, red-tinted, wooden, floral-bordered mirror beside the bed, Thelonious A. Peacock finally saw the perfect image of a man, but he saw no man.

How frightening it was for him then to think of the new position he would have regarding his wife, his children, his mirrors and his constituency. Only a whole human could fulfill the needs those relative positions required.

He then struggled to deny the truth of his greatest fear. The entire process was internal and might be considered unexciting or even disappointing to a shallow mind, but to their Mister Peacock, it was a horrifying reality: he himself had become merely an accessory to his costly collection of mirrors.

Thus with immense fear and great trembling, Thelonious A. Peacock turned away from that mirror to accept the truth, and he undeniably realized he could never again be... the man they all knew.

Till Death Do Us Part

April 1st had always been a terrible day for beginnings, and endings for that matter, but this April 1st was neither. It was a day for celebration. That particular day not only marked the fifteenth wedding anniversary for Sonya Freed, a perfect wife and wonderful mother, but it also marked the end of her twentieth year of service with the Peacock Marketing Division.

She had, in those two decades of dedication, manifested an uncanny ability for obtaining advertising accounts of phenomenal monetary order. For the past twelve years, Sonya was the firm's top producer and highest paid staff member.

Though the competition courted her, she was comfortable at PMD and loyal to the company. Sonya was about five and a half feet tall and of a medium build. Her silky dark brown hair, cut in a page-boy style, outlined a pretty face that beamed with uncommon beauty every time Sonya flashed even a casual smile.

She had large hazel eyes and soft smooth brown skin. But it was neither her long, shapely legs, her firm, ample breasts, nor her professional style of dress and comportment that drew the firm's most important clients to Sonya.

It was, rather, a certain practicality in her that left agape many a mouth. This level-headedness endeared her to husband, Sigmund, who, though he hated his name, felt honored to share it with Sonya.

It was on the morning of that fifteenth wedding anniversary that the couple renewed their wedding vows according to the wishes of Sigmund, who said proudest the words: Till death do us part. Tears in his eyes, he kissed the dazzling ring on her finger.

He asked Sonya to remain at home for the day so the couple might lovingly recall all the joy of the past fifteen years, but the practical Sonya, cognizant of her indispensability on the job, said an amorous goodbye and was off to work.

Sonya had started at the Peacock Marketing Division when she was scarcely eighteen, and the company had been wonderfully accommodative by assigning her working periods around her college class schedules.

Upon graduation, Sonya accepted a lucrative full-time position offered by Mrs. Peacock in person. Even though the modest Sonya would never admit to it, she had contributed in key ways to the company's great success.

Many believed she excelled, in part, because she was so well-ordered. There was a definite structure to Sonya's working day: she arrived every morning at precisely seven thirty-nine; her first appointment convened at eight-thirty sharp; if she was in the office, her early break began at exactly ten-thirty and lasted not a second longer than ten forty-five.

At ten thirty-three, Sonya always ate an old-fashioned buttermilk donut with coffee at the same table in the same chair, a habit she had held for the entire twenty years. In fact, by means of simple multiplication and company records, it could be determined that she had eaten exactly four thousand, eight hundred, and seventy-nine old-fashioned buttermilk donuts on her breaks before that day.

As fate would have it, the company manager and a group of camera-flashing admirers from the newspapers and business magazines interrupted her break on that April 1st morning.

Her manager, in a stentorian voice, presented her a certificate, a thick stack of company stock and a gold company ring. Sonya was surprised and flattered, but she thought the ring was quite ugly, and she decided to try it on only for sake of politeness.

Without thinking, she thought to remove her wedding ring, but it would not budge. She laughed. Again she tried to remove the ring but had the same result. Everybody laughed.

Joking, one man told her that she had perhaps gained a little weight in the past fifteen years, and that perhaps she should "lay off the buttermilk donuts."

An embarrassed Sonya tried the ring on another finger and all rejoiced. They sang in her honor, and after cutting a cake and pouring her a glass of French champagne, they left her to resume her structured routine.

Sonya hardly touched her lunch that afternoon. The wedding ring bothered her more every time she looked at it. Why wouldn't it move? The twisting and pulling and wrenching only made her more frustrated. A waiter, noticing some problem with this regular customer, asked her if the food was to her liking. She hadn't even touched the presently-cold Salmon Florentine. She had him take it away and ordered a stiff drink.

Sitting there, reflecting over the past fifteen years, she finally came to the conclusion that she had never removed the ring since Sigmund had slipped it around her finger on that first wedding day. Strangely, as if that fact made any difference whatsoever, Sonya felt all the more resolved to remove the ring.

Sonya's eldest daughter, with the help of her grandmother, had prepared a special anniversary dinner for her parents that evening. Then all the children spent the night with Sonya's brother's family so that Sonya and Sigmund could have a romantic night, but Sonya would eat nothing.

She had convinced herself that she had gained weight, and she wanted to slim down in the hope that the ring might release its grip. Sigmund, believing his wife's story about an oversized lunch and consequential indigestion, politely excused her to the bedroom.

Even in bed, Sonya ignored Sigmund and continued to assault the ring beneath the sheets, while he, resigning romance for the night, read a witch doctor story by African writer Camara Laye.

Sigmund's sporadic laughing made his wife wonder if he was, in part, responsible for her problem. Had he and some African witch doctor colluded years ago to produce the strange ring? No. Sigmund did not believe in magic. It was their anniversary night, but that fact had been eclipsed by her passion for the ring.

Consequently, when the lights went out and Sigmund closed in to do that thing he did one night each week, Sonya demurely excused herself to the bathroom. In the secrecy of the bathroom, she made numerous soapy and lubricated attempts to free herself of the ring, but nothing worked. Exhausted, she went to bed just as the sun was beginning to rise.

She messed over the Eggs Benedict the youngest daughter had prepared. She simply could take no food into her system on that following morning. When it became seven-thirty, she decided to call in sick for the day.

In her entire twenty-year career at PMD, she had never missed a day of work for any reason, but she really did feel sick that day—sick of everything around her. At the heart of this illness was the thing wrapped stubbornly about her finger.

Frustrated, she ran to the garage, pried open her husband's toolshed, used wrenches and pliers and vise-grips in an attempt to remove the ring, but the eerie object still clung to her finger.

Then she abandoned all control and did not worry about damaging the precious ring. She tried caustic chemicals, metal cutters, files and myriad other tools before her patience was exhausted and her finger throbbed with pain, but the ring remained without a scratch!

Feeling defeated, she went back to the kitchen and stewed in her favorite chair. The youngest daughter probably had no idea how viciously her mother would react upon being offered an old-fashioned buttermilk donut at ten thirty-three that morning and will probably never offer one to anyone again.

Sonya's pixilated apology was accepted more from fear than from understanding. Her entire personality seemed to have changed overnight. In any event, Sonya resolved to herself what would be required to effect release from the ring: It was necessary to fast to lose any weight she may have gained over the years.

She did not eat so much as a raisin for the next twenty-two days, and she lost a tremendous amount of weight. In fact, there were even times when Sigmund failed to recognize his wife in the distance for her slighter appearance. She became gaunt and poor.

The PMD executives and working associates were at odds about what had happened to their "woman of practicality." Some suggested she had possibly been infected by an exotic intestinal parasite introduced to her system when the Freeds took a Brazilian vacation four months earlier.

Her immediate manager arranged a complete physical for her, but the brilliant Dr. Nelson could find no bug of South American origin attached to Sonya. If there was a bug, it was coiled around her finger—a South African gold species with a single marquis-cut diamond, surrounded by six tiny alternating chips of ruby, emerald and an unpronounceable stone.

In spite of the loss of thirty-one pounds, her wedding ring still lay frozen to her finger. Then Sonya began to tip the scales of reason. She decided to abandon all conventional means for removing the ring and put her faith in the workings of other worlds.

The first leg of Sonya's trip, her flight to Miami, was comfortable enough, but the prop plane and subsequent swamp-boat journey into the secret places of the steamy Everglades left little to be desired. Miz Nona's small village hut lacked all the conveniences of home: There was no running water, no electricity and no *Wall Street Journal*.

There was, however, an assortment of spider-like creatures, snakes and grotesque life forms Sonya had never seen before. There was an animal Miz Nona called the "undoo," a seemingly reptilian creature covered with coarse, jet-black hairs. Its head was three times its body size, and it subsisted solely on alligator eggs.

Miz Nona was a voodoo woman whose ritual magic came with her family from the people of the Congo River basin. She had agreed to "exorcise" the ring from Sonya's finger. Hanging from a braided leather cord around her neck was a dreadful fetish with demonic glassy eyes.

Its body was pierced with nails and tacks of varying sizes, and it was shrouded in cloth and leather garments. Miz Nona sat Sonya at the base of her two obese legs, which resembled gnarled tree trunks, and muttered some African chant in her gruff and coarse voice.

The room stirred with invisible movement and a rank, bone-cutting odor gagged Sonya to the point of nausea, but as instructed, she did not move. Malevolent, unseen voices and chilling laughs were heard before the door flew open, and then all was still.

Into that village hut walked a chicken of incredible proportions. The bird was almost seven feet tall! Certain the gimmick was that this was a man in a chicken suit, Sonya almost laughed aloud, but all at once, Miz Nona leaped onto the giant chicken and with much effort held it down by her sheer gravity alone while the undoo attacked it with its razor-sharp teeth.

A moment later, blood covered everything in the room, including a terrified Sonya, and the chicken fluttered one last time.

Quickly, Miz Nona split the bird's abdomen with a sharp knife and cut away a yellow, dripping mass of fat. She had to act fast, because no sooner had the chicken died did its flesh begin to boil and evaporate so that, in the end, only the heap of adipose tissue in the bloody, sweating, exhausted Miz Nona's arms remained.

After paying fourteen hundred dollars for the service, Sonya left with a handful of putrid chicken fat, which she was to hold in her hand for two weeks "at all costs." Miz Nona assured her that the ring would loosen its grip when the fat disappeared.

The only thing worse than the terror of Sonya's experience in Florida was the smell of that chicken fat. The odor was unbearable even from great distances. Sigmund, the children, and the dog stayed in a hotel for two the weeks to avoid the smell and an additional twelve days to air out the house.

The top brass and fellow associates at PMD were not so accommodating. A mere five minutes after Sonya entered the building, the odor pervaded all thirty-nine stories. She was fined for air-cleaning fees and loss of production time due to evacuation and was forced to take a mandatory leave of absence pending a mental evaluation by a psychiatrist.

The chicken fat disappeared in two weeks just as Miz Nona had promised, but the ring shone there, unaffected. Miz Nona refunded Sonya's money, and she admitted that her magic was no match against the power of the ring.

By this time, Sonya was frenetic, desperate. She was determined to escape the ring at all costs. She no longer cared for Sigmund or the children or even the dog for that matter.

In a frenzy, she decided she would have the finger amputated! Amputation seemed like the one sure solution, but there was even a problem in that: She could find no doctor who would perform the procedure for her reasons. Further, digital amputation was a calculated risk because the ring was situated on that particular finger in such a way that a fatality could result. If it had been any other finger, the amputation could have been performed.

Unwilling to give up easily, Sonya went from doctor to doctor from California to Maine, but no one was willing to assume the risk. She paid a lawyer to draw up papers releasing doctors from any blame or legal repercussions, and she offered ridiculous amounts of money, but she was finally advised to seek psychiatric help.

At last, she convinced herself the doctors were lying and decided to sever the finger by her own power, but she temporarily lost courage and resolve after nursing her son's broken and bleeding nose after a bicycle accident.

With renewed strength, she set an actual self-amputation date for herself and would have carried out the task if she had not read about a doctor in Mexico whose specialty was in removing rings. Using unconventional methods and new, untried techniques, he had yet to be foiled by a stubborn ring. Sonya prepared to travel to Mexico.

Sigmund finally put his size ten-and-a-half foot down. He was tired of his wife running all over the country to satisfy her outrageous passion. He told her she absolutely could not go to Mexico and that she would have to see a psychiatrist and go back to work at PMD.

A bitter argument ensued in which Sigmund revealed all the hurt and pain Sonya had put him through in her obsession to remove the ring. He tried to recall the love they once felt and reminded her of the promises they had made to each other.

Finally, she broke. With much crying, she apologized for the changes in her behavior and confessed that she didn't understand what had happened. She begged to take this one final trip to Mexico and promised it to be her last.

The smiling, ever-accommodating Sigmund loved his wife and wanted to see her happy, so he decided to accompany his wife to Mexico. He viewed the trip as something of a late anniversary celebration since their last had not been memorable.

Mexico City was warm and spirited and expensive as always. The couple enjoyed a cozy dinner of native entrees with the company of mariachi strings. It was the most romantic evening the couple had ever had. They talked. They giggled like kids. They made love. Sonya would go see the doctor in Pachuca the next day and, hopefully, the ring would come off.

Pachuca was quite a piece from Mexico City, and the ride seemed much longer than thirty miles on those uncomfortable mules. The doctor was an American, Chet Walker, who had come to Mexico because his practices were not yet accepted by the American Medical Association.

He was knowledgeable about rings and medicine, and he had handled many patients like Sonya—with a one hundred percent success rate! He went to work with acupuncture needles, drug injections and even goose grease. He had worked for four days before he realized all his efforts yielded no result, and he believed he could charge the Freeds nothing for his first failure.

Finally, after all that had happened since she first tried to remove the ring on their fifteenth anniversary, Sonya smiled and accepted the fact that the ring was there to stay. She would never again attempt to remove it.

Sigmund, however, had developed a terrible case of indigestion from eating contaminated food. He was flown home to Los Angeles and hospitalized at once. The nefarious virus swept through his weakened body. He experienced so many chills that his nerves themselves were tired of firing. He screamed in seething pain even at Sonya's gentle touch.

Dr. Nelson said there was nothing she or anyone else could do. Sonya did not even take note of the moment that the ring began to loosen its grip. No, she was too busy realizing the foolishness and vanity of her actions during the past few months.

Sigmund became delirious as many do in the last moments. He confessed his great love for Sonya with his dying breath. She agonized on feeling the very spirit of life leave his body. Weeping, Sonya remained beside the bed until a minister came in to escort her out.

Leaving the bed, she chanced to glance upon her hand. How bare and ugly it seemed! The ring! It had fallen off in the bed at the very moment that Sigmund passed away.

Now in a state of shock, Sonya Freed looked at the minister who reminded her of those words Sigmund had always said so proudly: *Till Death Do Us Part.*

ANTHROPOPHAGI

Though the world will never know it, JC would have been an excellent marine biologist. It was his dream. But he had been forced out of San Francisco University in the middle of his senior year. Not long after, he started work as a community service officer and, after working and advancing for eleven years, he had become a common detective assigned to the marina in the remote northern California coastal town of Syracuse.

At five feet eight inches tall, this curly-haired, olive-skinned man of thirty-three years was handsome in an odd way. He was impossible to miss even in a large crowd and possessed great personal charm and presence.

JC Ransom was the son of an impoverished South San Francisco fisherman who had entered the University on an Educational Opportunity Program, and he had maintained the necessary grades.

Yet despite his hard work and a genuine love of life in the sea, he was disliked by most of his professors. This was because, instead of focusing on the theories and notions of his teachers, he invented his own and held his own untested ideas in higher esteem than theirs.

He rejected evolution as a plausible and accurate depiction of change in favor of what he called "a higher and baser law," claiming "life on Earth had always pursued a sentient, intelligent direction."

Further, he held romantic notions about sea monsters, sea serpents and other creatures that did not exist. His bold rejection of all conventionality caused even department heads to worry. This "loose canon" could someday be an embarrassment to the school.

During his senior year, a loose confederacy of professors conspired and determined he would never graduate from USF, taking the necessary action of flunking him in their courses. As a result, he was ultimately expelled from the school for academic failure. While he appealed to the University for clemency, the professors even challenged the appeal. Frustrated with the school, he gave up his ambition for a career in marine biology and went up north to make a new life for himself.

Ironically, the waves at the beach rolled in gently on the morning of April 1st. The winds seemed to sing a symphony to the glory of a brilliant sunrise as mousse-capped ripples lapped the gleaming gold-speckled sands.

It was as if the tiny swells carried the form of the goddess Aphrodite herself, but the goddess who actually sprang from their foam would change JC's life beyond recognition and lead him to his eventual destiny.

In the two years before being appointed detective at the Syracuse Marina, JC had been on loan at the Tides Marina in Bodega Bay a few miles south. He hated the new job at Syracuse for its predictability.

He hadn't seen a single day's excitement in three years on the cool beach of the little-populated community where crime was non-existent. A phone call from a hysterical city mayor on that April 1st morning would change all that.

It was teenager Will Hurt who discovered the body, or more precisely, the half-body of an attractive girl swaying back and forth in the cool, frothy tide pool, and even then the multitudinous scavengers of that delicately structured community had begun filling their bodies with the fortuitous meal. Will had added to their feasting with portions from his own stomach.

Within the hour, a great crowd had assembled around the little pool, each person horrified, yet no one could avert unblinking eyes to less disturbing sights.

JC arrived with the small town's bravest and most important men. The sheriff would check the nude half-body for fingerprints and the mayor, who would put a robe on the girl so the children would at last be allowed to view her. Finally, she was transported to the hospital laboratory where experts would attempt to determine the cause of death.

JC perused a copy of the lab analysis as he examined the girl's lovely body. Because the water hadn't yet penetrated her soft, tender skin, it seemed that she had only recently been killed. Her beauty had been preserved intact: while her face captured all the grace, refinement, and delicacy of the classic ideal, the subtle roundness and richness of her body was a romantic marvel. At once, he fell in love with the girl, but he wouldn't dare show it.

The townspeople had countless questions and theories about the girl and cause of death. Most people concluded, however, that the girl had been killed by a shark "like the one in that terrible movie."

Some could remember another such incident from a warm day in May of 1959. As a teenager and his girlfriend were swimming and gamboling not far from the Golden Gate Bridge, a vicious great white had attacked, killing the boy and mangling his body.

In examining this girl's body in greater detail, JC noted that it had been severed cleanly in the area just above the waist, but there were no other wounds or abrasions on the rest of the body.

Anyone even vaguely familiar with sharks and their methods of attack would know the girl was not the victim of a great white or any other shark, as shark bites result in jagged wounds. JC could not help but come to the conclusion that the sea held no creature capable of such a deed.

This murder was the wicked working of man. This woman's voluptuous body had been divided by a very sharp knife. JC felt angry that any person could be so crass and callous to kill this beautiful girl; he felt aggrieved that he would never be able to know her, never be able to kiss her.

But why had she been murdered and hacked in half like this? Had some pervert raped her and later divided her body to carry it away and continue satisfying his sick desires? The very thought was repulsive. JC stayed with her until two attendants arrived to transport her to the morgue where she would be examined more carefully.

In the town, JC questioned Will and other bystanders about events of the past few days. No one could identify the victim. No one had ever seen her before. She was unknown in this tightly knit community were everyone knew everyone else and everyone else's business. No one had seen any strange teenagers hanging around town or on the beach.

Occasionally, in the summer months, those weird, artsy-type teenagers dressed in black came up from the big cities to sully the otherwise tranquil beaches with drugs, sex, and loud rock music, but this was April; the teenagers were still in school. Not a one had been sighted in months. Syracuse was a small, peaceful place where violence was unheard of and murder, until then, was literally unfathomable.

While the sheriff looked to his detective to do the investigative work and catch the murderer, JC didn't know where to begin. He had neither suspect nor motive. Finally, he thought he would have to take a hike a little ways up the coast to visit an old black man whose name was Claude Crabbe, but Claude was a strange one.

Reluctant to confront the old man, JC put the trip off for another day. Yet if anyone could possibly shed light on this bizarre and extraordinary event, it would definitely be the strange old man, as no creature or action of the sea could escape his ever-searching, cold, black, shifting eyes.

JC arrived at the morgue after the examination by the coroner was through, and the foul-odored troll of a man, whose hand felt even colder than death, left after eating a meal that smelled far more wicked than any of the rotting corpses decomposing on the tables in the small room.

JC had attempted to get Claude on the telephone earlier, but there had been no answer. No doubt, he was out fishing again. Everyone knew he fished on every day of the year, rain or shine.

The murdered woman's naked body rested on a smooth marble slab before the obsessed detective in the pungent refrigerated room. JC covered her with a silk robe before rescuing that half-body from the unnaturally cold environment. No one saw him carry it out of the building, and no one saw him load it into his car.

In the privacy of his remote beach house, he removed the robe to look on the woman's nakedness in more detail. Fortunately, the fiendish coroner had been loath to do anything to ruin her.

All the men who had seen the girl were captivated by her beauty, but she hypnotized JC. His eyes were transfixed on her for two full hours before he gathered the resolve and sense to remember his plan. How nice it would have been to kiss her lips! JC had become obsessed with her. He closed his eyes and forced himself to look away in order to prepare himself for what he had planned to do from the first moment he saw her.

It was Will Hurt who, unknown to the busy detective, had peeked into the tiny room to see what JC was doing to the half-body of that poor murdered girl. Thus it was Will, who in a paroxysm of uninformed horror, streaked out into the briny bay breezes to call for help.

JC eventually finished with the dead girl's body and was prepared to deliver it to the morgue when persons began to appear around the small beach house from the deeper shadows of the night. In a little while, the entire population of Syracuse stood around the house.

As a minister called down evil on JC and condemned him by citing Bible texts, several strong men busted into the house and dragged the seeming perverse detective out. They spat in his face, pounded him with heavy fists, and tied him to a tree.

What was happening to their town? First a murder, and now this unthinkable act of depravity! Even the elders of the community, those most opposed to violence, approved of any punishment visited upon JC.

Many questions were posed during the informal tribunal: Why had he taken the body? What unnatural thing had he done to it? Was he the murderer?

When he was finally allowed to answer, he explained that he had taken her to perform a few medical tests on the body. He said he had discovered that a deadly virus—a virus unknown to the medical world—that had afflicted the girl's body.

Naturally, the simple Syracuse townsfolk did not believe him. Instead, they insisted he had sinned against Nature. A "virus" indeed! The idea of such an imaginary death-dealing organism was beyond their comprehension.

They did not believe in education and took great pride in their self-proclaimed "righteous" and "unspoiled" community. After all, Syracuse was unafflicted by the problems and challenges facing all the so-called "advanced" and "hi-tech" communities.

But this wicked and unnatural outsider would change all that! This demon spoke of unseen killers and witch's brews and potions and blinking instruments that challenged and opposed the very law of Nature!

All creatures on Earth must live and die by the law! And this perverted detective! Had his utter contempt for morality caused him to do the gross and unnatural things he had done to the dead girl's body? How horrendous! This worldly man had lived a life of ignorance and indifference toward any sort of decency, and now he would die for it.

The crowds cheered as his shoulders, heated from the whipping, swelled with blood and finally flowed scarlet rivulets down his chest.

As the beatings continued, JC lost consciousness. A sudden darkness of the sky followed, and a violent storm began to rage against the fearful community. Cringing in the rain, the most troubling fears of the townspeople were confirmed. What manner of fiend *was* this JC?

In sheer panic, the trembling town elders moved the crowd to action and JC's body was taken to a high precipice and pitched into the roaring, growling, and loudly bellowing sea. In the "trial by sea," this spoiler would do battle with the invincible law of Nature itself, but JC had been born to thwart that Law.

It was Will Hurt who pulled JC's body from the sea under a bleak sky three days later, and it was Will who gawked at the specter in utter amazement as JC drew in troubled breaths. In reality, Will had always admired JC and hoped he would survive the trial.

Not long after the detective sat up, however, the truncated body of yet another unclothed woman materialized in the suds of a puissant swell, and she smelled as foul as she appeared.

Her flesh had been eaten to the bone in places and was still being consumed by a greenish-brown fungus that seemed a bit moldy after its slimy casing yielded way. Her teeth were razor-sharp, serrated, and in need of cleaning to remove the rotted and stinking chunks of spoiled flesh from between them.

This girl's face, unlike the face of the other victim, held an expression of sheer terror, pain and agony. Surely the final scope of her presently waterlogged eyes had held the sight of the monster that had, with a metal blade, hacked into the slender abdomen to rend asunder her body.

By this time, Will had fallen to the ground, and his body was charged with uncontrollable muscle spasms of such intensity that JC, exerting all the strength his weakened body could muster, was barely able to hold him down.

Another dead half-body seemed to crawl up the gloomy beach under an overcast sky as the last series of convulsions ran through Will's form. The teenager shivered there, his eyes glossy and his skin becoming blue; he was in a state of shock and needed shelter and warmth.

Scanning the shoreline, JC spotted a cabin and recognized it as Claude Crabbe's. He wasn't sure he would receive any help from the mean old man, but the aegis afforded by the little dilapidated shack on the hill was absolutely necessary. With great effort, JC lifted the inert boy's body, cradling it between shaking shoulders, and slowly stumbled and tripped his way to Claude's door.

"I git cha a coupla blankets, but that boy cain't come up in here!"

The old man, unfortunately, would not have the sick or maligned in his mildewy abode and soothed his conscience by saying he was old and had no reason to invite Death into his door.

Claude was a squat, round-bellied, cantankerous old sort who had been known to scold individuals in the community for leaving broken bottles and coffee grounds in the garbage cans he raided so often. Little wonder because Claude, being the only Negro individual in that white, old-fashioned, bigoted community, had not lived the most pleasant of lives.

He had injured his left arm in an accident after his Caucasian wife mysteriously disappeared. There had been an investigation and Claude had been suspected of foul play, but his wife's body had never been recovered.

While there was no proof of it, some believed he had murdered her and had found some ingenious way of disposing of her remains. A few even suggested he had eaten her fatty flesh.

Not long after, he lost his left arm when his small fishing boat sank for some unknown reason on the treacherously rocky and little traveled shoreline of the foggy coast a few miles north of Syracuse. His left arm ended in a metal pincer, which he could open and close by flexing the muscles in his arm.

Consequently, his living as a fisherman had taken a turn for the worse in the twenty years since the accident. Presently, his table welcomed any creature he was lucky enough to gaff with his metal pincer—dead or alive.

His body was festered with bleeding sores, and brave parasites would occasionally cross the furrows of his wrinkled brow. Claude's large chest and potted stomach almost seemed humorous placed upon his stick legs, but no one ever laughed. In truth, there were many winters in which Claude nearly starved to death.

Waddling a little as he dropped the blankets at JC's feet on the porch, the old black man spat out his cigar and wetted his thick lips, looking down with contempt upon the unsteady young man.

"Ya shoulda threw im back out in the wata. There's trash out dere dat'll eat im up—crabs, squids, little ol starfishes. Mebbee deya grow bigga for it an we could eat dem. You messin up da cycle, boy."

The old man laughed, but JC knew he was serious. The young detective asked a question.

"This kid might die, Mr. Crabbe. He's in shock. He might lose his life. Don't you care about that?"

"There ain't no such thang as carin when you hongry, boy. Only thang ya cares about is some food. Carin ain't nevva been fa folks like me. It's only fa dem folks wanna make somethin outa nothin an starve fa it. A main's gotta eat for he kin thank ta do anathang else. It's a law a life!"

JC felt sorry for the old man.

"I think he'll be all right."

He looked deeper into the man's eyes and saw his father.

"How are *you* doing? You getting enough to eat?"

Claude did not want pity.

"You jus warry bout yaself, boy! Ah'm eatin fine! I gots me a good fishin place where Ah catches all the fish Ah want nah. Got ma freeza fulla em. But Ah tell ya, dey gettin all fished out."

He laughed.

"What's funny?"

"Well ya know, dey's da same kinda fish Ah was gettin at when ma boat sunk an Ah los ma arm. Dey schoolin fish, but Ah kin get em one atta time. Come'n take a look in ma frigerata."

Claude showed the younger man the large fish portions in the squeaking, meat-packed freezer. He offered to fry up some, but JC, concerned for Will outside, went to check the boy.

Upon re-entering the cabin, JC realized that he had been wrong in his assessment of the old man. While Claude initially seemed mean and uncaring, he really did have a warm, friendly side and a sense of humor.

JC took a seat by the fire and smiled at the old man.

"Tell me more about these fish you've been catching."

"Well nah JC, dey useta hang out in da rocks... till a white flagboat comin up outa Mexico or one a dem places down dere wrecked inta the rocks by em. Den dey all got weak an started swimmin by my boat like dey was sick or somethin, so Ah helped mahself. Dey *is* sick an rotten—mosta ems no good fa eatin, so Ah takes what's good an throws da rest away."

JC's interest continued to grow.

"Had you ever caught one before the Mexican ship crashed?"

"Nope. None. Useta be real tricky. Tricked me when Ah was a young sportin man like you—made me lose ma boat an eber'thang. One of em took ma arm. But dey cain't trick me like dat no more. Too old and too wise fa dat!"

JC watched as the old man took up a good-sized log in his pincer and gently placed it on the sizzling fire.

"What do these fish *look* like?"

"Gotta big, funny-lookin head. Kinda got antennas... like a gooseyfish."

"I see. Thank you, Mr. Crabbe. Thank you for everything."

With renewed strength, JC took the recovering Will Hurt by the arm, borrowed an old burlap sack large enough for one of the half-bodies and slowly headed off down the beach. Claude, for his part, was in the water, and he miraculously rowed the tiny boat over crashing breakers en route to his mysterious fishing grounds.

JC's lab would have been considered primitive and stone-aged according to standards of modern-day technology, but it was the most magical temple the young and impressionable Will had ever seen. In fact, it was this very magnificent display of beeping, blinking, lighted instruments and bubbling test tubes that caused Will to eventually leave Syracuse to become a brilliant research scientist.

In any event, JC and Will worked for fifteen days in the secluded laboratory before they produced an antibiotic solution. The redolent, decaying flesh of the half-woman had become glued to the table as it dried.

After culturing a strain of the pathogenic bacteria from her tissue and isolating the proper antigen from his own blood, he was able to produce two hundred milliliters of a greenish-brown, opaque, odorless liquid.

He monitored Claude for two complete days in an attempt to discover the hidden rocky fishing spot and the fish Claude was supposedly catching. In the end, however, an approximation of the remote, foggy location had to suffice.

Equipped with several syringes and a green liquid-filled flask, the detective paddled his boat for miles along the shoreline over a strangely white-covered ocean floor to no avail. Not a creature of earth, air, or sea could be spotted on a coast that once teemed with animal life.

While rowing along in the open water, JC was certain that on two separate occasions he had hit a rock or something. In one instance, he even thought that some creature had attempted to overturn the small boat.

Just as he turned the boat around to head for home, he heard a terrible scratching sound coming from under its hull. This sound grew constantly louder until... *Crash!* He was in the water and the little upturned boat was moving away from him against the current as it sank. By this time, the shoreline was at least a mile in the distance.

As his clothing and boots took in water, he struggled along and splashed his way to an ancient piece of driftwood bearing the inscription *Alea Iacta Est*. He was attacked by some manner of sea predator only seconds before Claude came along and finally dragged his shivering body from the water.

A jagged circular three-inch area of tender flesh just below his right hip had been shredded and devoured by some bold predator, possibly a small shark. JC grimaced and rolled from side to side in pain as he lay among the bloody, silvery, tiny-scaled fish bodies in the hull of Claude's boat.

"Went out fishin, did ja, JC? Almos got ate up yaself! Ya know, ya *ain't* no fishermain if ya don't know da law. Ya know what da law *really* is, Boy?"

He groaned a quivering reply.

"You saved my life! No, I don't know what the law is. Tell, tell me!"

"Aw, Boy! Like *you* gonna undastan! Ya do betta off jus goin on back ta dem white folks in dat gadammed honky town."

In the discomfort of Claude's dark, dank, moldy and smelly wooden shack, JC applied an herbal poultice to the animal bite to reduce the pain.

The blue-trimmed orange flames silently raged in the un-mortared stone fireplace while, on a set of stones within, a large frying pan filled with hot grease and thick fish slabs spattered and hissed in protest to the condensation of moisture dripping from the cut and hissing end of a green branch. As night fell outside the house, the bay fog had, like a living, breathing creature, slinked across the water's calm surface to engulf the shack.

Within, JC worried that the savage animal bites causing such a throbbing in his hip and leg carried the deadly flesh-eating disease that had so perversely affected life in the area.

Though he had lost everything in the boat, he had managed to save two full syringes of the green antibiotic cure for the virus, and he pumped the contents of one into a crooked vein in his shaking forearm.

"Hope ya ain't shootin up no drugs, Boy, cuz Ah don't go fa nunna dat in here!"

JC was taken by surprise.

"Uh, no! This isn't drugs. I just gave myself an antibiotic shot."

Claude stared at the young man who, self-conscious, put the syringe away. JC continued uneasily.

"I thought the wound might be infected and didn't want to take any chances."

"It's not drugs?"

"No, it's medicine."

"Medicine is drugs, ain't it?"

"I, I guess so."

"Den you takin drugs. Don't do dat no more in here."

After a moment, he smiled at JC

"Well, dinner's as ready as it's getting, an Ah ain't gettin no younga waitin fa ya."

Greedily, Claude and JC filled their stomachs to capacity with fish, bread and cheap wine. Then they stretched out like lazy dogs for a moment to feel the warmth of the fire. After thinking for a while, JC turned to the old black man.

"I don't know if I told you, but my father was a fisherman like you..."

Slowly Claude grinned.

"Den he didn't thank ta teach *ya* anathang?"

JC bowed his head.

"It's not that he didn't try. I just never wanted to learn. He useta beg me to go out with him, but I never wanted to. I wasn't a good son to him, Mr. Crabbe. I resented my father because he wasn't rich and successful. He never took the time to tell me things, to explain things about life to me, but that was only because I never let him. He tried."

His eyes watered as he looked up.

"Now I'd give anything to have gone fishing with him. You see, it wasn't just me. I had a rough childhood. My father was an alcoholic and my mother was—"

Claude interrupted matter-of-factly as he spat into the fire.

"Black. Yo momma was black."

"She was three-quarters black. How'd you know?"

The old man smiled, not looking at JC.

"By ma wife, Ah had a boy looked jus like you. Mebbee not as good-lookin and smart, but he was a lot like you round the eyes an nose."

Claude rose, went to the hearth and poked at the fire before putting on another log.

"*Ma* boy clownin round fell off da boat one day when he was bout fifteen. We all tried ta pull him back up ta da boat, but alla sudden, some kinda animal pullt him on down. Jus yanked im down like a bobbin on a fishin line. We looked all ova fa two, three days, but we could nevva catch up with his body. Disappeared. Musta got all eaten up in dat ocean."

Claude's eyes were fixed on an invisible screen in the distance; the cheek muscle under his left eye twitched as he watched a horrific rerun that had played a few times nightly since that day. A tear ran down his wrinkled face, filling his overlarge pores with brine.

"An ma wife—she nevva got ova it."

He paused.

"Naw, nevva got ova it."

Looking down at JC, he wagged his head.

"Ah didn't kill ma wife. Everbody wants ta say Ah did, but Ah didn't. Ah *loved* dat woman. She jus never got ova our boy's death. One night, she jus broke all down an gave up. Walked inta da wata."

He wiped his eyes and blew his nose on the sleeve covering his good arm. Another scene played on the invisible screen.

"A bad, rainy, stormy night. Big, wild waves crashin inta the rocks. Wind, lightnin. An she jus walked inta da wata. I nevva saw her again. Got eaten up out there."

Moving away from the personal revelation, Claude began to speak in more of a philosophical tone.

"Ah been a fishermain all ma life, an Ah calls mahself a fishermain cuz Ah do what dey all do. Ah makes nets, Ah sets traps, Ah harpoons, an Ah uses a hook an line. Ahya do anythang it takes ta catch em."

He took a swig from a half-full whiskey bottle that had been sitting on the floor by the hearth. Grimacing, he continued.

"Nah, creatures live in the ocean is the same way. Dey jus like me. Some use a bait an line, some use clamaflage, some jus outright eatcha up, some use tricks an some even use e-lectricity. Dey all do what dey does fa one reason: ta get em somethin ta eat. If ya don't rememba nothin else, Ah say rememba dis: all of em, an Ah mean *all* of em, is gotta eat somethin. Deya all kill ya ta eat ya if dey can. Dat's the lawa da ocean, da lawa life. You wanna eat them an dey wanna eat you. Nevva forget dat, Boy."

Claude was flattered by JC's interest, and his unpolished baritone voice rattled on throughout most of the night.

In the morning that followed, the fog still besieged the shack as old Claude prepared for yet another day of fishing. He had decided to allow JC to go along because, though he would never admit it, he really liked the young man's dedication to a higher purpose and enjoyed his company. JC was intrigued by the old man's fiery insistence on a practical understanding of life. That eat-or-be-eaten/man-as-nature attitude worked well for Claude, but to JC it lacked a sense of humanity, a higher sense. So, like old friends who had found a sense of completion in each other, the two set out for Claude's hidden fishing grounds.

The day was unusually foggy all along the California north coast, and it was beyond JC how the old man navigated along the treacherous and rocky shoreline. All at once, the boat got caught in a narrow but swift current that spun it three turns before releasing it into a lagoon as still and calm as a freezing lake. The fog, however, grew even thicker.

"We *made* it, JC. We's here! Nah, you paddle dis thang along slowly till Ah say stop."

Looking over the side of the boat, JC noticed that the sea floor in the area was a chalky white, something uncommon for northern California.

It was hardly distinguishable at first, but JC began to hear a sweet, faint sound that seemed to be the voices of women singing.

"Mr. Crabbe! That noise! What's that?"

"Be quiet! Dem's the fish! Dey make dat noise when dey been up outa wata fa too long. It's what dey sounds like when they's tryin ta breave. Stop rowin. We real close nah!"

JC plowed the oars into the water to slow the boat and sat back in wonder.

"It's the most beautiful thing I've ever heard."

By this time, Claude was readying his spear and harpoon.

"Ha! Don't be *stupid*, Boy. Dey only stay outa wata like dat when dey lookin fa somethin ta eat. Watch out! Don't lettus get too close ta dem rocks!"

Yet even as JC redirected the boat's course, the good-sized tail of a large silver fish broke the water's surface not fifteen yards from the boat. The fish was headed toward the shore.

"Git afta it! Don't let it make it ta da rocks! Fast, Boy!"

JC rowed the boat with all his might as Claude steered a course to intercept the quarry. The streamlined fish would have easily outrun the clumsy little boat if it hadn't been rendered weak by the virus.

Nevertheless, Claude Crabbe drove his spear through its back with great ferocity. The mortally wounded fish struggled for a brief moment, blew out a painful belch of foul air, and seemed to accept its assured death. JC could not see it struggling in the throes of death from where he sat with his head between two spent knees, attempting to catch his breath.

"Grab the *tail*, JC! Ahma dress it right here. Dis boat's too small. We got no reason ta be carryin aroun junk we don't need."

Complying, JC held the shivering tail as Claude drew a great blade that shined like a beacon in the fog before it fell with three bloody blows upon the twisting, agonizing body whose other half struggled in the water.

He thought he heard a scream that seemed human as the body fell apart and the fish got substantially lighter. A geyser of steaming blood spurted high into the air as the fish body writhed about in the boat. As Claude stomped on it with a heavy, red-brown, blood-caked boot and clawed it with his clasper, the steamy entrails of the fish spilled out into the boat's hull.

"Dammit! Dis one's sick, JC—almos rotten already!"

Claude's capable hand tore the heated, stinking, bleeding mass apart as he searched for a treasure.

"See dat! Dis one's fulla eggs!"

The foul, sickening odor of fresh, hot blood filled the air, and a moment later, crimson portions of tissue clung to the old man's face after he buried rotting teeth and thick lips into the translucent white membrane holding the promise of future life.

"Ya oughta try one a dese. Dey's good fa ya. Keep ya from gettin sick..."

After further coaxing, JC bit into one of the smooth, quivering spheres only after he had washed it clean in the cold seawater. To his surprise, it tasted delicious—not at all fishy. The mild flavor of the fleshy portion inside reminded him of veal.

JC thought he was beginning to enjoy "the thrill of the hunt." The men talked idly as JC washed the other eggs and Claude trimmed fat and rotten areas from the fish body, but both bolted up upon hearing a playful splash a few yards off the boat's stern.

"Let's go, JC!"

The strain of the rowing caused him to squint his eyes shut in sheer determination, but he could feel the shifting in the boat as Claude gained trembling balance and poised the spear for the kill. It was only then that JC heard the strange noise—the horrible, unmistakable scream of a child in fear. He stopped rowing all at once to look out into the sea.

A frightened, terrified human child struggled in the dancing waters. It was a beautiful little girl of about thirteen with wavy blond locks! Her skin was fair and unclothed so that her developing perky breasts pointed out above the surface of the cold water.

How like any other little girl she was! And yet, she possessed a wild and untamed quality about her. The virus had caused her to rub her nose and the area below it to the point of irritation as evidenced in an unsightly rash.

At present, however, she was more concerned with the impending doom of Claude's spear. She attempted to duck under the water, but it seemed her mucous-lined throat and lungs could hold very little air. She broke the water's surface seconds later screaming and sputtering and coughing up slimy, reddish-tinted seawater.

At first, JC thought Claude was positioning himself to rescue the child from the water, but the old man lashed out with his blade to split open the pale flesh of the girl's flaccid shoulder. She shrieked and pleaded toward JC as old Claude Crabbe closed in for the kill.

"*Damn* you, Boy! Hold dis gatdamned boat still!"

Finally, JC believed the sight before his eyes. This old man, in his dispassionate and unconscionable sense of life's basic realities, would actually murder a poor, helpless child.

"No! Mr. Crabbe! Don't do it!"

With that, JC grabbed the oars and reeled the boat around to prevent the slaughter, but the sudden inertia of the quickly turning boat caused Claude to fall out into the water.

The resulting shock waves caused by the unexpected plunge increased the distance between the old man and the boat. It all happened so fast that JC, in a panic, had dropped the oars into the water and could not manipulate or steer the boat toward Claude, who vainly clutched for a boat that drifted slowly out of reach.

Yet even as JC readied himself to dive into the sea to prevent the potential tragedy before him, he noticed a huge, flat rock that jetted out of the sea not more than fifteen feet from the suddenly turbulent, foamy, and agitated water surrounding Claude, and the trembling old man, seeing the rock, struggled toward and pulled himself onto it with his one good arm.

He was bleeding from a large gash on his right thigh where a golf ball-sized plug of flesh hung there, attached only by a shred of skin.

"JC! Ah'm *hurt*! One of em bit me! Ah'm hurt real bad! *Hurry*! Come git me!"

A shining, silvery tail spanked the water's surface to send one of the once lost oars bumping against the boat's hull, but even before JC could retrieve it, the beautiful blond woman-child, who seemed oblivious to the deep and jagged gouge in her left shoulder, made her way to the safety of the rock.

Claude's voice was desperate.

"Kill it! Git da spear an *kill* it, JC! What's wrong wit'cha! What're ya waitin fa, JC? Kill it!"

The young detective couldn't understand Claude's urgent and panicked behavior, but then he saw a sight so incredible that it seemed his heart stopped in shock, his eyes betraying all that he had ever known. As the sickly girl pulled herself onto the rock, JC realized she was no little girl at all.

True, her head, neck, shoulders, breasts, arms, and bloated waist were human, but she had no legs at all. Instead, she had the tail of a fish. And this fish body was covered with festering sores and parasites. Even a sea lamprey was attached to her near an abbreviated dorsal fin.

The should-be crippling effect of a split and bleeding shoulder didn't slow her much, and she sprang upon trembling Claude Crabbe with amazing swiftness.

Then, with great skill, and as if she had performed the task a countless number of times, she curved her index finger and delicately extracted one of the old man's eyeballs from its socket as he cried out in agony. Careful not to damage it and spill the precious fluid, she placed it in a watering, ready mouth. A playful tongue rolled it about for a moment before the sharp teeth sliced through it to spill the thick liquid over a red, irritated lip and chin.

Ignoring his horrible cries and slapping his frantic hands aside, she pinned him down and plucked out the other eye with a seeming sense of pleasure. His pitiful wails and groans were finally enough to disturb the creature who slowly slinked tail-first back into the sea, but his howls had aroused the attention of other fish-women.

"JC? JC! Help me!"

The first to arrive was a large, blubbery specimen that was missing the flesh from her wrist to midway through her breast. Dragging the worthless arm behind, she made her way up the rock.

A strange growth resembling a fishtail protruded from her waist, and JC concluded that the males of this particular species, like the males of the deep-sea anglerfish species, spent their lives as tiny parasites, their jaws fused with the skin tissues of their mates.

The creature chewed through Claude's shoulder so that it returned to the sea carrying his one good arm in its one good hand. The corpulent creature was a skillful diver who reached the chalk-colored ocean floor in seconds.

As JC watched her feast on the bloody limb, belching up a bubble of foul air, he realized why the ocean floor in the area was so uniquely white: it was covered with human and marine mammal bones!

"JC! Kill it! *Kill* it!"

Another feminine creature approached Claude's mangled, shivering body on the bloody rock. Her skin was black and wormy, while her thick, matted hair seemed to hold a gallon of dripping seawater.

This one split his abdomen open with a spur on her wrist that JC hadn't noticed on the other specimens. She was intent on what she desired and went for his liver. Then, after ripping away the ligaments attaching it to his pain-contorted frame, she took it into her slimy, dirty hands and bolted it down on the spot.

Throwing his pincer to the sky in a seeming appeal to a higher nature, Claude's body froze for an instant, and he finally relaxed in death.

Another of the gruesome predators climbed the blood-covered stone to claim a leg and his manhood, returning to the sea to devour them. This is the way it continued until Claude had, piece by piece, disappeared from the rock in less than two minutes.

The creatures next began to focus their attentions on JC, who stood trembling and mesmerized in the boat throughout the entire macabre episode. He did not quiver in fear. Rather, his body perspired and shivered at the thought and resolution for doing what only he of all humanity could possibly do.

At the bow there appeared a woman creature far more lovely than the first woman whose body had washed ashore, far more lovely than any creature JC had ever perceived. With a mere flip of her wrist she overturned the boat and sent JC flying for thirty yards before he splashed headfirst into the rocky shallows. He sat up, spitting into his hand two of his broken teeth and sputtering blood-tainted saltwater.

She swam toward him, and lifting him completely from the water, she examined him carefully. She smiled with delight, licked the blood trailing from a wound directly over his left eye and returned him to the water.

Continuing in the aggressive play, the creature, grabbing him by the front of his shirt and holding him close, opened her mouth and kissed him passionately, her tongue darting excitedly over the bleeding gums and broken teeth.

After the kiss, she took the index and middle fingers of his left hand into her mouth and sucked them sensually for a moment before clamping down with razor-sharp teeth to slice them away. He groaned aloud in shock and horror, gripping his wrist with the other hand while watching the blood spurt from the abbreviated appendages. The female animal chewed the fingers, licking her lips with delight, and spat the small bones into the water.

But even as she went after JC again, the other creatures had crowded around, and she was challenged for the right to him by another creature who was larger than she was, though not as attractive. Then the two, with the forty or fifty others forming a loose circle about them, moved to deeper water to do battle for JC's viscera, the choice section for eating.

Most of those who watched were sickly or wounded, missing limbs, and plagued with open sores and festering rashes; they were a motley lot. The virus, combined with the destruction of habitat, had decimated this endangered species, which JC as classified *Feminae oceanus*, in this the last pod of the creatures in existence.

Their numbers had fallen from over two thousand at the beginning of the century to less than fifty. In recent years, many weakened individuals had turned to cannibalism and infighting.

In the center of the circle were the pod leader and the challenger, who ranked second in status. Their anger and excitement was reflected in rapidly effected skin color changes: first bright orange, then dull green, then bright red with black splotching and finally bluish-black. With spurs extended and teeth bared, they made passes by each other, scratching, biting, and clawing at each other with each turn.

The sky seemed to darken over a sea that churned and foamed with blood as the struggle continued for a half hour. At last, the leader, more savage and more experienced at fighting, accomplished a roll under her rival during one pass and ripped her abdomen wide open.

The spectators became instant participants in the scramble to claim the entrails and other choice parts. They lashed out at each other, greedily gobbling up chunks of flesh until, in minutes, the loser's body had disappeared and the water was stained with the smell of blood.

Not surprising, the distinctive flavor and excitement of such a battle attracted the bloodthirsty phantom shadows from the distant reaches of the deep. The sharks only monitored the group at first, each selfishly seeking a scrap or shred of flesh, but the blood, like a powerful drug, made them grow constantly bolder.

Occasionally, one would bolt through the line to take a dangling hand or arm. Early on, the woman creatures, who had formed a circular barrier with their backs protected inside the ring, dispatched the most daring sharks.

However, the disease had rendered many of them weak and had, by relation, weakened the strength of the circle. The sharks, mostly blues with a few large whites, grew jerkier in their movements, more agitated and aggressive as their numbers increased.

Though they hardly worked as a team, a pattern developed in their attacks. Several would isolate and surround a weakened individual and one would suddenly strike, chewing off much of the victim's tail.

Others would rush in to take the arms, and finally the entire group would alternately go in and feed on the helpless and undulating body twisting on the sea floor. Remoras, morays and pilot fish joined in the feasting. So it went until the sharks had devoured nearly all the creatures.

JC had been able to watch glimpses of the scene from where he stood in the shallows, completely captivated and even ducking under water to witness the action. He hadn't even considered it would have been safer on the shore until the mangled leader of the creatures, in bright red phase, sprang up from the water hissing loudly and lunging toward him. In the shallows, he was able to dodge the first few attacks, but she was closing in.

Scrambling toward the shore, he tripped over Claude's murderous spear and, turning, grabbed it up just in time. The beautiful creature, teeth and spurs bared, sprang upon him only to be impaled on the wicked spear, and screaming loudly and lashing her tail violently upon the surface on the water, she fell to convulsions. Death quickly followed.

He believed he was himself dying as he crawled onto the shore. He wondered if he would ever leave the place. Strangely though, he heard a sweet voice singing in the quiet fog. Torn between a deep curiosity and the desire to preserve his life, he hesitated.

The voice was innocent, youthful, wonderful, haunting. It filled his eyes with tears, his chest with love and his soul with peace. It called to him. It comforted him. The appeal was irresistible. Ignoring the pain and blood oozing from his fingers and other wounds, he dragged himself toward the source of a song no man had ever lived to describe. Within moments he had reached the rock where the little girl rested.

To his surprise, it was the very girl he had saved from Claude's spear—the very same child who had so playfully taken and eaten both of the old man's eyes! And now it seemed that she was dying. He cried aloud as the song continued.

As he lifted the limp little body, his hands ran over the boils and carbuncles that covered her tiny back. Many scales were missing from her trunk and her stomach was bloated, but then he understood. A black, fishtailed growth was attached to her waist! Her pale stomach was stretched so because she was full of eggs. She was so pregnant, so young, so beautiful. Poor, fair blond child!

Though he was dizzy for having lost so much blood, he fought to stay awake and alive. Digging into the pocket of his trousers, he withdrew the last vial of the antibiotic solution strapped by masking tape to a syringe. Removing the cap and needle cover, he filled the apparatus and injected its contents into the girl's round, firm rump. Gently, he pulled her barely-alive body to his bosom, placing her head in his lap. She was so lovely. Poor child!

Her keen nose caught the scent of blood flowing from his fingers and his face. She opened her eyes.

"You're awake! Thank God for that. Don't worry. I'll take care of you."

He brushed her curly blond locks from her forehead to see the delicate, pretty, little face. He marveled at her.

For an instant, he had forgotten everything he had learned from Claude and he paid the price. In that moment, this seemingly harmless child bared rows of saw-like, razor-sharp teeth. Her mouth foamed and her eyes rolled back white in their sockets as the feeding frenzy began.

She was actually able to throw her jaws out of her mouth to take the first bite from an arm JC attempted to jerk away. Fingernails dug deeply into the detective's back to hold him as the child swallowed mouthful after bloody mouthful of living, quivering muscle tissue.

When she was finally sated, she had eaten eleven pounds of tissue from JC's thighs, chest, and shoulders and had taken a plug from his cheek.

The meal had renewed her strength, and she slid from the rocks to the ocean floor where she rested as her stomach adjusted itself to the oversized meal. After a half hour, she tested the currents and, feeling much better, splashed around the rock in front of JC.

Pulling herself up, she crawled toward him, smiling. She sipped ecstatically from a warm puddle of blood in a depression in the rock, and finally reaching him, pulled the shivering man to her nude bosom and stroked him. Tears flowing from her eyes, she began to sing. It was the most beautiful song he had ever heard.

JC was in shock as he shivered there in the cold breezes coming from the sea. He looked up at the beautiful, clear, twilight sky and sighed as he caught a glimpse of a shooting star racing across the heavens. He was dying, but he smiled as he thought his green antibiotic cure might save this rare species.

He thought then of Claude Crabbe and his primitive, pragmatic philosophy about life. Certainly there was more to life than eating and being eaten, more than simple survival. Certainly there was a higher purpose for man.

JC had sacrificed his own life to save a savage, brutal race of lower creatures who did not have even the sense to appreciate what he had done, but lying there in the little girl's arms, he did not care. He had saved her and perhaps generations of unborn creatures like her.

She paused from her singing to lick the blood from his face and then resumed the song with passion more profound than ever before, making him reflect on the observation made by Claude about the creatures' songs. As JC looked up toward the watery eyes of the tiny, blond, woman-child creature, he realized that, once again, she was hungry.

SYNCHRONICITY

There are some who believe that life originated billions of years ago in the seas, that millions of years ago, an amorphous but animated cluster of ambitious and sophisticated molecules, tired of an unending diet of organic soup, slung itself onto dry land to cast the first of the many bonds which inescapably link man to the sea and the sea to all life on Earth.

These self-same believers further contend that this discontented cluster, in time of course, acquired muscle tissue, bone matter, a complex spinal column, highly specialized organs, limbs, digits, instincts, a brain with some 100,000,000,000 odd neural cells and, in spite of itself, even intelligence. The result: the creature *man*—still not content, but forever fascinated by the watery world he abandoned so long ago.

After having spent most of his thirty-two years in the mid-western United States, Oklahoma born-and-reared Tobias Frye had never ventured to the seashore, or even a riverbank for that matter. He literally hated water and bathed as infrequently as his wife and friends in the township of Dusty would tolerate.

At six feet tall, he was a lean, awkward, intelligent-looking man with tawny-brown hair styled in a conservative manner. In spite of many freckles and a reddish sunburn on the back of his neck, he was handsome in the European-styled suits he wore.

At seventeen, he had received a scholarship to the Massachusetts Institute of Technology and almost turned it down because of its proximity to the ocean, but he reluctantly attended and excelled at chemistry, abstract math and computer software disciplines.

Upon his return to Dusty, he was something of a celebrity and local legend for being the only person *from* the town with a "real" college degree.

As the general partner in Dusty's only chemical and computer software research company, his incredible ability for identifying and establishing abstract co-relational relationships was lauded in the United States and Japan. It was Tobias who pointed out that a few dead houseflies given to a pesky ant colony was Nature's own method for population control, and it was Tobias who called NASA officials and warned that the spaceship would never make it out of the Earth's atmosphere on the chilly January morning in 1986.

As everyone remembered it, it was on April 1st that Tobias, along with his wife's cousins who were his business partners in the limited enterprise, received, as a gift from a thoroughly impressed and satisfied African client, a seventy-five gallon aquarium complete with stand, lights, pump and filter, rocks, plants, snails, and three rare fish. Even Gunther P. Doolittle, the small town's official licensed ichthyologist, was unable to confirm the customer's claim that all fish were male and that the particular genus and species were rare indeed. Gunther did, nevertheless, suggest that it seemed the fish would be "mighty tasty in a samwich."

Fortunately, no such fate would befall the fish, for Tobias, much to the amazement of his wife and business associates, was strangely drawn to the hypnotic gurgling of the aquarium. Even more incredible, this self-proclaimed hydrophobe began to spend hours away from the lab and his desk to sit on a small stool before the watery scene, his face utterly blank, his eyes transfixed, and his mind perhaps savoring the flavor of that rich organic soup digested so long ago.

Always eager to research, Tobias was interested enough to check out fifty-one volumes in a series on rare fishes at the local library, and he took a three-day leave from the business to consume the material. By this time his partners, Ken Wallaby and Friday Hughes, began to worry about their once-stable partner, but a lawyer's review of the partnership agreement provided no measure to check Tobias' aberrant behavior. After all, he paid for the expensive black caviar he fed the fish from his own pocket.

Having no education, specialized skill, or business savvy between them, Ken and Friday were only in the business because both were related to Ethel, Tobias' wife. The entire township of Dusty knew that, without such a connection with the higher-ups, "them two boys would be workin at the mill with all the other rednecks."

Many in the town's population resented Ken and Friday for being so lucky, and nowhere was that umbrage more evident than in the scurrilous gossip that followed the two. The subtly attractive red-haired Ethel always defended her "cousins" though.

Always dressed in formal black, Ethel was one of Dusty's most respected citizens and attended every funeral with an earnest zeal. She donated money to needy families and did volunteer work one day each week at the convalescent hospital. Though she was lacking in social refinement, she won people over with her genuinely warm and unassuming nature.

Late one Sunday night, Tobias called Ken and Friday to the office stating he had fantastic news. A little after four a.m., the two arrived, hopeful, cranky and bleary-eyed, and found Tobias camped in front of the aquarium as expected, ranting about a conclusive urine analysis, which yielded that all three fish were male.

He further revealed he had found a way to tell the seemingly identical fish apart and that it was logically appropriate to give each a name. The greedy fish with the caudal disorder manifested in occasional spinal spasms was called Ken. The one disposed to violent fits who could not see from its right eye in bright lights as a result of bumping it while attempting to attack passersby was named Friday, and the fish which seemed the most healthy, unflawed, and intelligent was called Tobias.

Even as Tobias elaborated on the similarity in personality betwixt man and fish did Ken and Friday whisper to arrange a clandestine meeting with an attorney who boasted he could disfranchise their unsound associate whose thinking had gone so suddenly askew. Both were prepared to take the necessary actions to eliminate Tobias from the partnership and seize the business had it not been for the lucrative merger proposed by a Japanese corporate giant.

His particular genius was praised and often published by the Japanese. Thus the completion of the merger made Tobias much wealthier than his associates, since he had originally owned a considerably larger share of the business. Naturally, Ken and Friday resented the fact that Tobias made more money and received such honor and praise. Nonetheless, even while they admitted his exceptional computer-like co-relational ability was the key to the company's success, he countered that the good health and growth of the fish were indispensable to the company's health and growth.

Ken and Friday, who were finally provoked to the threshold of action, they, conjunct with Ethel, who had all but lost her husband to the loathsome fish, devised an exigent way to cure Tobias of his piscine obsession.

According to Ken's plan, Ethel would lure her husband away from the aquarium with the promise of zucchini and sweetbreads for dinner since Tobias had discovered that meals of zucchini and sweetbreads were usually followed by periods of heightened intellectual activity. In the meantime, Friday would steal into the business and destroy the fish by feeding them black caviar injected with toxins. All agreed.

After having fed the poison to the fish, Friday hurried home and informed the other conspirators that the fish would soon be dead and that the Toby of old would return. Unknown to all three conspirators, however, the fish named for Ken was similar to his namesake for a markedly greedy disposition: it bullied the other fish so that it devoured every last envenomed egg.

With an aura of satisfaction, Ken sat at the table and unceremoniously bolted down his dinner and belched in satisfaction as his nervous wife, Lilly, studied him hard and long with careful, guarded eyes.

The telephone rang late in the night at the Frye home. Drunk with sleep, Ethel reached over and unplugged it thinking it was her husband who, at the office in a frenzy of intellectual activity brought on by the zucchini and sweetbreads, would irritate her with useless new information on the fish.

In her sleepiness, she had forgotten that according to the plan, the fish should have already been dead. Next the phone rang at the business and Tobias, perceiving who the caller was, answered only after twelve rings. His voice was sullen.

"Friday, you don't have to tell me. I already know."

Friday stuttered in confusion and nervousness.

"Ya cain't know, Toby! It just happened... and no one's been able ta get a hold a ya!"

Tobias interrupted.

"I *know*. Ken's dyin. I found him floating in the tank when I came. I, I've tried everything to revive him, but nothing's worked."

Friday had dropped the phone. Fumbling to steady the receiver near his mouth, his sigh was grief-filled.

"No Tobias! Ya don't understan! Ken *Wallaby*'s dead! *Ken*! Our flesh'n blood business partner! He's dead! I'm at his house now. He died just a minute ago!"

Tobias examined the slimy fish in his hand as it gasped a final time. He began referencing.

"So our *partner* Ken is dead? How?"

"They don't know yet. He got real sick an Lilly called the ambulance an then she called me. Fire truck got here real fast, but they couldn't do nothin ta save im. He's *dead*, Toby!"

Tobias stroked the fish thoughtfully, mournfully, and tossed it, mucous-dripping, into his trash can where it stuck to the green and white banded computer paper.

"They must have given you some indication *why*, Friday."

"Toby, Ken was healthy as a horse. You know *that*! They said they'll find out though, at the lab at the hospital."

"Well, when you find out, call me back and let me know. It'll probably tell us why his fish died."

Friday cursed a few words in anger.

"Toby! Forget them damn fish! Here our *partner's* dead an you're still talkin bout them damn *fish*!"

Suddenly, Friday reflected on the poisoning and remembered how one fish in particular seemed to eat all the toxin-injected caviar. He remembered Tobias had always been accurate in his uncanny abstract correlations, but this was just too incredible!

"Toby, only the fish what was named after Ken died? How're the other two?"

"Nothin wrong with them."

Tobias hesitated.

"Funny as it might sound, Friday, they look like they're real sad their partner is dead."

Friday exploded in anger.

"That's it! I've had enough of them gaddammed fish! Toby, now eitha you get ridda em or *I* will! Ken didn't axe ya ta name one afta him an I didn't axe ya eitha. You just a strange man, Toby. It's somethin wrong in your head! You an them gadammed fish could go ta hell for all I care!"

Tobias was finally able to interrupt.

"Friday, you don't understand. Isn't tonight proof of what I've been telling you and Ken for all these months? We can't let anything *happen* to these fish. Whatever happens to them will happen to us. Whatever happens to us will happen to them. We have to *protect* them."

"The *hell* we do, Toby! The hell we do!"

Friday slammed the receiver down and recomposed himself for a moment at the table before offering a few words of support and kissing Lilly tenderly before he left. The fish, he decided, would have to be destroyed. But even as he raced toward the office, he became less and less sure he would have the resolve to do it.

Tobias unlocked the deadbolt even before Friday could wiggle his key into it. The confrontation was solemn and deliberate.

"Friday, I'm sorry. I know he was your cousin."

"Get outa my way, Toby!"

In his irresolute hand he held a hunting knife that wavered as he spoke.

"I'm gonna *kill* those fish, Toby... for once an for all."

Tobias held his place between his partner and the aquarium.

"You'll have to kill me first. The way I figure it, I won't live for long if I stand aside and let you do it."

Friday stared curiously into Tobias' eyes. He was both impressed and frightened to think that Tobias was so certain of his correlation. There was only one way of finding out for sure. As immoral as it was, it was the only way he could escape the curse of the fish.

"Okay Toby, if that's the way it's gotta be!"

The blade sliced flesh and stuck in Tobias' collarbone, and the frenzied Friday would have freed it and struck again if the explosion of a gun had not been heard.

Four of Dusty's police officers entered after Friday heeded the warning to drop the knife and raise his hands. He was handcuffed and read his Miranda rights. Tobias, for his part, was confused by the unexpected entrance of the police. Even as an officer attended to his wound, he grimaced and spoke to understand.

"I'm glad you showed up, Freddie, but what are you guys doing here?"

The sarcastic answer came from the officer who carefully handled the knife as he put it into a plastic bag.

"Savin yer life. Your partner there wanted the business all to imself. The hospital lab called fifteen minutes after they got Ken's body. Ken Wallaby didn't die by no accident. He was poisoned, an guess who all the evidence points to?"

Friday still sat in the room. On hearing such an allegation, he bowed his head and angrily muttered a garbled phrase.

"I cain't *believe* it!"

Then he spoke aloud.

"I didn't poison Ken! Everyone who knows us knows we was *cousins*! He was like a brotha ta me! Even *you* know that, Freddie—"

Feeling the onerous weight of condemnation, he appealed to his languid and pale partner.

"I didn't kill im, Toby. You believe me, don't cha?"

The large, red, pot-bellied sergeant pulled a pen and notepad from his pocket and posed a question.

"Are ya gonna talk without waitin for yer lawya? After all, ya *did* try'n kill Toby here, a fine man whose only mistake was lettin the likes a you an Ken in his high-class bidness in the first place. We was suspicious a you all along! That's why we followed ya *ova* here."

"I *swear* I'm innacent! I don't need no lawya! I'll talk!"

The sergeant smiled.

"Really? Then where was you between the hours of seven-thirty and eight-thirty last night?"

Friday became nervous as he stuttered and fell silent. He remembered that he had been alone during that time, that he had spent the time trying to poison the fish.

"I, I changed ma mind—I think I betta wait fa ma lawya."

Though becoming faint for having lost so much blood, Tobias wanted to know more from the officers.

"Did they say *how* he was poisoned?"

The sergeant answered.

"Says rite here on this fax paper: *He ingested toxic waste.* Someone fed it ta im in a cuppa coffee... or a beer maybe. Someone *close* ta him—like a *cousin.* Lilly said when he come home from drinkin with Friday there, he looked sick and he was actin strange."

"That's a *lie*! It what'n like that at all! She's try'n ta set me up! Put it off on me! Ken was jus *fine* when he went home!"

Friday had stood to object, but the attending officers forced him to sit again.

"What're ya waitin for? If yer gonna take me ta the station an book me, then *do* it! Get it the hell ova with!"

The sergeant approached Friday, hoping to intimidate the man further.

"What cha so anxious about, Mr. Hughes? Seem like you're worried we might *find* somethin."

Just then a fifth officer came in with a glass flask contained in a plastic bag.

"Freddie! We *got* somethin here—looks like this is the poison he used. We found it in the trunk of his car."

Friday languished in the chair as he remembered that he had put the remainder of the poison used on the fish in the trunk of his car. The fat sergeant took the plastic bag from the younger officer and withdrew the vial containing the clear jiggling liquid. He removed the rubber stopper and drew in a deep breath. Next, he poured a drop of the liquid onto his finger and tasted it.

"Yep. It's toxic waste alrite. Get im outa here."

But even as guards guided Friday past the aquarium, the prisoner chanced to glance into the watery scene. In that very moment, one of the fish had viciously attacked the other, and the wounded fish bled from a place just in front of the left pectoral fin. Friday stopped to look back toward his dizzy, wounded, bleeding business partner.

"Do ya see that, Toby? Your fish's shoulder's bleedin jus like yours! You were right, Toby! That proves I didn't poison Ken! I poisoned his fish. Ethel knows! I'm sorry, Toby. I'm very sorry!"

The sergeant stepped between Tobias and a contrite Friday.

"Move on, Mr. Hughes. We're takin ya ta jail where you belong."

Shivering, Tobias looked pitifully on Friday's distressed expression for a last time as the officers forcefully shoved their prisoner out the door.

A guard led Ethel Frye down the dusty, smelly corridor and into a room that had booths all along the wall opposing the door.

"That'll be window eight, Ma'am."

She walked two uneasy steps and stopped. Her Halston dress was black and her bright red hair was hidden under a black hat because she had just come from the baker's funeral.

"Ta yer right, Ma'am."

She had been seated for nearly five minutes before she saw the door open to admit an unsteady Friday Hughes into the small glass tank. He was wearing the denim jeans and blue cotton shirt that were typical for the incarcerated. She smiled, clearing her throat and adjusting her hat as she sat.

"Well, hell, hello Friday."

He bowed his head to hide the shame and embarrassment in his eyes.

"Ethel, I'm *so* glad ya came. I cain't believe this is happenin. My own momma an daddy ain't been out ta see me yet!"

Ethel cleared her throat again and focused on the white knuckles of her cold, folded hands.

"Why'd ya call me here, Friday, when you know how I mus feel bout what cha done ta Toby?"

His non-verbal answer, demonstrated in a facial expression, was pitiful.

"Don't cha look at me like that. Ya *know* what cha did! Ya tried ta kill ma husband. Ya tried ta kill ma Toby!"

"Ethel, please!"

"What?"

"Ma arraignment's tamarra."

"So?"

"You're the only person alive who knew for a fack where I was at that night."

She sat back and fumbled through her purse for the cellophane-wrapped cigarette package and a book of matches.

"Ethel, you of *all* people know I didn't kill Ken. We was all in it tagetha. You know I was at the office that night. Ya remember? I was poisonin the fish jus like we planned!"

She spoke while lighting the cigarette.

"Ya know, Friday, I don't know *what* I know anymore. For all I know, ya coulda had it out against Ken, seein you was always jealous cuzza him."

His only witness seeming skeptical, Friday began to panic.

"It what'n me, Ethel. I *swear* it! It musta been Lilly! Yeah! Everbody in Dusty knows she never liked him afta he got all big an fat! It was Lilly!"

She blew out a cloud of smoke, shaking her head with disgust.

"An how am I gonna know *that*? What I do know is that you an Lilly was meetin at the Dusty Motel almos every other night. Maybe you was in on it tagetha. Maybe both a ya was out ta kill ma husban too."

Friday began to lose his composure.

"Ya gotta help me, Ethel! Ya *know* where I was! They're sayin they wanna sen me ta the e-lectric chair!"

He began crying aloud.

"Are ya gonna help me, Ethel? Come on, tell me! What're ya gonna *do*?"

She sighed and grabbed up her bag.

"I'm gonna do what I shoulda done a long time ago, a job you wasn't *man* enough ta do when I wanted ya ta. I'm killin them fish and gettin ma husban back."

"I'll kill you *first*, you whore!"

Friday did his best to attack Ethel as she sprung back, falling over the chair, but, misjudging his relative proximity to the glass in front of him, all he managed to do was knock himself dizzy by butting his head. Nevertheless, he attacked again and again until his face was a bloody mess and two guards came in to drag him out.

In one instance, he overpowered the guards and, in a seemingly murderous frenzy, bolted toward the frightened Ethel who cringed while she stood. He was knocked senseless by a painful collision with the glass. Exerting great effort, he struggled against the guards to call a final warning, his mouth gushing blood over his frayed lower lip to drip from his chin.

"Ethel! Wait! Ya don't know bout them fish! Them fish is *us*, Ethel! Me an Toby! When Ken's fish died, *he* died! Ya gotta believe me! Killin them fish'll mean killin me an Toby! Axe Toby, Ethel! Axe Toby!"

By this time, the guards had subdued the seemingly insane young man, who was foaming at the mouth. Ethel could only stare in horror from where she cringed in the dusty, uncomfortable corner.

"Kill them fish, and ya kill *us*! Me an Toby!"

Those words were his last as a guard, whose own nose had been bloodied in the scuffle, vengefully struck the struggling prisoner in the back of the head with a blunt stick. Ethel, for her part, was visibly shaken and embarrassed as she staggered toward her car, urine cooling and drying on her sticky legs.

After climbing into her car, Ethel did consider the import of Friday's assertions and reflected on her husband's incredible ability for making abstract correlations. She thought about Friday. He was probably the best-looking man in the entire state of Oklahoma. Of a medium height, muscular, dark, and sexy for his low and soft twangy voice, he may have even been the best-looking man in the entire Southwest. He did have a temper, though.

On a whim, Ethel decided to drive by Ken Wallaby's home. Maybe there was some truth in what Friday claimed, maybe it was Lilly who poisoned her husband Ken. She noticed a squad car and an unmarked police detective vehicle outside the house as she crept down the street in her luxury Japanese sedan, stopping a few houses away so she could watch. After some time, the young officers and the middle-aged detective left the Wallaby home, but the detective returned to the door briefly to kiss Lilly and whisper something into her ear.

Determined to find the truth, Ethel climbed from the car, approached the house, and knocked curtly. Lilly opened slowly, solemnly.

"Lilly, I'm *so* sorry bout Ken... Is it anythang I can do?"

Nervous, she paused and continued, as Lilly did not invite her in.

"Uhm... This is real embarrassin, but I, I kinda *peed* on myself. Can I come in an wash up?"

The door swung open to reveal a very skeptical Lilly, who was curious.

"Ya went ta the jail. Friday *told* ya somethin, didn't he?"

Continuously jawing a wad of stale gum, she studied Ethel's reaction.

"Ya don't have ta say nothing. Face says it all. Ya *know* where the washroom is. Go on."

Though it was four in the afternoon, Lilly was still nude under her bathrobe. She was vain, though not without good reason. She had beautiful round breasts, firm shapely legs and smooth, soft, creamy white skin, which contrasted with her wavy jet-black hair and large, almond-shaped dark eyes. The wonderful shape of her behind caused some of Dusty's older residents to gossip that Lilly probably had some Negro in her somewhere.

When she met Ken, he was a high school football legend destined to greatness and maybe even Oklahoma University. Unfortunately, a back injury aborted his career and sidelined him in Dusty. Lilly, though, hadn't the courage to abort the child, so the two were married after she finished the eleventh grade.

In retrospect, she would have gained that needed resolve had she known that Ken was going to eat so greedily and become so repugnant and obese. On those rare occasions his back was capable enough for sex, he literally crushed and suffocated the petite Lilly, who was all too eager for the episode of usually forty-five seconds to end.

She waited the normal five years before she began having affairs though, and she limited those only to people both she and Ken knew—no strangers and no itinerants just passing through Dusty.

Waiting in the parlor for Ethel to come out of the washroom, Lilly opened a new stick of chewing gum as she heard the toilet flushing. She put on lipstick and waited for this uninvited guest to reveal her purpose for the visit.

"*Find* everthang alrite, Ethel?"

"Sure did. Thanks."

Ethel sank into the couch across from the new widow.

"Ya need any help on the funeral arraigments or anythang?"

Lilly sighed.

"Aw naw. Not at all. We're still waitin for the casket ta come in. Hadda special order a real big one! Side from that, everthang's done. Ken had good insurance."

Beginning to relax, Ethel sat back, thinking, and lit a cigarette.

"Did the police say anythang more bout what kilt ol Ken?"

"Toxic waste."

"What's that?"

"Toxic waste? Oh, ya know—it's that kinda real bad pollution junk that big business an the government an the Japanese are always dumpin out in the ocean an sky an in our drankin water."

She eyed the smoking cylinder between Ethel's fingers.

"Scuse me, Ethel. Ya know I really *did* give up smokin a month ago, but with Ken dyin and all, it's been real hard. Can I have a drag off your cigarette there?"

After taking it from Ethel's fingers, Lilly took a long hit, held it, and blew it out slowly, blissfully.

"I thank toxic waste'll kill us all before it's over with."

Ethel subtly motioned for her loaned-out cigarette, but she was ignored.

"Lilly, of course ya heard about it. Uh, they arrested Friday last night. Said it was *him* who poisoned Ken. Whadaya thank of that?"

Lilly sucked in another long drag and answered while exhaling.

"Maybe he did."

Ethel caught Lilly's eyes in a reproachful stare.

"Maybe he didn't. Maybe someone *else* did—"

Abruptly and maliciously, Lilly flicked the burning cigarette toward Ethel and, in a fit of rage she turned over a table to send a lamp crashing to the floor.

"Why don't cha come rite out an *say* it, Ethel! Ya know ya wanna say I killed ma own husband! Ain't *that* why ya come on ova here?"

Ethel was caught off-guard by the anger and emotion. She stuttered in her reply.

"Uh, well uh, no! I never said it was you*!* I said maybe it was someone else*!*"

Lilly was standing over her cringing guest, a large enameled vase in her hands.

"Someone else like *who*? Like me!"

The vase shattered against a masonry wall. Ethel stuttered in fear.

"Ya, ya know I didn't say that, Lilly, but, but ya *did* know about the toxic waste!"

Knowing she had terrified her guest, Lilly lingered a moment over Ethel and backed away, laughing malevolently. Then she began crying, went to the bar, and poured a double-shot of Southern Comfort into a snifter before continuing.

"I'm sorry..."

She gulped a large tingling mouthful of the shimmering liquid, contorting her face.

"It's grief I guess."

She recomposed herself and paced as she spoke.

"Ya see, Ethel—the only reason *I* know bout toxic waste is cuz I'm *educated*. I didn't go ta college fa it or nothin, but I'm bout as educated as ya can get round here. See, I don't knit an bake an clean an help ol folks an go ta bingo an funerals like you. Sometimes I read, but mostly I watch TV. You kin learn a lot from TV—Jeopardy, Price Is Right, even Oprah. It's alotta learnin on them shows. Yep, I figure me an Toby is bout the only educated people in this town. Now *that's* why I know bout toxic waste and you don't."

Ethel regained her resolve and pursued her purpose.

"Lilly, I *know* you an Friday was havin an affair. Everbody in Dusty knows it."

Lilly laughed.

"I know bout *you*'n Friday too, Ethel. Ya thank he didn't tell me bout that time you two did it out in the rain cuz ya knew Toby hated water an y'all knew he wasn't gonna come out an see what y'all was up to."

Ethel blushed.

"That was one time only! And it wasn't a real affair like it is with you two."

"So what *about* it. I was havin an affair. So what?"

"Aren't cha worried bout im? I mean, ya cain't believe he *did* it?"

Lilly sighed, rolling her eyes.

"Heck yeah he did it! They fount the toxic waste in his *car*. An by the way, if ya only 'did it' with im once, why are *you* so worried bout what happens ta im?"

Ethel stood to make her case.

"It's *natural* for me ta be worried about im. He's ma cousin."

"Friday ain't yer cousin!"

"He is. He's ma step fourth cousin on ma uncle's second wife's side, thrice removed."

Lilly just stood there a moment, chewing her gum in puzzlement.

"Oh, I see. But I thought *I* was yer cousin."

"Ya *are*. On ma Mamma's side, yer ma illegitimate third cousin by ma grandfather Homer who whored around with his fifth cousin by marriage twice removed. On Daddy's side, ya're ma fourth cousin even though ya Mamma is ma fourth cousin, cuz ya Daddy is ma fourth cousin too... one half removed. All in all that makes us third an a half cousins by marriage and fourth cousins by blood."

Nervous, Lilly crossed her eyes, perplexed.

"And me'n Friday?"

"*Sixth* cousins—but it don't matter after fifths, cuz ever'one knows you an Ken was fifths."

Lilly sighed and smiled, at ease.

"Talkin bout Friday, ya *did* go'n see im in jail, didn't cha?"

"Yep, an he's in real bad shape. But he's been tellin the police an everbody he's innacent. Says maybe it was *you* who poisoned Ken."

"That's a lie! A white-faced lie!"

Ethel studied the very nervous woman who sat, stood, sat again, crossed shapely legs, and fumbled for another cigarette. She would know more.

"Welp, that's what he's been screamin ta the detectives an everbody. He's tellin em ya killed Ken ta get the insurance money an his share a the bidness."

Irritated, Lilly glanced toward smug Ethel who seemed to derive pleasure from watching her squirm, so she launched her own offensive.

"Well, Ethel, that's not why the police came ova here taday. They think we was *all* in on it. Me'n Friday an you'n Toby too. *Say* they got reasons ta believe we was all—"

A sudden insistent knock at the door startled both women to their feet. Lilly deftly tipped around the window and peeked up from the lower right corner. She whispered wildly across the room.

"Oh no! It's the police again! Detective Ford Bray!"

This time the knocking was louder and it was Ethel who panicked.

"Lilly! Ya *gotta* hide me! Ya cain't let im know I'm here! It'll look real bad fa us if he finds us meetin like this!"

At the next urgent series of knocks, Lilly was caught up in the contagion of panic. She called out nervously.

"Justa, justa minute, Detective! I'm just, just puttin somethin on—"

She whispered to Ethel.

"I know he'll think we're up ta somethin! Hurry! You hide in the bedroom closet! I'll get ridda Ford!"

With Ethel gone, Lilly took a deep breath, ran fingers through her hair to appear a bit disheveled, and opened the door.

"Detective Bray? Come in. Didn't thank ya'd be back so soon."

He entered, removed his hat, loosened his tie and salaciously ogled her behind as she moved across the room to the bar.

"I told ya before, Lilly. Ya don't hafta call me Detective. It's *Ford*."

Swiping fragments of the broken vase from his path with a well-worn Frye boot, he grinned suggestively, eyes never averting from his target.

"An Lilly, ya didn't hafta go an put nothin on fer me."

Accustomed to such innuendo from men, Lilly's practiced and flirtatious response encouraged the detective.

"Ya know, Lilly, I'm startin ta think *you* wasn't in on this bidness of killin Ken at all. Hadda be Toby'n Ethel. Anybody in Dusty'll tell ya Toby knew Ken what'n good for that bidness in the first place, that Ken was makin twice as much money as the resta us decent folks fa doin next ta nothin. Hell, I woulda worked twice as hard as Ken, but Toby didn't give *me* no partnership. But Toby finally saw it, saw ol Ken fer what he was, and that's why he'n Ethel got tagetha an poisoned im."

Lilly served a Jack Daniels shot to Ford and as she sat, she let her gown fall open to reveal the way she crossed her beautiful legs.

"What bout Friday?"

Ford gulped the drink, anxious to see more.

"Aw, that dumb hick—he's too *stupid* ta know bout toxic waste. That's why it was Toby'n Ethel. They're the smartest people in this town. They'd know."

Lilly resented that the town people thought Ethel was so smart, but suddenly realizing Ethel might be listening from the bedroom, she closed the gown and stood.

"Well... What's gonna *happen* ta Friday?"

"I don't know. He could still go ta prison fer what he done ta Toby—attempted murder an all—but I *will* tell ya one thang. If he keeps flappin his jaw bout cha like he is, we might have us a federal investigation here. Ya need ta go talk ta him and shut him up."

Immediately sensing a way out of the awkward situation, Lilly responded instantly.

"Oh, I'll shut im up, alrite. I'll jus head on down there now!"

She feigned anger and appeared to recompose herself.

"Ford, Honey, lemme jus throw somethin on an I'll be rite back out. You will take me on down there, won't cha, honey?"

She slipped into the bedroom and closed the door, leaving Ford confused and suddenly let down out in the parlor. Angry, Ethel met her inside the door, whispering in the darkness.

"You're not gonna put what happened ta Ken off on me'n Toby! We had nothin ta do with it!"

Scheming, Lilly breathed a reply.

"Didn't ya hear Ford? Nobody'll blame you! Ya know how everbody in this town jus loves you. Ethel, ever'one in Dusty knows Toby ain't nevva treated ya rite, nevva cared bout cha. So be smart fer once in yer life! Let im put it off on Toby. Just thinka all the money an freedom you'll have if they get him fer it!"

"Are you *crazy*, Lilly? I don't want—"

Ford's timid fidgeting with the doorknob sent Ethel scurrying for the closet. Lilly stalled.

"Don't come in, Detective. I'm not changed yet."

Ford opened the door and stood in the light flooding into the dark room.

"Not so *fast*, Lilly! Now out there I said it *might* be Toby'n Ethel, but then again, I might be wrong."

He closed and locked the door and then flicked on the light.

"How bout I jus let cha *convince* me. Come on, let's see what's unda the robe."

Lilly teased, opening the robe wide to let it fall off her shoulders onto the warm wooden floor where it lay gathered around sexy ankles.

"Oh ma flippin Gawd!"

She approached the detective.

"What's wrong, Ford, honey? Don't cha... like what cha see?"

Coming close enough to barely brush her soft smooth body against his, she sat back onto the bed, first crossing and then rubbing her legs and thighs.

"Ford, why don't cha, uhm..."

Naughty, she smiled, licking her lips.

"Show me yer pistol."

It was only after Ford's dusty Wrangler blue-jeans and boxer shorts fell to his ankles that Ethel grew disgusted enough to burst out from the closet.

"Cousin Ford! What on God's Green Earth da ya thank ya're doin? Now I jus cain't *believe* Auntie Minnie raised no, no sexual harasser! Look at ya! You're a sex pervert!"

In the desperate struggle to pull up his jeans, Ford fell over sideways onto the floor. He stuttered.

"Cousin Ethel! You're unda arres fer the murder a—"

There was a sudden explosion causing Ford's body to jerk one violent time and then he lay still. Both Ethel and Lilly recoiled at the second of the gunshot, but it was Ethel who was brave enough to check the body.

"Cousin Ford?"

She rolled him over.

"Oh ma God, Lilly! He's dead! His pistol went off, like prematurely!"

Ford Bray lied there, a trail of blood oozing from his faded heart-embossed boxer shorts. The expression on his face was one of surprise and definite discomfort. Lilly, afraid to look directly, glanced sidelong and turned away.

"Ethel? Did he, did he shoot imself in the... you know what?"

The braver woman, cringing, nodded in the affirmative.

"Well, what're we gonna do now, Ethel? They already thank we got tagetha an kilt Ken. They'll *swear* it was us who shot Ford ta cover up somethin!"

Ethel, in a daze, went out to the parlor and sat on the couch. Lilly followed.

"Let's thank bout this a while, Lilly. Ya know, if ya thank bout it, no one has ta *know* I was here. Ya could tell everbody it was jus you an Ford here an he wanted ta do it an his pistol jus kinda went off by accident."

As she looked over at Lilly, she could see the wheels turning in the woman's head.

"I mean, that *was* the way it happened, *right* Lilly?"

Lilly smiled.

"*Exactly* the way it happened."

Ethel stood, relieved.

"Gimme fifteen minutes ta get outa here an call the police, okay?"

Still nude, Lilly answered with confidence.

"Oh, they'll *buy* ma story alrite—hook, line, an *sanker*!"

The next day, Lilly, sporting a grief-worn sheer black body suit with stiletto-heeled pumps, appeared at the jailhouse to visit Friday only hours before his arraignment.

"Can anybody hear us talkin?"

His sweaty fingers stuck to the glass as he reached to touch her.

"Uh... Naw, it's against the *law* ta spy on people."

She smiled sadly, touching the glass opposite his fingers.

"Well Friday... How ya been?"

His eyes swelled with tears.

"It's been real *hard*, Lilly. Police beat me up most ever'day, jus like that Rodney Kang. An ma asthma—it's gettin real bad. Sometimes I wake up an jus cain't breave. Feel as like I'm suffocatin."

She studied his eyes and tortured expression with suspicion.

"Friday? What's this I hear bout ya tellin people I kilt ma husban?"

He could not hide his culpability.

"Lilly, Baby, that was when I thought ya was gonna let me take all the blame."

He looked toward her, pleading.

"Well, what was I *sposeta* thank? Ya didn't call me back an ya wouldn't come'n see me. Ethel's the only one come'n see me."

She glanced aside, hoping no one could hear.

"I was bein *watched*, Honey. I couldn't. I, I jus cain't believe ya turned on me like that! I *loved* ya! I thought we was in it tagetha."

"We *was*! I mean, we are!"

"I don't know if I kin trust ya anymore!"

He cried.

"Please Lilly! Ya kin trus me, ya really can. Please believe me."

He wiped his eyes with his left sleeve and blew his nose on the right sleeve.

"Listen, Lilly. Once I'm outa here, we'll go afta Toby'n Ethel and it'll be all ours. We'll have the whole bidness ta ourselves."

Her eyes sparkled with a new greed.

"Maybe I *will* let ya take all the blame. Rite now, I dunno if I really *need* a partner."

Friday panicked at such a thought, though he stilted his voice and tried to appear calm. He spoke while sneering.

"Lilly, whether ya want it or not, we're still in this tagetha—ta the death. If I'm goin down, I'm takin you with me."

He remembered something else.

"Besides, I got a little ol plan."

"What's that?"

Confident he had her attention, he sat back.

"Well, I know how we kin kill Toby without touchin a hair on his head."

"Oh yeah? An how's that?"

"First of all, no mora that talk bout ya not needin no partner."

Lilly flirted, undoing the top two buttons to reveal voluptuous cleavage.

"Aw Friday, ya *know* that's not what I meant. I said what I said cuz ya hurt me tellin people all them bad thangs bout me. I was really hurt by that."

He felt ashamed.

"I'm sorry."

She undid the next two buttons, revealing full breasts.

"Come on, Honey. What's yer plan?"

He leaned toward her and whispered into the screened hole in the glass.

"Way I figure it, all we gotta do is kill his *fish*. We do that an he'll die all on his own."

Disappointed, she sighed and fell back into the chair, disgusted and incredulous.

"Friday Geronimo Hughes! Don't tell me Toby's got ya believin his nonsense bout them fish!"

"Then howdaya explain it? When Ken's fish died, *he* died!"

Lilly pounded the glass with a tiny frustrated fist.

"Friday, you dumb redneck! If I could belt ya one, I would. Both of us know what happened ta Ken, an it didn't have nothing ta do with no fish!"

Friday pressed on.

"No Lilly, ya gatta *lissen* ta me! Now ya *know* Toby! Tell me—is he ever been wrong bout those relationship thangs he does? Them *Japanese* pay that boy a million dollars a year ta do it. An we all know them Japanese *ain't* exactly dumb people!"

She began to consider the possibility. Friday continued.

"There's somethin else. When I hurt Toby's shoulder, ma fish hurt his fish's shoulder. It ain't no accident. Toby knows somethin."

His furtive whisper interrupted her daze.

"One problem, though."

Newly inspired, she was interested.

"What problem?"

"Fish look just *alike*. It's almost impossible ta tell em apart. What that means is if ya kill the wrong fish, ya *could* be killin me!"

Even as Friday spoke his concern he was overtaken by an ominous, sinister fear. His face grew flushed. Reluctant, he stuttered on.

"Ya, ya see, ma fish has got bad vision in one eye, so he's always bumpin inta the glass'n stuff."

Smiling eagerly, her eyes grew more inspired.

"Friday, don't you have bad vision in one eye?"

"Yeah, it's what I told ya. That fish'n me go tagetha. That's why ya gotta watch em real close an kill *jus* the otha one, jus Toby's."

Nervous, he swallowed.

"This is life and death fer me, so we cain't afford no mistakes."

She smiled to reassure him.

"Trust me, honey. I'll watch em real close an make sure I kill the right fish!"

Intimately familiar with Lilly, he grew fearful for her apparent excitement. He knew exactly what she was thinking, so he called out as she rose.

"I don't *want* any of the money, Lilly."

"What?"

"You kin have the money. I don't want it. An you kin have the bidness, the whole thang. Don't want that neitha. I jus want outa here."

She sat, smiling.

"Now don't that beat *all*! Friday, honey, what's come ova ya?"

He had trouble hiding his newly-founded dread. He wagged his head.

"Nothin, baby. I jus hope ya don't kill the *wrong* fish."

He hoped his fate had not already been sealed.

"Aw heck, Lilly! Goin ova it all again, I thank Toby was *wrong* bout that relationship thang he said bout them fish. Ken's fish had nothin ta do with what happened ta him. You and I both know that. Even Toby kin be wrong."

He forced an awkward laugh.

"Ya know, Lilly, when ya thank bout it—how's killin a *fish* gonna make a man die?"

He stood, trying to discern her intentions as he looked down into her eyes.

"Tellya what. Let's jus *forget* all about messin with them fish, alrite?"

She smiled sweetly.

"What's wrong, Friday, honey? Ya don't trus me? We're still partners ta the death, ain't we? Don't tell me you think I'd kill yer fish on *purpose*. Is that what ya thank?"

"No! No, I didn't say that!"

She flirted, undoing two more buttons so that she exposed her supple, contoured flesh down to her bellybutton.

"Don't worry, honey. I wouldn't let anythang *happen* ta ya. We're partners, right?"

He called loudly as she turned to leave.

"Waitaminute Lilly! Where're ya goin?"

As she turned to face him, her silky, shimmering body suit was open to the panty line.

"I got bidness ta take care a."

With that, she turned and swished away, never looking back.

"Waitaminute Lilly! I ain't done talkin ta ya yet! Lilly! Lilly honey! Please come back. Please!"

Once again, he had slammed his face into the glass and bled from the mouth, and once again, in came the guards who hit him with sticks and dragged him away.

"Mr. Ito, it's very nice to finally meet you. As you already know, I'm Tobias Frye, and this is my wife, Ethel."

The delicate man bowed.

"Mrs. Frye. I am honored to meet so handsome a lady..."

He bowed again.

"Mr. Frye. I am greatly honored. Your genius at the abstract correlation is esteemed and studied in all of Japan."

As the couple bowed, Ethel was impressed by Mr. Ito's formal manner. She whispered to her husband between clenched teeth.

"The man's a *Japanese*, Toby. Why'd ya tell me he was a Oriental?"

Standing erect again, she sighed and relaxed her own manner.

"Uh, Mr. Ito? Did anyone ever tell ya we're gonna be cousins?"

While he appeared confused, she smiled and continued.

"Yeah, your nephew Toshi who's here in town is marryin ma second cousin's niece. That'll make us fifth or sixth cousins at worst dependin on how ya look at it."

Even more confused, Mr. Ito bowed again and affected a ceremonial smile.

"Thank you."

Ethel left thereafter to attend Friday's formal arraignment, giving her husband and Mr. Ito the privacy to discuss business. Mr. Ito worked for one of the world's largest Japanese business interests. He was in Dusty because he was currently working with the Japanese and American governments on a covert project that involved the concealment, disposal, and final disposition of toxic and nuclear wastes.

Tobias had recently advanced an outline on a theory with reference to an abstract correlation on *The Heightened and Accelerated Deterioration of Methanols, Arsenics, Concentrated Solvents, Chromium and Lead Compounds, and Spent Uranium and Plutonium Rods in the Sustained and Temperature-Altered Presence of Unusual Combinations of Rare Elemental Isotopes.*

The Japanese secretly hoped to buy the information and intelligence and sell it to the rest of the world, this only when the need for such technology had reached critical levels. Because Mr. Ito's company owned the affiliate that had bought shares in Tobias' business, he was sent to access the viability of the man's theory.

Amid a detailed discussion on radioactive half-lives, Mr. Ito stopped at once, distracted by the aquarium. His eyes grew large.

"Do you know, Mr. Frye, what you have in this tank?"

Tobias was unnerved by the usually phlegmatic man's seeming excitement.

"To a degree, but I haven't been able to identify the species."

"They are rare, Mr. Frye. Until this very moment, I didn't believe they existed."

"Yes, I *assumed* they were rare."

Mr. Ito removed his thick glasses.

"Mr. Frye? Would you like to, would you *sell* these fish to me?"

Tobias was firm, though he hid his resentment and suspicion.

"No. That would be out of the question, Sir."

"I would be willing to pay any price you ask up to twelve million dollars."

Tobias was impressed at such an offer. It made him reflect on his recent concerns for the security of the fish. He had already taken detailed precautions for their safety by purchasing an alarm system, surveillance cameras, and hiring an armed security guard for the infrequent times he left the office, but even all this did not seem to be enough. He was still forced to pray and worry every day.

Perhaps, he thought, Mr. Ito was some noble humanitarian who could ensure the safety of the fish. Surely a man who could pay twelve million dollars for two fish could afford and would devise an unadulterable security system, regardless of the cost. Such an investment would receive the best protection money could buy.

Still, Tobias would know more.

"Mr. Ito. These fish mean more to me and my business partner Friday that you could ever know or believe."

He paused a moment in irresolution.

"I mean, Mr. Ito—in consideration of your offer, there are some things I must know. First of all, why would *anyone* pay so much money for two fish?"

The little Japanese man forced a smile in a deliberate attempt to diffuse the younger man's obvious suspicion.

"A good question, Mr. Frye. The answer lies in ancient Japanese values and beliefs that perhaps *you* would not understand. The many myths and legends associated with your rare fish have caused them to be revered and sought in the courts of emperors and noble men, by warlords, priests, and men of great age and knowledge. So esteemed are these fish to us, that great men and even dynasties have risen and fallen at cause of their possession. The fish may bring great fortune to the owner, and yet, it is said, they may also bring great doom."

Tobias' abstract correlation about the fish was becoming clearer.

"Where do these fish come from?"

Mr. Ito lit an American cigarette before answering.

"We do not know for certain. In history, we have tried over many generations to breed them, but never with success.

Many believe they are like the truffle of Western Europe. They come naturally from the Earth. How? We do not know. We only know that, over the past nine hundred years, they have become more and more rare, and handsome."

"How many are left?"

"As far as I know, Mr. Frye, these which are yours are the only two in three hundred years."

Tobias was saddened by such a thought, and yet, he grew even more determined to guard the fish. In light of the new information, however, he felt himself an inadequate curator for so rare a creature and resource. Perhaps Mr. Ito could afford to provide the indubitable security required.

Nonetheless, there was something in Mr. Ito's speech, something in his voice, something in his countenance that belied his air of benevolence, something in these that made Tobias distrust the smiling man.

"I regret to say, Mr. Ito, that I am unwilling to sell these fish even though you are able to offer so much. I'm sorry. Maybe more fish will turn up somewhere."

"Not in Japan or anywhere. The ocean is becoming too warm and defiled. Perhaps you are a shrewd bargainer, Mr. Frye. I am now willing to pay up to eighteen million dollars for the fish."

"No thank you, Mr. Ito, but if I ever decide to turn the fish over to someone, I'll let you take them for a fair price provided I can name certain conditions."

"And these *conditions*?"

Tobias returned to his desk as he concluded.

"The conditions are irrelevant because, for now, I'm not at all interested in letting my fish go for any price."

After unbuttoning the coat of his American-made suit, Mr. Ito followed and sat in the hand-sewn chocolate-brown leather armchair facing Tobias.

"Very well, but if you ever change your mind—"

Tobias interrupted.

"I'll let you know."

The discussion then shifted to the Tokyo Stock Exchange. Using correlations to reference world events juxtaposed with various economies, Tobias was able to predict market fluctuations with uncanny accuracy. Despite an irresistible desire to inquire on his own American market interests, the Oriental man remembered his assignment and sought other information.

Though respected in Japan as a shrewd manipulator of human resources, Mr. Ito was unable to extract from Tobias the substance of his theories on the accelerated reduction of toxic and nuclear wastes. After several exhaustive attempts, the thoughtful Asian decided he'd stay in Dusty longer than expected so that he could try again on another day.

There were certain legal matters regarding the merger's completion that required execution, so, after Tobias stationed an armed security guard by the aquarium, he and Mr. Ito left to see a lawyer in Oklahoma City.

In her brand new Japanese station wagon parked near the building, Lilly ducked as she watched Tobias and the foreigner drive away. Slipping on her four-inch spike heels, she slinked from the car and into the building, her silky black body suit shimmering in the bright florescent lights of the lobby.

Gently, she undid the pin in her hair to let the wavy jet-black tresses fall around her shoulders, and she sprayed a provocative, spicy *parfum* onto her wrists and between her breasts before entering the elevator. As part owner of the business, she had no problem going past the office receptionist and into her husband's office where she would have indirect access to Tobias' suite and ultimately, the aquarium.

Lilly knew about the armed guard and was prepared to face him. As she eased open the door between the adjoining rooms, the guard snapped straight up from the *Hustler* magazine, his hand on his pistol.

"Who *is* it? Who's there?"

The door swung open to reveal a bawdy Lilly, her body suit unbuttoned and snagged on a delicate, moisturized shoulder. In one hand she held a bottle of Andre Cold Duck Champagne, while in the other she held two good-quality fluted plastic glasses—long, slender, and contoured.

"Lilly? Lilly Wallaby? Is that you?"

"Hello Rhett, I been waitin fer this moment fer a long, long time."

"Are ya nervous?"

"*Heck* yeah I'm nervous! They say I'll get the chair if the judge don't believe me—"

Annoyed, the short, skinny, balding bailiff approached Ethel and Friday, his hand on his pistol.

"Y'all gonna hafta keep it down. Y'all know the judge—he don't take kindly ta people whisperin in his court."

Both sat up. Friday wore a tan polyester suit with a white shirt. The wide coffee-stained paisley tie and butterfly collar spoke for how infrequently he dressed up. Ethel sported another of the fine black dresses the townspeople had grown accustomed to seeing her wear. Many of these same people had converged on the courtroom that day to glean some gossip from Friday's arraignment.

The judge was an African American, or in Dusty, a Negro. Judge Hezekiah Howard had a reputation for being draconian in his sentencing. The severity of his punishments was best illustrated when he sentenced a visiting California blonde to eighteen months in prison for littering in Oklahoma. Because Hezekiah was from a small segregated railroad town nearby and not Dusty, the fact that he had Howard University undergraduate and law degrees didn't count to most folks.

Thus Tobias was still considered the only Dusty home-grown resident with a college degree. Hezekiah was a brilliant though embittered man who unapologetically used his judicial power to punish the same people who, because of their prejudice, had limited the degree of his successes.

After first glancing over a shoulder, Friday whispered to his cousin as the judge severely criticized a man for pecuniary irresponsibility toward his estranged family.

"He's gonna have me fried, Ethel, I jus *know* it!"

She smiled to comfort the nervous, sweaty, twitching young man.

"It's gonna be alrite. Don't worry bout the judge. I'll talk ta him. He's ma cousin."

Friday was incredulous.

"*Him*? But he's a nigger! I, I mean a Negro!"

"Third cousin on ma Daddy's side."

Friday sat back, whispering.

"Well, I guess I *gotta* believe ya. I mean, no person would wanna make up somethin like that... I, I mean... That's good!"

It wasn't long before he made the connection. By that time however, the short bailiff was calling his name.

"Friday Geronimo Hughes!"

He stood up.

"Uh, yeah, that would be me, Judge."

The judge eyed him with contempt.

"Mr. Hughes, my courtroom is *not* a brothel or tavern. You will speak only when spoken to, and you will answer in formal speech. 'Yeah' is unacceptable. You will answer 'yes' or 'no.' Do I make myself clear?"

Friday stood at attention, rigid, saluting the judge.

"Uh, yes! Yes Sir, Mr.— I, I mean? Judge, Sir!"

The judge sighed in disgust and rolled his dark eyes in deep, wrinkled sockets.

"How do you plead, Mr. Hughes?"

"Not guilty, Sir. An I brought a witness ta stand up fer me."

"A witness?"

"Yeah, an she's yer blood-rite cousin if she ain't been puttin me on."

The judge removed his glasses to see Ethel better.

"I don't *believe* this! Ethel? Ethel, what is it?—Frye now? How are ya? It's been years!"

She rose.

"I'm fine, Cousin Zeke. And the reason I came here was ta tell ya that Friday Hughes here was on an errand fer me when Ken Wallaby was poisoned. Couldn'ta been him."

He hardly heard her.

"Really? And how's your mama? I heard she had the fever real bad at one time a few years ago."

"That was a long time ago. She's fine now. An ya know *her*—she's still got her garden till this day and she still—"

Friday was amazed. Hoping to ingratiate himself with the judge, he made a clumsy interruption.

"Ya know, Judge, seein as I'm kin ta Ethel here, an she's kin ta *you*, well then I figure I mus be kin ta *you*, too. Me'n you is *gotta* be cousins somewheres!"

Sobered by the thought, the judge looked toward Ethel who nodded.

"Fifth, once removed. Your Aunt Martha was his auntie too."

Friday grinned in triumph.

"I jus *knew* it!"

The judge fell silent and wrote something on the papers before him. He paused in seeming contemplation before addressing Friday.

"Mr. Hughes, in light of the fact that, despite our *profound* differences, we're..."

He hesitated.

"We're *related*. And because you have such a credible witness in cousin Ethel here... And because Tobias Frye insists no charges be pressed against you, I've decided to dismiss all the charges leveled against you. In the future though, I would advise against you—"

Suddenly Friday's hands flew to his throat and he gasped for air. In a seeming seizure, he flipped onto the table and then down to the floor in front of the judge's bench where he writhed and twisted about.

"Mister Hughes! I *will* have order in this court!"

So panicked was Friday that, when Ethel rushed over attempting to calm him, he punched her in the stomach to send her flying backward.

"Ethel! The *fish*! I! I cain't breathe! Ma fish! Ma fish is outa water! Lilly! It's, it's Lilllieee!"

The judge could make no sense of what was going on.

"Bailiff! Subdue that violent man!"

Friday's next blow sent the bailiff soaring, his mouth and nose bleeding.

"Ma *fish*! Ethel! Please help me! It's Lilly! She's tryin ta kill ma fish! Help me!"

Ethel already knew. By the time Friday could look to the place she had lain sprawled on the floor, she had disappeared from the courtroom.

"Lilly! Now yer way outa *line*, here, Baby! Ya betta put that damn fish back in the tank!"

The shapely, semi-nude woman sighed with dissatisfaction.

"Aw Rhett, you're such a *wimp*! I ain't gonna hurt it. I was just testin somethin out."

The inhibited, naked man just stared at the desperately flapping fish, afraid to go near it.

"Lilly! Come *own*, now! Yer gonna cost me ma *job*!"

She tried to grab the wild, distraught fish, but it struggled away.

"Oh leave me alone, Rhett! Cain't cha see I'm tryin ta *catch* it?"

The fish had bounded into her face, slamming its cold, hard, spiny body into her forehead.

"Ow! That hurt! Rhett! Ya gotta help me! Ow! He *bit* me! I'm bleedin!"

Though unnerved at the sight of Lilly's bleeding face and hand, Rhett grabbed his shirt and thought to wrap up the fish to subdue it, this according to his most recent security guard training seminar.

"Be careful, Rhett! That fish is crazy!"

The nude man was not prepared for an attack as he tip-toed toward the violent fish, so he nearly fainted when the fish, in a sudden burst of panic, flipped toward him and clamped resolvedly onto his "nakedness."

"See to the injured people, Bailiff! And try to keep him away until help arrives!"

Friday continued in his violent seizure. While wildly staggering about the room gasping for air, he had struck and wounded a half-dozen gossipers and knocked out a photographer. The bailiff approached him, stick ready to strike, but Friday could not be subdued. He unintentionally broke the bailiff's right arm and tossed him eight feet into the air before trampling him in a path that led directly toward the judge. Hezekiah Howard, sensing the danger, climbed onto the bench.

"Bailiff! He's headed right for me! *Do* something!"

The bailiff's battered face and bald head were smeared with blood. He cringed in extreme agony as he reset his right arm and spat two of his front teeth onto the old, worn wooden floor.

"What? Whadaya want me ta *do*, Judge? The man's insane!"

"*Shoot* im! Shoot im if you have to! Just do something!"

The bailiff stumbled to a knee and drew his pistol. His shaking hands aimed as Friday reached the nervous judge cowering on the bench.

"He's *got* me, Lilly! Help me! He's got me real good!"

She tugged hard on the fish, much to Rhett's pain and displeasure, but it would not release its grip.

"He won't let go!"

"*Do* somethin, Lilly! Please do somethin!"

Looking around, she found a golf putter leaning against the wall, and she smacked the fish solidly with it, but this only increased Rhett's anguish. The fish held on.

"I'm *tryin*, Rhett! Whadaya want me ta *do*?"

"*Shoot* im! Get out ma gun an shoot im!"

Panicking, she located his pants and holster and withdrew the gun. Trembling, she aimed at the fish.

"*Shoot* him, Bailiff! Now!"

"*Shoot* im, Lilly! Now!"

The guns exploded twice, simultaneously, and bullets tore concurrently through the backs of man and fish. Both froze for an instant in a final all-consuming spasm before falling lifelessly to the floor.

Unfortunately, the judge had been in the bailiff's line of fire and the second bullet had wounded him mortally. Just as inopportune for Rhett, his "nakedness" had been in Lilly's line of fire, and as he lay on the floor fatally wounded, he spoke a final line.

"I, I didn't get ta axe ya before, but ya gatta tell me, Lilly, was I *good*?"

She sighed, smiling.

"Ya were the *best*, Rhett."

Lilly rose and examined the dead fish. She wondered if and how Friday might be dead also. With Friday dead and no heirs to his estate, her profit and share in the business would no doubt increase. And yet, there could exist an even more profound eventuality. There was still one fish left in the tank—Toby. If Toby and Ethel should die, Lilly would own everything.

Still mostly nude, she re-gripped the pistol and approached the aquarium. Leaning over it, she aimed at the last of a species, the last of a kind. Yet even as she steadied the gun, she did not notice the remarkable coloring of the fish, nor did she notice its strength and grace, nor its uniqueness, nor its rarity, nor its environmental impact.

As she followed the fish with the revolver, eager to squeeze the trigger, she did not even notice the person who had crept up behind her. The room seemed to resound with a thud and then the ping of the putter as it rebounded off the back of her head and into the overhead light fixture. Instantly unconscious, she fell face down into the aquarium and did not move again.

Though the result was pleasing to all parties involved, the meeting with the lawyer in Oklahoma City was marked by uncharacteristic fits and starts from Tobias who later apologized. He claimed he felt "uneasy" and "in great peril," but he could not understand why. Returning to town, he left

Mr. Ito at the Dusty Inn and hurried to the office to check the fish.

The police had blocked all entrances to the building with bands of wide yellow tape, but because Tobias had graduated from MIT, he was allowed to pass through the barrier.

When he reached his office, two officers were pulling Lilly's semi-nude body from the aquarium. The less attractive of the two was fat, unkempt, and his face was tattooed with acne scars and still-bleeding sores and scabs. He furtively tugged at her top until the two firm, plump, perfectly-formed breasts jiggled there, exposed.

"What a waste! What a *gadammed* waste!"

Rhett's nude body lay on the floor, his hands grasping the gunshot wound, his expression uncomfortable, while Friday's fish cringed there beside him, a bullet hole through its back.

In shock, Tobias approached the red, pot-bellied officer in charge and stammered his question.

"What? How did this happen, Freddie?"

The sergeant coughed blood into his handkerchief before responding.

"As far as *I* kin tell, Toby—an I *am* a trained detective— Mrs. Wallaby and my nephew Rhett were havin some kinda *weird* sexual ronda-vous here. Apparently, she wasn't exactly *satisfied* with how the boy was takin cara his bidness an she shot im. When she realized what she had done, she went over an drowned herself in the aquarium. We fount the gun at the bottom of the tank."

"And the dead fish?"

The sergeant sighed in a disgusted manner.

"Beats me. But cha know young people taday! They have some strange ideas on sex. Strange indeed! She got little teeth marks on her face, and Rhett—Lord only knows what they was doin with that poor fish."

Tobias watched an officer put Friday's fish into a plastic bag with laboratory tongs.

"Oh, by the way Toby, I dunno if ya heard it yet, but yer partner Friday was killed in court taday by the bailiff when he just went all out crazy and attacked Judge Howard."

Tobias looked toward his own fish.

"You didn't have to tell me that, Sergeant. I already figured as much. But, just from the look of things here, I'd guess the judge was killed too, by accident?"

"That is *exactly* what happened. How'd ja know?"

"Just a guess. A crazy guess, but there's something else going on here. I think there was another person involved, but I don't know why."

The sergeant coughed again, inspecting his handkerchief for blood.

"Don't, don't *thank* so, Toby. We've covered all the bases. If ya thank a somethin or fine somethin, though, ya let me know."

"I will, sergeant. Thank you."

Tobias had waited in the office, enduring sixteen hours of investigation, before the last officer disappeared. Desperate for the security of his fish, he reluctantly called Mr. Ito over that he might announce conditions with reference to a deal.

"Number one: No experiment or test will ever be performed on this fish."

The older man was uncomfortable and hesitant in his reply.

"Mr. Frye, perhaps we can come to a compromise in our terms. If you give me also the fish that died today, I will agree to whatever you demand."

Mr. Ito's eyes searched the room.

"Now Mr. Frye, Where is this other fish?"

"The police have it."

The hopeful smile showed stained and crooked teeth.

"Perhaps they will *give* it to you."

"I don't think so, Mr. Ito. It's being held as evidence, indefinitely. What do you want with a dead fish anyway? What *I* want to know is what guarantees you can give me on the security for my fish if I sell it to you."

The Japanese man thought for a long moment and sighed.

"I am willing to pay thirty million for the fish, but I fear to say I offer no guarantee."

He rose from the armchair and approached the aquarium with Tobias following.

"I'll be honest with you, Mr. Frye. There is something I did not tell you when we discussed your fish before..."

Skeptical, Tobias carefully monitored his fish as he spoke, never looking at his guest.

"And what would that be, Mr. Ito?"

The older man studied the fish as well.

"It is also believed in Japan that this fish can bring great wealth, good health and long life to the man who truly possesses it. A ten-fold increase in wealth is not uncommon, and yet, some men have grown more wealthy by one hundred times. To truly possess it a man may also increase his life by fifty years."

An indefinite phrase stood out in Tobias' mind.

"I'm sorry to interrupt, Mr. Ito, but what do you mean when you say 'to truly possess it'?"

The Oriental smiled and answered.

"'To truly possess it' is to *consume* it. If I buy your fish, I will have it finely sliced and prepared as sashimi and sushi. Half I will consume myself, and I will sell the remaining half to other wealthy men for considerable prices. But for you, you may 'possess' a portion of mine and enjoy the wealth and health it brings for nothing."

Tobias did everything he could to control his physical rage and to still a tongue that sought to hurl a racial epithet.

"There are things in life, Mr. Ito, that money just can't buy. I think you better leave. I think you better leave *now!*"

While Ethel went to all the funerals, she was not the woman she had formerly been. She lost weight and stopped working at the convalescent hospital. Her every waking thought was consumed by her concern for the fish. Consequently, she and Tobias became close and seemed to fall in love with each other all over again.

In spite of the generous offers and numerous attempts at discovering Tobias' theory on the accelerated reduction of nuclear and toxic wastes, the Japanese were forced out of the business. Nevertheless, neither Tobias nor Ethel was prepared for the surprise return of a former business associate, and neither imagined a man of such intellect, discipline, and honor could commit such an extreme act.

"Come on! Put the gun down, Mr. Ito!"

"Do not come any closer, or you might be hurt!"

Ethel's voice quivered with fear as she spoke.

"What do ya *want* from us, Mr. Ito?"

"I want the fish! You must sell me your fish!"

Tobias dropped his arms.

"Mr. Ito, Sir. You may or may not know this, but I'll die if you kill that fish."

"And I'll die if I do not!"

He coughed violently so that, even after wiping with a tissue, there was blood on his lips.

"I have cancer. Many of my friends have cancer. We are dying and we don't know why for sure. Some say we are the final casualties of America's bombs on Hiroshima and Nagasaki. Environmentalists say it's toxic waste. The doctors nor anyone can do nothing for me now. Your fish only will save my life."

A sense of disgrace caused Mr. Ito to order Ethel from the room. Never would it be said that he threatened a woman with a gun. To simply *use* a gun was disgraceful enough.

Once outside the suite, Ethel hurried toward a phone to inform the police what was happening. She had not gone far, however, when she heard the loud explosion of a gun discharging. Afraid to enter, she stayed outside the door and listened, but nothing stirred inside. In horror, she imagined scenario after scenario, all boding tragedy.

Finally, the police assault team arrived, eager to get the gossip, but on kicking open the door, they found a seemingly contrite Tobias sitting on the little stool in front of the aquarium, his head bowed and discharged revolver hanging from a stiff, curved index finger. Mr. Ito lay twisted beside the tank, a bullet hole through his contorted face.

While the officers nervously aimed rifles and shotguns at Tobias, it was Ethel who was brave enough to approach him and take the gun.

"Toby? Honey! What happened?"

He turned toward his worried wife.

"I'm sorry, Ethel."

He took her hand.

"I tried to stop him. He shot himself. He just turned the gun on himself, and he fired."

Cautious, the sergeant approached.

"Then what're you doin with the pistol in yer hand fer, Toby?"

While Ethel surrendered the weapon, Tobias answered.

"I took it from him."

The sergeant coughed blood into a napkin while scanning the room.

"Why? He was *dead* if it happened like ya say. He couldn'ta done no more harm with it. Why take it?"

Tobias slowly looked up at the man.

"You're right. I don't know why I took it."

"Or maybe ya *had* it all along. Everybody *knows* that damn Orientals don't carry guns. They do *karate* an all that."

By this time, Ethel had grown angry. She grabbed the sergeant's arm, turning him.

"What're ya sayin, cousin Freddie? That me and ma husban're lyin? Are ya tryin ta say Toby killed ma cousin, Mr. Ito there?"

He took Ethel's hand.

"You wasn't in the room when it happened, Ethel, an neitha was I. Neitha of us knows nothin fer sure."

He withdrew his cuffs.

"What I *am* sayin is I gotta arrest Toby here on suspicion a murder."

Tobias finally spoke on his own behalf.

"But Freddie, I've never even owned a gun! The man committed suicide! I saw it with my own eyes!"

"Then why the heck didn't he do it in Japan? Don't take me fer no fool, boy! I been watchin war movies fer years. If he was gonna do that hara kiri thang, why would he pay fer a ticket an come alltheway out ta Dusty, Oklahoma smack in the middle a nowhere ta do it? It don't take no fancy college degree an a high-class bidness ta figure *that* out. Somma us uneducated folks round here ain't *stupid* as ya thank we is. Poirnt blank: yer alibi just don't add up. That's why I'm arrestin ya."

He forced Tobias against the desk, searched him, and handcuffed him.

"Ya have the right ta remain silent. Ya have the right ta a lawya. If ya cain't afford a lawya—an I know you can—the court'll appoint one for ya."

When Ethel tried to intercede again, he cut her off.

"Tell it ta the judge, cousin Ethel. Tell it ta the judge."

While he awaited his trial date, Tobias received a visit from Toshi, Mr. Ito's nephew. The thoroughly-Americanized

Japanese young man told Tobias that, while he knew without a doubt his uncle's death was probably the result of a suicide, there were certain provisions for exclusion in his uncle's life insurance policies that would be adversely affected by such testimony.

Toshi explained that, even though he was an American, the Japanese beneficiaries of the policy were family. To testify and deprive family of needed benefits would disservice his uncle's memory. After apologizing, Toshi begged Tobias' forgiveness and departed with great guilt.

In his death, Mr. Ito had become a hero of sorts in Japan. The press eulogized his life, fashioning him as a shining example to the youth and ridiculing the allegation of suicide as a ploy fabricated by a seedy American lawyer.

In the meantime, the Japanese government strongly urged the speedy trial and punishment of a man who had murdered a national treasure. While conscious suicide had once been an honorable option to disgrace in Japan, in this case it had seemed a cowardly and ignoble evasion of responsibility. It was more expedient to believe that Mr. Ito was slain by hands other than his own, regardless of the truth.

"The People of the Sovereign State of Oklahoma verses Tobias Frye, the Honorable Judge Justice Price presiding!"

To Tobias' lawyer, Ira Kafka, the proceedings were an abomination of the justice process. Ira was a Californian who lobbied for and defended environmentalist concerns in the northwest United States. Upon reviewing Tobias' story in the newspapers, he offered his defense free of charge. Besides that, he was Ethel's sixth cousin on her mother's side, three-eighths removed.

According to the national newspapers, Tobias was a lunatic who had murdered a powerful Japanese businessman as a result of an obsession with a rare fish. Many witnesses from

Dusty came forward and attested to the sudden changes that had occurred in Tobias' personality after receiving the fish as well as his paranoia about the fish.

They elaborated about the expensive Beluga caviar he had flown in fresh twice a week, the forty-five thousand dollar security system, and the armed guards who, after failing, were replaced with specially-trained attack rattlesnakes so that, by the time the prosecution was through making its case, Tobias seemed unstable, confused, and dangerous at best.

Skilled at perceiving jurors' proclivities, Ira suggested a defense based on a plea of insanity. Tobias, however, was undeterred.

don't understand the games you lawyers play. Whatever happened to honesty and truth?"

Ira removed his glasses, ran his fingers through curly brown hair and countered.

"What are you doing here in the first place? You told the truth back at the scene. You were honest, and see what it got cha!"

He sighed, turning his back.

"Tobias, honesty and truth are irrelevant. Winning, and, in this case, winning your life, is what's important. The justice system has no respect or use for truth anymore, and the public wouldn't believe it if it knocked em down, trampled em an bit em in the ass. They'd all rather believe a lie!"

Tobias stood there a minute, confused.

"And reality?"

"Reality is boring, Toby. Even if it is recognized, it doesn't sell, and it doesn't win cases. Blame the media. But jurors are the public, and the public believes the best constructed *story*, which is generally also the best constructed *lie*."

Returning the glasses to his nose, Ira reassumed the air of a lawyer giving advice.

"It's all a little ironic in your case, Toby. Your job will be to actually tell the truth. All you have to do is tell the jury what you believe. Tell them your whole crazy fish story. Then let me do my job. I'll prove insanity in your case, which is the closest anyone ever gets to reality anyway."

Ira was fired immediately, and, although Tobias made calls to attorneys in nearly every state in the union, he remained bereft of counsel because not a single honest lawyer could be found.

Finally, he stood alone before the judge.

"And where is your counsel, Mr. Frye?"

Tobias answered.

"I fired my lawyer, your Honor. 'Truth' and 'Reality' will serve as my counsel."

The judge removed his glasses and stared at Tobias.

"Do you realize that you're on trial for *murder* here, Mr. Frye?"

"Yes, your Honor. I do."

"Do you also realize that this is a capital case? Do you realize the consequences which will likely result if you're convicted?"

"Yes, Sir."

The judge's eyes studied the confident man before him.

"The court would be willing to recess to give you the time to hire another lawyer or at least have legal counsel advise you on the great peril you take up by attempting to defend yourself..."

Tobias looked toward Ethel sitting behind him whose expression pleaded with him to accept the court's gesture of goodwill, but he turned back to the judge.

"A recess is not necessary. *Truth* and *reality* should serve adequately as my counsel."

Disgusted, the judge muttered sarcastically under his breath before continuing.

"Very well, Mr. Frye. Now... Do you have any witnesses in your defense?"

"No I don't, your Honor. But I'd like to make a statement."

"A statement?"

The judge sat back in his seat.

"Mr. Prosecutor, do you have any objection to Mr. Frye making a statement here?"

The district attorney was a man in his fifties with white hair who bore an uncanny resemblance to Mark Twain. Twisting at his moustache, he strained to suppress his laughter as he answered.

"Uh no, not at all, your Honor. No, Sir. I cain't have no objection ta that."

The judge shook his head.

"Well then, Mr. Frye, we're prepared to hear your statement. You may begin."

Tobias cleared his throat loudly before speaking.

"Your Honor, Ladies and Gentlemen of the jury, I stand here accused of murdering a former friend and former business associate, but the truth and reality is this: Mr. Ito committed suicide."

He sensed the skepticism in the courtroom.

"It's true. You see, he was already dying. He was dying a slow, torturous death, of cancer. He told me he lived about a hundred miles from Hiroshima when the bomb fell in August 1945. To him, the bombs were the beginning of a great cancer in Japan. And he told me that more than once. Anyway, he also believed, according to Japanese legend, that my fish could save his life and the lives of many of his friends. He offered me thirty million dollars for it, but I couldn't sell it to him. When he finally realized he would never get the fish, he put the gun to his head, and he pulled the trigger."

At that point, Tobias paused, withdrew a handkerchief, and wiped the emotion from his eyes.

"It is true that when the police came, I had the proverbial *smoking gun* in my hand, but that was because I took it from him after, you know, after the suicide. I don't know *why* I did it, but I just took it. It didn't make sense, but I think that most of you, if you were unwilling witnesses in unnatural situations that didn't make perfect sense, most of you in panic might do some things that do not make perfect sense. The police never checked, but if they had, they would have found no gunpowder marks on my hands. Any gunpowder stains would have been found on Mr. Ito's hands."

He looked from his notes and into the confused faces of the jury.

"I did not kill Mr. Ito. He was a man I respected and a good friend. I have told you the reality of what happened. It is unsensational, it is not incredible, but it is the truth."

Ethel alone applauded the statement as Tobias sat, while the rest of the courtroom sat in quiet contemplation. Only after scribbling an outline for himself, the district attorney rose and faced the court. Approaching, he smiled, sat on the table, and put a hand on Tobias' shoulder.

"A very well-prepared statement there, Mr. Frye. Covered all your bases, spoke up, looked us all in the eyes, wasn't too nervous. Tell me something. Did you and your invisible friends Mr. Truth and Mr. Reality there learn all that fine lawyerin at MIT?"

The courtroom erupted in laughter. Pleased with his own humor, the district attorney rose and faced his audience, though he addressed his remarks to Tobias.

"I just got a few questions for ya here, now either three of ya can answer."

More laughter. Smiling and confident, he took up his notes.

"First of all, thirty million *dollars* for a fish? Now that's a heap a money! He offered it ta ya, an ya still wouldn't sell it? Why?"

Tobias thought before answering.

"The fish is extremely rare. It's the last of a kind. Besides that, the fish is very important to me for personal reasons."

"Thirty million *dollars* important! Well, I guess that's pretty darn important, isn't it?"

"Very important."

"Important enough ta *kill* for, Toby?"

"No! I mean yes! No, wait! I did not kill Mr. Ito!"

The judge intervened in Tobias' behalf.

"Mr. Prosecutor, I know you're having fun, but I have to warn you—"

The district attorney interrupted.

"I'm sorry, Judge. Please forgive me, Mr. Frye."

He paused, biting a pencil butt before continuing.

"Ya know, Toby, didja ever think ol Mr. Ito coulda taken better cara that 'last of a kind' fish than even you could? He coulda maybe bred it? Ta be able ta offer thirty million, he musta been a wealthy, wealthy man!"

Tobias tensed, took a breath and answered.

"Mr. Ito would have killed my fish, Sir. I know that."

"Really? An how would ya know that?"

He crossed his arms and spoke.

"He *told* me. He told me he wanted to make my fish into sushi."

The judge's gavel was required to end a sudden loud session of commenting and whispering in the courtroom.

"Sushi! Why wouldn't ya jus figure that! An the thoughta your fish on that little Jap's plate an on his little chopsticks made ya pretty damn mad, didn't it?"

"Yes! No! I mean it was an insult! It was a complete disregard for life!"

"Did ja two have an argument?"

Tobias calmed himself and answered.

"No. No argument. But I ended our business dealings at that point."

"I see."

The prosecutor returned to his table to retrieve a written note.

"You're a pretty smart man, ain't cha, Toby? Graduated from MIT an all?"

"Yes, I went there."

"Get good grades?"

"Okay grades."

"Graduate with honors?"

"Yes."

"Truth is, ya graduated first in your class. Number one! Highest honors out of everbody! Is that true?"

The answer came with some reluctance.

"Yes."

Flipping through a notepad and then returning to his desk, the prosecutor displayed a sheet of paper.

"Here I've got an article about you, Mr. Frye. *Time* magazine says you got one of the top IQs in the world. Is that true?"

Tobias thought a moment.

"It's in the magazine, though I'm not sure how the reporter, or anyone is qualified to make such a statement."

Mischevious, the district attorney smiled at the jury.

"I see. And in spite of alla your smarts, is it true ya believe, if your little fishie dies, then you'll die too?"

Tobias answered after the laughter subsided.

"It isn't a matter of belief. It's a reality. My business partners also had fish. Ken was poisoned when his fish was poisoned; Friday was shot in the back when his fish was shot in the back."

The district attorney laughed to mock him.

"Now what a coincidence! That really *is* interestin! *National Enquirer* interestin!"

He laughed, twisting the moustache again, and spoke toward the jurors.

"I really like lookin at that *National Enquirer*—I just can't seem to resist them incredible, sensational headlines when I'm at the supermarket checkout line. But, ya know, if ya really read the stories in that silly paper an look at only the facts, those incredible stories seem ta fall apart. Happens every time."

He turned back to Tobias.

"You *say* whatever happens ta the fish happens ta the man, but did ja know that jus last week they found the toxic waste used ta kill Ken at his house an proof positive in a letter ta Friday that Lilly poisoned im? Did ja know *that*, Toby?"

"No. The police reports aren't public—"

The prosecutor interrupted.

"Are ya sayin Lilly then went down an poisoned his *fish* with toxic waste too?"

"No, I'm not saying that. I—"

"Toby, I know there's sposeta be *some* fish with lungs, but do those fish y'all had have lungs?"

"No."

"Well did ja know that in court, Friday suffered a severe asthma attack that provoked the violence, which led ta his shootin by the bailiff? Did ja know it was asthma?"

"I knew he suffered from asthma, but—"

"Did his fish also have a asthma attack?"

There was no answer though Tobias' eyes displayed latent anger.

"What's that stuff you're so famous for? I'm just a simple country boy who don't understan those high concepts. What is it? Abstract *what*?"

"Abstract correlations."

"That's it! That's rite! Abstract correlations! And a 'correlation' means 'somethin havin related parts or elements'? Is that rite?"

"Yes."

"So how're ya gonna relate a man, a human bein, ta a fish or anythang else fer that matter?"

By this time, Tobias' rage had grown to the point of exasperation. He stood, shouting.

"Is it that hard to understand? *Everything's* related! That's what nobody understands! That fish is me! I am that fish! And *somewhere* out there in Nature, something is *you*! All of you! But look at you! You're either blind or don't care! You'll keep on until it's too late!"

The judge's gavel and voice rose above Tobias' diatribe.

"Mr. Frye, I *will* have order in this court! I'll put you in jail and throw away the key if you continue in this manner!"

Tobias stopped and turned to the judge. His voice was ominous.

"You can do anything you want to me. You have that power. But Judge, somewhere out there there's a fish with *your* name on it, or a salamander, or maybe a lizard. And when someone out there thoughtlessly deep-fries it, fishes with it, or squashes it, then you'll finally believe me."

"Environmentalist!"

The district attorney's slur was followed by other terrible epithets rifled from the crowd of witnesses who hurled vegetable matter and other objects while threatening greater violence. Even the jurors jeered so violently that the guards quickly escorted Tobias away for his own safety. The astute prosecutor capitalized on the emotion in the room.

"Your Honor, I submit that Tobias Frye is a unstable maniac and a threat ta society. I further submit ta you that he has lied in your court taday. He took that gun and blew a man's brains out because he believes he's intamately related ta a *fish*! The prosecution strongly recommends the maximum penalty for this heinous, horrible crime. We rest our case."

It took only eleven minutes for the jury to get coffee, eat a few donuts, to discuss the day's weather and to reach a unanimous verdict of "guilty" on the charge of murder in the first degree. The judge, according to the Court's graces, asked Tobias if he'd like to make a statement before being sentenced. Slowly Tobias stood, wondering how events had turned so bad so fast.

As he looked out on hundreds of hate-contorted, jeering faces, he wondered if there was any *meaning* in the entire experience, he wondered if any purpose had been served. Then he looked to Ethel who was weeping silently, her heart broken and her spirit crushed.

Of all the things he could have changed in his life, Tobias would have treated Ethel differently, he would have treated her better, he would not have taken her so much for granted. She had been devoted to him since they first met as fifteen-year-old Dusty High sophomores.

After having married him at seventeen, she endured the MIT experience and the post-graduate work, as well as two active sons and countless science projects that kept him constantly away from home. It didn't seem to matter to her that he had never told her he loved her—she had given up the hope for romance in her life.

It didn't seem to matter to her that Tobias never remembered her birthday or their anniversary or that he had never showed her concern or affection, but in his heart, he knew it *did* matter. For years, on those rare occasions he was at home, he knew that somewhere in the wee hours of every night, Ethel would slip away from the bed and cry bitterly behind the locked bathroom door. Her life was miserable and he knew it, but she was a dedicated, caring wife.

Sometimes though, Ethel felt a little intimidated at being married to a man the world described as brilliant. Yet his genius at abstract correlation was commonplace at home, and she saw nothing remarkable about a man who constantly forgot to lift the seat before urinating and always sprayed the last few drops on the floor.

Recently however, during the trial, he had surprised her with small though genuine displays of affection. Just before returning for the verdict, he had smiled at her and kissed her cheek, and in the evening before, he even held her hand for a few minutes after dinner. As she sat there in the courtroom weeping, she was the most beautiful and wonderful person in the world to Tobias.

When the judge tapped on the gavel, she raised her eyes to look on her husband who stood across the courtroom in the splendid black suit, his face simultaneously displaying anger, resolution and grave concern.

Sitting at an opposing table, the District Attorney, pleased with his work, twisted at his bowtie, then smiled and winked at Tobias. The judge's seeming stern face belied his own concern as he thought that perhaps there *was* a salamander out there with his name on it, yet he was resentful that Tobias had made him consider such a thought.

Focused and solemn, Tobias cleared his throat.

"I am not an environmentalist like you say, but I respect Nature. I also have respect for the relationships I do not understand. Everything existing is in some way related. Everything is interdependent. We don't always know how, but we should realize that, in spite of our ignorance, we *still* have a responsibility to those relationships. Whether it's cancer, AIDS, serial killers, high school shootings or toxic waste, the lasting solutions are not legal, moral, or chemical, but *relative*. Man's solutions lie in understanding relationships."

The judge was gentle and empathetic in his interruption.

"Your words were fine, Mr. Frye, but ironically enough, you have said nothing 'relative' to your case. Please try."

Tears of frustration welled in Tobias' eyes.

"Can anyone even *hear* me?"

Warm, briny rivulets streamed down his face as silent, he looked over the throngs gathered around, their stony, Neanderthal brows set against him.

"I did not kill Mr. Ito, and yet you want to kill me. Sadly, what Mr. Ito didn't understand, what none of you understand, is that we can't lastingly benefit ourselves by hating or destroying, we do it by preserving, by analyzing, and by understanding."

He assumed a place in front of the judge as he faced the listening crowds.

"There are reasons for everything that happens, and these reasons lie in relationships that occur every day right under our noses. We only have to look. We have *all* made abstract correlations at one time or another. We've observed and made conscious links between an agent and an event, between an abstract cause and a seemingly unrelated effect."

He paused.

"But because we haven't understood the *nature* of these relationships, we've passed them off as superstitions, hunches, and old wives' tales. These same relationships, whether believed or understood, are *realities*. I *know* there is a fish out there with my name on it. I know I am responsible for protecting that fish. Whether or not I would have killed Mr. Ito to protect it, I never found out. Suicide was his escape. In spite of this, a jury of my peers has found me guilty of murder."

By this time, the district attorney, his bushy white moustache twitching, was pondering the possible truth of Tobias' words.

Tobias faced the judge.

"Your Honor, you can sentence me to what you will, but I am confident that, as long as my fish stays healthy, nothing can happen to me. If by chance, my fish and I die, you will all lose out somehow. In both of us you will have destroyed the last of a kind."

Tobias went back to his table and paused in thought for a moment.

"I'll close with this, a relationship you will all come to understand in time. You see, in spite of what even the environmentalists believe, Nature has a way of protecting itself. Consider all these cancers and AIDS as nothing less than a polite warning. If man continues to disregard the abstract correlations in his environment, then that environment itself will manufacture his destruction."

As Tobias sat, the judge took a moment to scribble something on a legal pad before stammering his first few words.

"Uh, thank... Thank you. I have heard enough, Mr. Frye. I'm sufficiently convinced that you are *indeed* an environmentalist though you say you are not. I'm just as convinced that you're a madman. You should have pleaded insanity, but you didn't. I afraid you've tied my hands. And for that reason I'm forced to do something I've never done before. Although I'm ideologically against it, I'm sentencing you, Mr. Frye, to the penalty of death."

In spite of being fired by Tobias, Ira Kafka had followed the trial closely as it was reported in *The Dusty Dish*. He phoned Tobias on the eve of the final appeal with news of a planned trip to Japan to visit insurance companies that might prove Mr. Ito's suicide, thus absolving Tobias of the murder charge.

Minutes after the appeal, Tobias and Ethel sat quietly in a private room, awaiting a decision. He nervously grasped her hand.

"How's my fish?"

"Healthier'n ever. Seems kinda lonely though. How're you?"

"Fine."

He shivered though he wore a sweater.

"I think you should check the water temperature. I've been so cold lately."

There was an uncomfortable silence before Ethel spoke.

"You afraid?"

"No! Not at all. I'm not afraid."

She bowed her head.

"I am!"

Overcome with new emotion for his wife, he took her in his arms and held her heart close to his.

"Don't worry, Ethel. I'll be fine. Nothing can happen to me as long as you take care of my fish."

She was crying.

"That's just *it*, Toby! I dunno if I'm capable a that! That's makin *me* responsible fer ya stayin alive. Me! An there's so much can go wrong. What if somethin happens?"

"Nothing will happen, Ethel. We just won't let it."

Thirty-one seconds later, a prison official barged into the small room, his expression somber and his gravelly voice grave.

"Cousin Ethel, Mr. Frye. Yer final appeal was denied. Yer execution date has been finalized fer two weeks from taday—that's exactly fourteen days a life ya got left. Enjoy em. I'm sorry, Mr. Frye. Ya jus betta hope yer rite bout that fish."

Toshi too, had been monitoring Tobias' case as reported in *The Dusty Dish*, but not without a profit-inspired motive. A consortium of powerful Japanese businessmen had offered him enormous wealth and a secure position if he could "acquire" and "deliver" Tobias' theory on the accelerated reduction of toxic and nuclear wastes. Because he was related to Ethel, Toshi often went to her house and begged her to sell her husband's work, but she was more concerned with Tobias and the fish.

On one such occasion, Toshi glanced over at the huge salt-water aquarium and was enchanted by the brilliant, colorful, exotic creature within.

"And what kinda fish is this, cousin Ethel?"

Even as she spoke, she flicked a switch, which drew a curtain that began to surround the aquarium.

"It's, it's a toby, Cousin Toshi, a toby."

The curtain was Ethel's contribution to the protection of the fish, but this time, as the black runner circled the tank, it caught the cord of an electric auxiliary pump and drew it toward an opening in the aquarium's top.

"Your husband's *theory*, Cousin. Name a price and it will be paid. Money is no object."

She was beginning to grow tired of him.

"Now Toshi, I got a husban on death row not ta mention a million other stresses in ma life. The *last* thang I wanna do is talk science with ya. And if I knew what'n where the damn theory was, the last thang I'd wanna do is talk bidness bout it! So jus forget it, will ya, Toshi!"

Toshi remained undeterred as he scanned the office.

"Does he keep it in this room?"

"Oh *I* don't know! Yeah, I would thank he does."

She went to and opened the door.

"Now, if ya don't mind, Toshi, I need some rest. Ya gotta leave, and frankly I don't thank I want cha comin back for a while. Ya're really startin ta *bug* me, Toshi. Bye."

She slammed the door. In the thirteen days since the final appeal, Ethel had grown very tired running back and forth between the prison, the office and home—so tired in fact that she did not notice Toshi's nervousness as he stole her office keys.

Ira Kafka arrived early in Oklahoma City the next morning, and he raced his Japanese sportscar toward the prison with proof positive that Tobias was probably innocent. As he arrived at the guard's desk, he was told that Tobias was out getting a haircut and a shave in preparation for the execution. When a bald Tobias and distressed Ethel finally appeared ninety-one minutes later, Ira was nearly hysterical.

"Toby! Where have you been for so long? You're scheduled to be *executed* in an hour."

Tobias and Ethel were confused and yet hopeful so that excitement rang in Ethel's voice as she spoke.

"What *is* it, Ira? What happened in Japan?"

"Toby's innocent! I've got *proof*! Mr. Ito did have cancer. Here I've got eleven signed affidavits from people who'll testify if necessary that he said he was going to kill himself! *And* I have a note Ito wrote to his own family saying the same!"

"Oh Cousin Ira, that's *great*!"

The three, with the guard, ran the papers up to the warden, but he was a man of rules and regulation. He refused to even examine the documents, claiming that in doing so he'd be overstepping the "paramadors" of his office.

"When I execute, I'm justa pawn carryin out the ordas of the *executive* man in the State of Oklahoma, the Governor. I do what he says. Now, if ya git *him* ta tell me ta hold off so everone kin see ya papers, I'll do it. Hearin out these kinda thangs is his *job*. So I suggest ya give *him* a call or go ta his office or somethin, cuz in fifty minutes, I gotta do *ma* job."

Ira flew to the phone and called, but the Governor was in a meeting with Japanese business and couldn't be disturbed.

"Come on, Ethel! We've gotta get *over* there!"

Though anxious to leave, she was shocked when she looked back toward Tobias. It was only the second time she had ever seen him cry.

"Toby?"

"Ethel, I *love* you, Ethel—I love you so much."

Now weeping herself, she rushed to his embrace.

"Oh Toby! All ma *life* I've wanted ta hear ya say it. I always wanted ta believe it. I wanted ta feel it, ta live it!"

She kissed his mouth.

"Oh, I kin feel it now!"

Impatient, Ira dragged her from the embrace.

"Oklahoma City's a forty-five minute drive! We've gotta hurry, Ethel!"

Tobias launched a desperate plea as Ira and Ethel reached the door.

"Ira, *you* go to see the Governor. Do everything you can."

He looked lovingly toward his wife.

"Ethel, I want *you* to go watch the fish—just in case Ira doesn't get there in time."

With the wetness of Tobias' kiss still on her lips and a new fire burning in her heart, Ethel hurried with Ira out the door.

The metal bell clanged loudly as Ethel, in her car, raced to beat the train to the intersection, but the crossing arm impeded her passage and brought her to a screeching stop that spun the car one hundred forty-seven degrees. Heavy breathing was one of her body's reactions to the sudden adrenalin surge, but she pulled herself together enough to notice that the train had four engines. So many engines usually meant more cars and a longer wait. She began counting the cars to control her impatience but ended up slamming her fists on the dash and steering wheel in frustration.

As she looked back up, she wondered for a first time, "What on God's green earth!" the train could be hauling in so many cars. Squinting her eyes, she trained her vision on the white lettering printed on a car that approached and passed: HAZARDOUS WASTE. The next car read the same, as did the next and nearly twenty others that she counted. "Hazardous waste," she thought, "oughta be bout the same as toxic waste."

But what puzzled her most of all was the quantity: two of these trains passed through Dusty each day carrying at least as many hazardous waste tanks, and trains like this one had been passing through for as long as she could remember. The question was: where was all this toxic waste *coming* from? And even more eerie, where was it going?

She could hear the sound of the sound again as the caboose passed and the crossing arm raised itself. Tires screeching over the tracks and onto the road, she heard the pager's high-pitched and steady beeping. She punched a button on the top right corner, resulting in "911" on the display. This meant, without a doubt, that something had gone wrong at the office.

The motor hummed as the black curtain steadily re-gathered itself on the track to reveal the huge aquarium standing against the back wall of the office. The short man who crept carefully toward it had in his hand a thick notebook.

This intruder was Toshi Ito, and he had illegally entered the office with the hope of stealing Tobias' renowned theory on the reduction of nuclear and toxic wastes, but the great body of work could not be found. What Toshi *did* find, however, were notes on Tobias' new theory on "Relativity" and his notes on the fish, complete with details on conversations with Mr. Ito.

Whether Toshi wanted the fish to sell it or for personal consumption was unclear, but he had gone to the tank and was chasing the fish with an oversized net when the eleven-foot-long guard Texas western diamondback attack rattlesnake latched onto his lower leg.

Panicked to the limit of sanity, he lashed wildly, and, finally concluding that the consumption of the fish would cure him, he thrashed violently into the water with a hand desperate to grasp the fish. On the floor the reptile recoiled and prepared to strike again. In one poorly aimed stab at the fish, Toshi accidentally flipped the switch that drew the circular blind.

The motor hummed as the black curtain steadily extended itself along the track to engulf Toshi, the rattlesnake, and the suddenly agitated watery scene.

Ira fared well with the Governor. The mere mention of Tobias' name brought the administrator's instant response. The Governor himself had been closely monitoring the case in *The Dusty Dish* and had been actively searching for a way to stay the execution. Ira's revelations and testimony would give him sufficient grounds. Consequently, it was the Governor who made the frantic call to the warden, and it was the Governor who assured Ira that the State of Oklahoma was literally incapable of executing an innocent man.

Simultaneous with the Governor's call to the prison, Ethel screeched to a halt in front of the Frye building. It was only after she got into the lobby that she realized her keys to her husband's suite were missing. As she tugged the unlocked door and entered, the edifice held a sense of foreboding, a sense of tragedy.

A power spike or failure had caused the computer on the mezzanine to shut down while the building's digital clocks' LCDs blinked 12:00 continuously. She hurried up to the office and pounded on the door.

"God help me! I gatta check that fish!"

Frantically, she grabbed the doorknob only to find it wasn't locked. Panting, she stumbled into the seemingly empty room. Feebly, she forced her paralyzed legs to move her toward the aquarium. From her purse she withdrew the small black remote that operated the aquarium curtain.

She pointed and pressed the button. Nothing happened. She mashed it again with the same result, and then she realized something she had missed initially: The aquarium pump was not working. As a matter of fact, all the electricity in the office was off. The backup auxiliary pump wasn't even working.

She rushed to the aquarium, and without thinking, she ripped the curtain from the track. Her scream was horrific. Staggering backward toward the desk, she fell onto it while gasping for breath in order to scream again. She closed her eyes, hoping the vision of terror before her was unreal, but as she opened them, she only reacted with a nauseated, guttural groan.

Toshi's body sprawled there dead, an arm and face in the water. His expression, through the glass and salt-water, was still adjusting itself to death. The attack rattlesnake was stretched out its full eleven feet, dead and attached to Toshi's leg. Apparently, it had bitten the young man in the very instant that the black curtain finally dragged the auxiliary pump into the water and both were electrocuted.

Saddest of all, Toby's fish floated at the water's surface. It flapped a fin feebly and gaped for oxygen. Clinging to the hope of saving her husband, Ethel hurried over, unplugged the pump, and lifted the fish from the water, but the fish only looked at her with an expression of sadness, of pity and of great love. It seemed to wink a final "goodbye" and died in her hands.

She was startled enough to drop the fish when the phone suddenly rang. Ira's voice was ecstatic.

"Ethel! Great news! The Governor called over to the prison and stopped the execution!"

She drew in a languorous breath and sighed with relief.

"Oh Ira! Praise the Lord! Please! Please tell me again."

"Toby isn't going to be executed! The Governor saw all the documents I brought and he stayed the order!"

"Oh! *Thank* you! Ira, thank you! I'll be rite on down."

Slowly, a sense of foreboding began to grow again in her mind as she glanced at the fish.

"Waitaminute Ira! Where're ya at?"

"I'm still at the Governor's office, why?"

"Do ya know for a fack they didn't carry out the execution?"

"Ethel! Why are you stressing yourself out? I know the Governor ordered it stopped. What is wrong with you?"

A dial tone was the only answer he received.

"Hello? This is Ethel Frye, Toby's Frye's wife. May I speak with the warden?"

She turned away from the tragedy of the aquarium and the fish.

"Hello Warden. This is Ethel Frye. Where's ma—"

The voice on the other end said something to make her hang up. She sat a minute before she began to cry, and she wept for an hour before she began carrying out one of Tobias' last wishes. First, she tore pages from a notebook randomly found in the aquarium stand and placed them in a metal trash can, then she lowered the fish into the can, and finally, she added more pages and lit it ablaze.

Soon, she could smell the stench of flesh burning as the fire crackled and hissed in the center of the room. It was in the fluttering light of this conflagration that her eyes caught the name on the notebook's label.

Quickly, she rushed to the can and tried to salvage some of the pages, but they had been burned too badly. Her charred hands and fingers and later her face were black as she fell to the floor and wept into her palms.

"I'm sorry, Toby! I'm so sorry!"

In scrambling for the pages in the can, she had knocked it over, and quickly fire tiptoed across the carpet to the black curtain and to the window drapes where it raced toward the ceiling. Ethel still lay on the floor, clinging to the notebook that had once held the only copy of Tobias' theory on "The Reduction of Toxic and Nuclear Wastes."

"I wanna die! I jus wanna *die*!"

Fortunately, the sprinkler system came on and the room was instantly obscured in an artificial high-pressured water-storm.

Ira walked toward the shrouded woman in black who stood in the breeze on the starboard deck of a chartered fishing boat that bobbed in the briny waters north of San Francisco Bay. The Golden Gate Bridge stretched from rock to rock in the distant background with a skirt of fog which made it seem all the more picturesque and surreal. It was chilly, though the sky was a patchy blue.

"Is this a good place?"

As she removed the shroud, he saw she was crying unabashedly. She was beautiful. She answered.

"No. Not yet. I jus cain't leggo yet."

In her hands she held the decorative urn—blue, white, and delicately cameo-laden. The funeral director said it had been filled with the incinerated remains of Tobias, his fish, and his lost theory.

"You have *got* to let go, Ethel. It's what Toby wanted. You promised you would leave him here, in the sea. By the Golden Gate. Let *go*."

She nodded slowly in agreement, pried the lid from the urn, and, listlessly, let that cover fall into the ocean. Turning her head, she tipped the vase and let the ashes spill into the water, and when the urn was empty, she let it tumble over the side of the boat.

It floated for a moment, filling with seawater, moved to a vertical position and sank. Her eyes searched for an instant landmark so she might remember the place, a place that with each passing second, became a smaller and lighter stain in the swelling blue-green seawater. Whatever her husband had been, his love, his ideas, and his genius, just drifted away, dispersed and faded into the profound enormity of the sea.

The on-board barometers fell as the winds arranged gray and black cloudbanks in the sky and a cold breeze began to blow. Nevertheless, the boat's captain continued seaward hoping to make a rendezvous around Cordell Banks before noon. Ira approached the weeping woman whose swollen eyes were lost sifting for traces of Tobias through the briny swells of a seemingly eternal, unyielding, and sentient sea.

Her bottom lip trembled as she thought of being alone, bright red hair outlining a plain though pretty face that seemed wonderful and vulnerable at the same time. Clutching her shoulders from behind, Ira turned her and kissed her. Her struggles to free herself only made him more excited. Finally, she tore away, stumbled toward, and fell onto the pitted, scratched, and scarred cold-steel fish cleaning station in the center of the trawler's stern, sputtering an angry complaint.

"Ira Kafka! What! What the *heck* has gotten inta you?"

He rushed toward her, his hands groping her breasts and firm behind, but she parried by striking a knee-blow to his center of gravity.

"Ira! I don't know what's wrong with ya, but I'm warnin ya! You stay away from me!"

She watched him rise, groan, and lean painfully onto the cleaning station.

"Ira, now this ain't like ya at all. Please, please tell me what the hell is goin on!"

Nodding in acknowledgment, he lunged toward the rail to stand beside her and spoke between labored breaths.

"Ethel, I know. I know what you've been up to. I've known it all along. You, you aren't sorry about Toby bein dead and you know it."

She eyed him incredulously.

"I dunno what you're *talkin* about!"

"Yeah you do, Ethel. I've know it all along."

Now she was insulted and irritated.

"*What* do ya know, Ira? Go on. Tell me what cha know."

"I know about Lilly. Everybody else was fooled, but I know you outright killed her."

He smiled, studying her reaction, before continuing.

"It's all right. I'm the only one who knows for sure, though I think Toby knew, but he's gone. Everyone *else* thinks she drowned herself."

Nervous, Ethel began.

"Ira, I swear ta ya I didn't want—"

He interrupted.

"The putter. You bashed her head with that golf putter. And you might just get away with it."

Her look was a culpable one.

"Ira, ya don't understan—"

"I do, Ethel. And I know you were in on the plot against your husband all along—you and Friday, your sometime lover. But then so were Ken and Lilly. But only you succeeded at getting them all out of the way."

She looked away and turned back, angry.

"Horse feathers! Can ya offer any proof a any a that?"

Ira smiled as he stroked her face.

"You *underestimated* Toby, Ethel. He was a shrewd man. You knew he had everything on videotape, so you pulled it and destroyed it, but what you didn't know was that Toby, as neurotic as he was, had a second, hidden camera. I found his cache of hidden tapes and got it all: Lilly and Rhett doing it three times, Lilly experimenting with Friday's fish, her making Rhett a dead eunuch and all."

He turned her face toward his.

"And then there's the image of you savagely cracking Lilly in the head with that expensive putter."

She pulled her face away to hide seemingly contrite eyes as he went on.

"And that's not all. Friday, your lover and partner in crime—he wasn't too bright. He ran off his mouth to a lotta people. Toby knew you tried to kill his fish the first time and knew you'd try again. He had notes. He knew about all of you."

When Ethel looked back up, her eyes, attitude, and even her complexion had changed.

"Alrite. Whadaya *want* from me, Ira?"

"It's really simple."

Her eyes surreptitiously scanned the stern for options.

"Well, what *is* it?"

"You."

"What?"

"Don't act so surprised. You've known it all along, and you've used it to your advantage. I know it's crazy, but I *love* you Ethel, and now that Toby's gone, I want you to be my wife."

Skeptical she eyed him, searching for a deeper motive.

"That's all very nice, Ira. But if I'm a murderer like ya say I am, why would ja wanna marry me?"

He took her shoulders, looking into her eyes.

"That's just it, Ethel. You're not a murderer. When you killed Lilly, I'd like to think that a part of you wanted to protect Toby. I guess I'm a fool for believing it, but I do."

He caught her eyes.

"Marry me, Ethel."

"An if I won't?"

"Then I'll tell. I'll tell everything I know. I'll have to as a sworn officer of the court. But then, on the other hand, a husband can't be forced to testify against his wife."

She pulled away and sighed, looking away.

"Oh, alrite Ira, I'll marry ya. But we gotta give me some time ta grieve for Toby. Dusty folks'ld be gossipin more'n ever if I married too soon."

"Not if we got married here in California. Who cares about those ignorant, white-trash, dumb-as-dirt Okies in Dusty anyway. We can go to the justice of the peace as soon as we get back to San Francisco."

As her eyes continued to scan the stern, she focused on a large gaffing hook mounted on a wall and moved toward it.

"This is all so sudden, Ira. I'm really lost fer words. What about ma boys, ma sons?"

"We'll send for them. They're better off in California where people chew their food."

She approached him with a cigarette between her lips, and he lit it for her.

"Thank you."

Smiling, she took his matches. He took her hand.

"Tell me one thing, Ethel."

She blew smoke into his face.

"What, what's that?"

"Toby. as strange as he was, he wasn't a bad man. Why would you wanna do him in? I mean, were you in love with Friday or what?"

"Of course not. Friday was great between the legs, but he was a idiot."

She led Ira to the outside wall of the cabin and she sat back onto a raised crew seat under the huge blood-encrusted gaffing hook. Her voice and expression were rueful.

"I loved Toby, but then I hated im too. No one would ever believe it cuz they wasn't married ta him, but he was cruel in a kinda innacent way. Ya see, I, I was just somethin he had ta do. He never *cared* about me. He coulda never belonged ta me an he knew it. He knew it from the start, but he married me anyway. That's why I hated im. He shoulda known. He shoulda cared I'd be miserable, but he married me anyway."

Tears flowed from her eyes as she looked down on Ira.

"That selfish bastard! He gave me a miserable life. He was always gone, or workin! Heck, even when he was flesh'n blood right with me he was gone or workin! It didn't make me feel good about myself or anythang. It made me feel ugly an dumb an unwanted. Might not seem like it ta anyone else, but I had a miserable life, Ira."

Looking up, his eyes welled with sympathetic tears.
"Ethel?"

"Let me finish, Ira. That's why I kilt im. *I* set up that
pump ta fall in an electrocute that damn fish! *I* did it! An I
swore a long time ago that if Toby was gone, I was gonna never
let nobody make me miserable again."

There was an ominous tone in her voice. As her eyes
darted aside again, Ira, with her, focused on the pole behind
her with the terrible hook all smeared with blood. Her voice
trembled with resolution.

"An that's why I could never marry ya, Ira."

He wavered between panic and anger.

"You, you have to marry me, Ethel! Or you'll go to jail!"

"The *hell* I do!"

All at once Ira was soaking wet. Ethel had doused him
with liquid from a bucket sitting near her feet. He was angry at
first, and then he noticed his skin had a characteristic itch he
couldn't quite identify. The terror struck all at once as his
sinuses and lungs reacted to the inhalation of petroleum
distillates.

"Ethel! Nooo!"

The tiny, violent, flaming match sailed and flickered
surrealistically toward Ira and ignited the fumes reeking from
his clothes even before reaching him. Instantly consumed by
fire, Ira's figure, which at that moment appeared as merely a
shadow in the brightly burning flames, turned, fled three steps,
and dove toward the water only to be sundered and shredded
by the boat's huge propeller. Minutes later, gulls and brown
pelicans scavenged for bits of Ira occasionally roiled to the
surface in a sea that grew more agitated.

Ethel was startled by a loud and sudden splash on the
boat's starboard side near the bow. She rushed along the
trawler's edge on the narrow walkway that passed the cabin,

and she looked over the railing. In the water there was a lifeboat, and in that lifeboat was the trawler's captain.

The captain was a nervous old man who had watched Ethel set Ira on fire. He had called the Coast Guard to report the incident just before untying and lowering the lifeboat.

A retired banker who navigated for purely recreational purposes, the captain thought it would be better to abandon ship than be possibly forced to shoot a woman. Taking up the oars, he heaved, steering away from the forty-two foot fishing boat.

She called after him.

"Captain? Captain!"

The man would not even raise his eyes.

"Ya cain't leave me out here! Please! Come back!"

The sixty-two-year-old had achieved a comfortable rhythm with the oars. Never once did he even hesitate.

"Come back, Captain! Pleeease! I'll *die* out here!"

She was crying.

"Ya don't undastan!"

Ethel continued begging and crying until the small boat became a speck obscured on the watery horizon. By this time, strong winds were whipping salty spray into her face that stung her cheeks and burned her eyes.

As Nature grew more violent, the white-capped waves and water became choppy at first, before a certain synchronicity produced monstrous and irresistible swells. The boat would suddenly rise twenty feet on a swell and plummet with a crash just as suddenly. On two occasions, the un-piloted boat nearly capsized.

Ethel crawled back to the stern and clung to the cleaning station as she watched thousands of gallons of seawater racing onto one side of the deck and off the other.

"God! Help me!"

The entire sky grew gray-black before the downpour began. Straining her eyes to look out, Ethel couldn't tell where the sky ended or the water began. She thought, however, that in one brief instance, she saw a small light out in the blackness, and then it was gone. Her belief in that light inspired her to use the radio in the cabin.

"S.O.S! S.O.S., dammit! This is Ethel Frye! I'm lost out here all by mahself!"

The loud static that followed held the hope of vague voices interspersed with high-pitched frequency signals. Drenched, she brushed the soaking mess of scarlet hair from her face and called desperately into the transmitter.

"Hey *you* out there! Hey you! I'm a woman lost on a boat out here!"

The voices grew louder and more distinct with time as the signal became stronger until finally the officer was understood.

"Mrs. Frye, this is Lieutenant Michaels of the United States Coast Guard. You're going to be all right. We're headed right for you."

"Oh! Thank the Lord!"

"Just keep your radio set on, Mrs. Frye, and stay inside."

She looked through the window out into the ominous storm, skies darkening.

"Okay, but please hurry! Seems like it's gettin worse!"

"We'll get there as soon as we can, Mrs. Frye."

"Please do!"

There was a brief pause before the serious Lieutenant's voice broke the silence again.

"Mrs. Frye, this is highly unusual, but we have a civilian peace officer here from Dusty, Oklahoma. He says he has some important information to share with you."

There was some mumbling before he continued.

"Go on, Sergeant."

"Ethel?"

The voice was immediately recognizable.

"Cousin Freddie! What the heck are ya doin out here?"

The sergeant coughed into the bloodstained handkerchief before responding.

"Cousin Ethel, well. I thought I was gonna come out ta California ta tell ya some good news from Dusty, but if what I'm hearin bout ya burnin up a man is true, then—"

"It's not what cha think, Freddie! I swear! It was self-defense!"

Her voice was strangled in mucous and tears as she continued.

"Besides that, I'm distraught. Ya know I jus lost Toby."

The sergeant stammered and muttered a garbled phrase to the lieutenant before responding.

"Ya, ya see, that's jus *it*, Cousin Ethel. Ya ain't lost yer husban."

For a moment, Ethel forgot the storm.

"I beg yer pardon—"

"Toby's *alive*! He was never executed. That jewboy Ira Kafka got some information ta the Governa that saved his life."

Her mind raced through memory and possibility with remarkable swiftness.

"But it cain't be! I jus poured out his ashes this mornin!"

"As it turns out, ya didn't pour out Toby. Ya poured out that colored boy named Black Jack McCain. He didn't have no family left alive an Toby said he wanted ta be rested at sea too. He was Toby's cellmate on Death Row. They was sposeta die at the same time."

"But the warden an everbody said it was *him*! They said Toby was dead!"

"I know. Toby set that up. Set up a deal with the Governa and the warden so they'd tell everone that. Said he had his own reason fer lettin folks believe he was dead."

She sobbed, hanging her head, before continuing.

"That's, that's cruel! It's wicked, Freddie. I *grieved* fer that man! An here I am, rite in the middle a this *hell* grievin fer him! And now I find out he's up ta somethin! What about me! What does he care about *me*?!"

Screaming hysterically, her hoarse voice played a medley of profanities before the sergeant interrupted.

"Ethel! Please! Ya gatta calm down! Lieutenant says we're almost there!"

Her hysteria was stilled by a perplexing thought.

"Waitaminute! He was wrong! Toby was *wrong*! I was always so sure it couldn't happen, but he was wrong!"

She was laughing maniacally.

"What're ya talkin bout, Ethel?"

"The fish! His damn fish! It died! I saw it dead. Held it dead, but he's still alive! He was wrong!"

This time the sergeant stammered for being guilty of his own part in the deception.

"Well, uh Ethel. Now that ain't alltagetha true eitha."

He cleared his throat.

"Ya see, Toby didn't trust ya. He said ya tried ta kill his fish twice before an said he knew ya was gonna try again, but he wanted ta give ya the benefit a the doubt, ta see if ya really would try it again."

"What're ya sayin, Freddie?"

"Uh. When Toby was in jail, he arranged fer me ta *switch* his fish in the tank fer anotha that looked kinda close ta it."

The frustration showed in his voice.

"Goddam truth is, Ethel, it whatn't his fish what died. It was the kinda, kinda look alike. I had his fish in a special protection program the whole time till the Governa took ova."

The fishing boat carrying Ethel rose on a swell and suddenly free-fell fifteen feet to send her crashing into the ceiling. She shrieked in horror.

"Ethel! Ethel! You alrite, Ethel?"

Her mouth and nose were bleeding as she struggled with the overwhelming inertia in order to search for and find the transmitter.

"I don't believe it! I don't believe any a this! What on God's Green Earth am I doin out here?"

She watched as a violent river of black water surged through the broken cabin door and spread to cover the floor up to her ankles. The sea outside raged even more furiously than before.

"I'm gonna *die* out here!"

"I see the boat!"

The sergeant's voice cracked with excitement.

"Ethel! The lieutenant says he kin see ya! Waitaminute! I kin see ya too! Jus hold on a lil bit longer."

She looked up at the cruel ceiling as she smeared blood on her face while wiping her runny nose. The boat suddenly free fell again throwing her body across the cabin and into a counter. Books and supplies fell and splashed around her head as she rose, sputtering seawater.

"Ethel? Ethel can ya hear me? We're almos there!"

The radio set popped, sparked and shorted from being drenched with water so that transmission and reception were intermittent at best. As Ethel finally clutched the transmitter, she once again saw a light in the furious raging blackness outside.

"I! I kin *see* ya! Here I am! Right here!"

She sighed, closing her eyes.

"Thank Goodness! I'm comin out!"

The lieutenant muttered a phrase that the sergeant quickly repeated.

"Ethel, the lieutenant says ta stay in the cabin! Whatever ya do, do *not* go out on the deck!"

There was no response.

"Don't go up outside! It's dangerous out there!"

Still silence.

"Ethel? Ethel!"

The lights from the Coast Guard cruiser located Ethel standing on the boat's stern deck screaming something and waving her arms frantically.

"Oh no!"

The lieutenant's trained eye could accurately predict the mood and movements of the sea.

"Here it comes! I hope she can hold on!"

The huge wave abruptly sank and the boat fell twenty-six feet onto a surge that was rising even faster and powerfully than the first was falling. The sudden stop in the fall combined with the brunt of the new wave caused a shock wave that sent anything not nailed down flying toward the sky. Ethel's body left the stern deck at breakneck speed and rocketed nearly forty feet before plunging headfirst into the water, putting Ethel at odds with an agitated sea.

The sad, depressed man studied the delicate, frantic fish swimming about the large glass bowl. He followed it with a little green net. Careful not to injure it, he scooped it up and transferred it to the smaller bowl. Here the nervous fish swam, twitching, uncomfortable with the limited space and contour of the bowl. It disappeared for a moment and returned in a piscine state of panic.

The searchlights on the cruiser systematically scanned the rough surface of the turbulent waters, stopping on occasion to examine irregularities in the pattern. The Dusty police sergeant risked injury and life itself as he braved the stinging, salty winds and watery whips and lashes in order to stand on the deck with a flashlight while conducting his own search. It was the sergeant who located Ethel thirty-one feet off the starboard bow, her crimson hair in tangles as she struggled against the forces of Nature.

"I see er! I see er, Lieutenant! There she is!"

Even as the cruiser's crew organized and devised a method for extracting Ethel from the water, a subtle current carried her further and further from the boat. Out in the water, Ethel contemplated the entire set of circumstances that caused her to be at odds with Nature.

In spite of all her grief over Tobias, the revelation that he was alive didn't surprise her much after she got over the initial shock. In that moment, she realized she knew her husband profoundly better than she had believed before, more profoundly than she had known anyone or anything.

For the moment, she could feel his presence, she could read his thoughts, and, in that instant, nothing around her mattered: not the cold, cruel, dispassionate waves that tossed her about, nor the hulking, shadowy phantom of a dark ship that moved toward her, nor the bright, blinding seemingly divine light from above, nor even the rope and preserver tossed to her from the cruiser.

"Grab the rope, Cousin Ethel! Get the gaddamed rope!"

It did not matter. The truth was clear: she could not escape Nature, the sea being its most potent symbol. Regardless of their arrogance, humans were subordinate to Nature, subject to its laws, its whims, and its abstract correlations.

She reflected that Tobias' understanding of Nature was incredible, and she realized that this moment and circumstance for her had been planned. It was no accident. While Tobias did not know exactly how, he knew she would eventually be in such a position: at odds with Nature. She knew he, and not the frantic efforts of her would-be rescuers, would decide her fate.

"Please grab the rope, Cousin Ethel!"

Slowly Ethel looked toward two bright, brilliant lights in a surreal sky that seemed to have the shape and sentient expression of god-like eyes, a look of terror distorting her face as she finally realized what Tobias was contemplating.

"Pleeeease! No Toby! I'm *sorry*! Nooo! *Pleeease don't do it!*"

At that very moment, the current carrying Ethel along gushed into an opposing current of even greater force. The result was a spontaneous whirlpool that spun Ethel around faster and faster before sucking her deep into the bowels of the ancient, insatiable sea, which in that moment reclaimed the life and energy it had relinquished so many million years ago.

"*Gadamned* you, Cousin Ethel! Ya shoulda grabbed the gadamned rope!"

Tobias wiped the tears from his eyes with tissue paper as he watched the delicate little fish struggling in the bowl. He knelt, and raising the seat, took one last look at the beautiful red fish. Closing his eyes, he pulled the lever and listened to the coursing of the water. When he looked again, the bowl was empty.

Returning to his steel-reinforced computer-monitored sanctuary underground, he took a seat before the gigantic aquarium. He sighed. It was not long before the fish appeared and hovered in front of Tobias, not a foot from the tip of his nose. In an apparent stupor, Tobias Frye intently watched the fish who, just as intently... watched Tobias Frye.

THE LOVE TRAGEDIES

STORY FOUR

HERE TOLD THE STORY OF

The Man Who Wore a Splendid Coat of Black

For once upon a time within an ancient world there lived a royal, princely man who, for his noble and judicious mind, was chosen by the King to judge a land so vast and wide as minds could see, for he did arbitrate in all the cases that the King himself was slack of time and age to rightfully adjudge. He was a man who always wore a splendid coat of black and one whose piercing eyes were seeing deep into the hearts and minds of men.

It happened that one day, e'en while the princely judge was resting with some honoured guests within his home, his children came to him: They had been speaking with the children of his guests and so it seemed they were disturbed by differences betwixt the many youth who roamed about the place. It seemed the other children were disturbed as much by them, and so the oldest son belonging to the judge at once spoke his complaint aloud.

"My father and his honoured guests: Now we who are the children of a father who is judge in all the land are different than the others here and do not like them much at least, for some do wear no clothes and others wear too much. Some say they eat the things which are to us unclean, while others say our food is fit for none but animals. Thus all these youth are different than we are and thus the Judge's children hate them all, but not so much as they hate us for reasons much the same."

Well now, the Judge at once did call the other children forth to ascertain if what his son had spoke was true in ev'ry case, and so it was that when each youth had spoken up, there seemed to be divisions based on slightest differences from youth to youth. Much grieved by this, the Judge remembered that these were but youth who thought this way, and so he did recall a plot to bear consideration otherwise.

"Come up!" he said, "Yes, all of you!" with gentle kindness in his speech, and all the children crowded 'round with open ears and hearts. "Come take a place by me, and let me tell a story that will surely teach you how to see as I have learned to see."

Then earnestly the children did incline their hearts to listen to the judge as so he spoke:

For there was once a boy I knew who had no father, mother, sister, brother, cousin, kinsman, neighbor nor yet friend—no house, no home, no land, no servant man, no wealth that could be touched with human hand. This seeming worthless naked boy would sleep in any place where warmth was found, for sometimes did he make a bed out in a field and other times he'd find a cave that was not by another occupied. In all the land the people knew of him and pitied him and gave him food and threads so he might piece together rags to cover his indecent nakedness.

Well then, it came about one day that as this nearly naked boy was sleeping in a field of hay, here was an envoy from the King! This stately servant read pronouncements that were surely royal and magniloquent, for there were 'thees' and 'thous' and 'whereuntos' in what was read. So splendid was the style and lyric verse of what the man did read that brilliant-coloured flowers blossomed all while stunning, graceful butterflies began to dance about the two.

Alack, unlettered that he was, this naked vulgar boy, he could not understand a word of what was spoke, but yet at last he understood that he should follow after this so noble servant of the King. All while he walked he thought, "What evil have I done, to be so called to stand before the mighty King? What would he want of such a lowly, vulgar, insubstantial peasant such as I?" He thought to run or hide away or cover what he was: He was a nearly naked boy who owned not pride, nor any item that could make him proud.

'Twas noble to be brave and so he put on fearlessness to march into the court awaiting entrance of the mighty King, when much to his surprise, yes, when this magistrate arrived, the King himself was but a boy, and younger than the humble naked child! And deep within, he laughed and thought,

"Is this a king? This boy who seems too small for even his so royal clothes! Who seems to be unlearned by virtue of his tender age, whose head does tremble and seems foolish under such a royal, golden, weighty crown?"

But even more amazed was he that when this child-like king did speak, the composition that did flourish forth was eloquent and indeed wise. He was not what he seemed to be! Then next this youthful king, whose piercing eyes did see into the mind of that astonished naked boy, he called him forth. Ashamed for being quick to judge, the nearly naked boy went up and humble bowed before the King who smiled and helped him to his feet. As all the court looked on, the King spoke to this humble naked boy:

"I am a child, but will not always be. Still I was born and I will always be a king, for kings are kings for what they are, and not for what they wear or seem to be, and it should be the same for any man in spite of what he seems or wears or does. I've called you here because my father knew your father well and promised that you would receive a splendid coat of black when you had reached a proper age.

"Your father seemed as poor as you, but he was rich in other ways that only princes understood. He sacrificed to give to you his legacy. He had no thing to leave you but this splendid coat of black. For it is said that if you wear it all your life and never take it off, you'll benefit in wisdom far beyond the best of ordinary man. If you are brave enough, son of my father's friend, take please this splendid coat of black and put it on and go into the world. Then when you've gained this wisdom e'er profound, return to me, and, on my word, I'll honour you and put to use your wisdom even in the farthest reaches of the Earth."

The royal boy had spoken like a king, for in those days what made a king was greatness in his viewing things, for kings were searching into matters, weighing them and rendering decisions that were best for all, not for the seeming privileged few, for they were meant to rule in areas where it was ruinous for man to rule himself. The child-like King called forth the naked boy and put into those dirty, trembling hands that splendid coat of black.

"Do you accept this gift from me?" so said the youthful King.

Well now, the nervous naked boy had never spoken to a king before, and so the best that he could do was nod his head in the affirmative. He took the handsome coat and put it on, and, after bowing low to thank the King, he gladly went his way into the world. All while he walked away he thought,

"How is it that a simple coat of black can make me wise? For I was wise enough with nothing on, yes, wise enough to find me food and drink and place to rest myself in sleep. What other wisdom should I need?"

He stopped a while, and, after thinking there, he finally remarked,

"O well, it is a handsome coat of black, and given by my humble father through a winsome king. I'll test it out to see if I shall benefit for wearing it."

Not minutes later, as he walked about the city of the King, the former naked boy was stopped by several other youth who took exception to his splendid coat of black.

"Now cast it off!" they said, "lest we should do to you not what we ought. Take off at once that horrid coat of black!"

Well now, this boy, who never owned a thing until he had this handsome coat, he quickly answered them to say,

"It is a seemly coat of black and it is mine! What right have you to think to make me take it off?"

"We have no coats of black to wear!" they said, "And so it seems that you should not, for wearing such a coat may seem to make you better than we are, but we shall heed to that: we'll make you take it off or find such fault in black that you will seem the worse for wearing it. Now you must take it off or suffer injury!"

Well now, the boy who wore the coat seemed still surprised.

"It is a coat, no more! What difference does it make? I am a youth no less or more than any one of you! Are we so full of ignorance that we are judged for what we wear?"

On hearing this, at once the other youth grew full of rage, for they believed that he had called them ignorant, though he had not. They beat this boy with heavy hands and rigid sticks and other instruments of pain until he called out, "Please, no more!" yet never could he be persuaded to remove his hated sable-coloured coat.

As years went by and he became a man, the hate that others held for him because he wore the coat of black grew ever more profound, for he was not allowed to eat or drink or visit publicly in places where no others wore such coats of black, and since it seemed that only he was given such a coat to wear, he was without companionship in all the world.

Alone with saddened, heavy, mocking thoughts, that wisdom which the King had spoke the coat would bear began to grow, and, thinking on unfounded fear and hate that he'd been shown since he put on the coat, he came to this:

"When I was young I did not fully ascertain the value of my coat, but wore it as it was the only thing I owned. The others tried to make my coat a wicked, worthless thing, that I, for shame or to conform, might cast it off, but this is where the wisdom of the coat began: I learned to love myself for who and what I am... in spite of what the others say or make me seem to be. For what we wear is never so important as that which we are within."

As time continued in its ceaseless gait, the man in black grew wiser still. Alack, wise as he was, he dared to love a woman fair in all the world, yet she was wise and fair. For she was sought as wife in courtyards of the greatest princes of the world and spoke in depth at length with prominent philosophers. O how at first she loved her handsome man in coat of black! O how he loved this woman fair!

But in the world were those who would not let them so profoundly love, who simply did not like the man for what he wore and seemed to say by wearing such a coat. With subtle poisons was this woman gradually persuaded to detest the colour that he wore. To his dismay, before she perished she was speaking as the thoughtless world did speak. At last, unto her splendid man in black she spoke,

"I am a dying entity!" she cried. "I realize I am undone by worldly ignorance, and yet 'tis said that if you on this day remove your wretched coat of black, at once my face will be restored. If not, I'll perish, never seeing you again. O stubborn man! Why must you keep it on? Is wisdom such a better thing than earthly happiness? Please now remember me. If ever you have loved me, you'll forsake that horrid coat of black—you'll take it off for me!"

Well now, this man, he loved this woman very much, and so at once he went about removing it, but then he chanced to see his nakedness and he remembered then a life before he donned the hated coat, a life of insubstantiality and void of higher purposes. With saddened heart he stopped and to the woman fair in all the world he said "goodbye," confessing his great love a final time. The woman fair in all the world did strangely disappear as he leaned close to kiss her pouting lips and she was gone.

Alone again and saddened more than e'er before, this man set out to change the hearts and minds of ign'rant men

who never gave him rest, but as it was in ev'ry case, they did
not hear him but they saw and e'er despised his splendid coat
of black.

At last, this tortured man, he brought his case before
the King to sue for peace all while he wore the coat. The King,
since last the man in black did look upon his face, had grown
to be a handsome personage whose royal bearing was by
earthly man unmatched.

The man in black bowed low to look on such a king,
who, noting who he was, commanded him to stand. How full
of wisdom seemed the eyes of King! O how his stature 'spoke a
mighty confidence! But how he seemed to scowl and frown a
mighty frown when in his court he saw this man in coat of
black. At once the royal ruler whispered something to a
learned counsellor who, after seeming searching through a
book of law, he spoke these words:

"The law is clear: You cannot come before a king and
wear that coat of black. That you have sought the audience of
King so dressed is sure a sign of disrespect; it seems to bode
not well with him. If you were wise, you would at once cast off
that foolish coat of black! It seems the King, who wears not
such a coat, despises you for what you seem to say by wearing
it. Take now it off!"

The man in black remembered then the words the King
had spoke when but a boy, the weighty words of promised
wisdom e'er profound for wearing such a coat of black.

"Will even kings forget themselves," he thought, "to
legislate against the truths they surely know by virtue of their
being kings? I'll take my chances with this king!"

At once the man in black approached the royal
magistrate but was by frightful, fearsome guards with bloodied
swords and sharpened spears restrained. The learned
counsellor to King looked in the legal book again and seemed
to read these words:

"If any man in foolish coat of black should come to make a case before the king, the law provides that he may speak, but only after putting off the awful coat. When asked to put it off, if he should dare to keep it on, then he should be imprisoned all his life at best, or with his fam'ly killed at worst."

And looking up, this learned counsellor addressed the fellow there:

"What will you do, O foolish man in coat of black?"

Determined even more to make his case, the man called out and spoke directly to the King.

"So many years ago when we were young, you, for my father, gave to me this precious coat of black to wear, and yet before that time I never understood just why I had no family. For in your world and mine are ever foolish men who seem to fear all what they do not understand, who've learned to hate a boy or man for simply being different than they are. To let them carry on this course would be unjust, for there are differences in all of us: Some on their foreheads wear a mark, while others pass their lives with ever bloody hands; some serve their flesh or soul for who can pay the highest price, while there are some who are emasculate for God, and still, within the world, are even seeming women living in the frames of men. How we are different all!"

With nod from learned counsellor, a guard withdrew his blade to slaughter violently this man in coat of black, but quick the King called to the guard these words:

"You must not murder him, for fairness does proclaim that he must speak his piece!"

This being said, the guards released the man who spoke again with such authority as he had never spoke before.

"The reason that I have no family is sad indeed, for each of us were given coats of black to wear. At cause of pressure from the fearful, senseless world, my brothers cast their coats away, and I will never know just who they are, for they were weak. Yet sadly still they are not loved by that same fallow world they sought to please; they sacrificed their splendid coats for naught. My sisters either for their husbands or a seeming higher place disguised the coats of black they wore. I do not know them, cannot see them, neither do they know and cannot see themselves. At last, my father and my mother were destroyed by laws that were unjust, by seeming learned counsellors who wrote those laws, by judges who had eyes but could not see. O greatest pity in the wicked world! That they were killed for simply wearing coats of black!"

He wiped the tears that issued from his face.

"My father had a friend who was a noble king, who tried as would a goodly king to change those laws, but even he for all his royal might could not for ignorance and fear that seems to rule the world. My father left to me a coat of black to make me wise and O what wisdom I have learned: Unfit is common man to judge another man, for in this world there is no better or no worse. But we must make the best of what we wear and what we are; we must appreciate and seek to understand the differences from man to man. O King! I've learned that as for judging man, 'tis best to look into the crimes so charged for what they are, not into the so-charged man for what he wears and merely seems to be."

The King sat back and thought a while, and he remembered all the things that passed before his ever-searching eyes. And after many hours sitting thinking there, he stood to greet this seeming lowly man in coat of black. Well now, all precedent aside, he hugged him long and hard and finally proclaimed first to his learned counsellor:

"For many years you've been my royal counsellor, and many years before were counsel to my father King, but throw away your book of Law, for it is old and is to truly honest men unfair. This man in black was brave enough to challenge, yes, and even change the Law. And thus I'll have him write another book, and one inspired by the wisdom he has learned."

And finally, these words were for the man in black:

"Your father was my father's dearest friend and you'll be mine, O man in splendid coat of black! For truly wearing such a coat has made you truly wise. Just as I promised as a boy, I'll use your wisdom well. The duty even of a judge is not to judge, but first to hear a matter fully through, to spy behind those sometime false appearances, to think with careful mind, decide upon a matter for the matter that it is, not what it merely seems to be or was a time or times before. For from this day, you'll be the greatest judge in all the world, to rule for man who cannot rightly rule himself. For from this day, a judge will always wear a coat of black. And from this day, your story will be told to teach our youth to see and understand, but, being youth, not but a few will pay attention so to hear the wisdom being spoke. And now, come let us join our hands and hearts and souls as friends!"

And so the story has been told for many years for generation after generation born, for this is how was told the story of the man who loved to wear a splendid coat of black!"

Well now, the story being done, the Judge looked out and Lo! Behold! The children were asleep; not one had heard the story fully through. And there, beside the place he sat, his grown-up friends were all asleep as well. With saddened heart and soul he stood and stroked his splendid coat of black a moment there.

"How vain!" he cried and O so sad began,
"How vain are all the earthly works of man!"

THE LOVE TRAGEDIES

STORY SIX

HERE TOLD THE STORY OF

The Tragedie of Those Who Dare to Think

For once upon a time within a very modern world, a child was found who seemed himself Imagination though personified, yes, born in flesh and blood and seeming as a youthful man of grace and intellect and beauty rare and looked upon and praised at first by all the world.

Yet even as this man who dared to think, yet even as he sought to flourish by solutions and ideas untried in times before, when he did seek to right a wrong or cure the ign'rant disposition in the world of man, against him came a multitude determined more with every incident to bring about his death by painful enterprise.

Alack, wise as he was, he never could believe or understand that thought was never meant for man, nor was imagination such a welcome citizen in man's society. Yet fort'nately this man who dared to think, he had a friend who seemed himself the fleshly form of Wisdom born, and *Wisdom* always spoke at length disparaging plain the thinking man because he dared to love and sought to help society of man, society that by its history had persecuted even to the death all those who dared to think or bring imagination to an undeserving world.

Though *Wisdom* spoke as would a bearded, white-haired father to a son, the man who dared to think did vehemently argue and assert that he would go into society to teach man how to, by imagination, mend his ills and solve the problems plaguing him. Yet even as the man who dared to think did leave, did *Wisdom* offer carefully advice that sounded much like this:

> *"My son who dares to think to better man,*
> *'Tis noble though a certain poisoned drink;*
> *But soft, know you that ever since the world began,*
> *Man's persecuted those who've dared to think.*
> *To better man is vain, as time has shown—*
> *You'll learn that man is better left alone."*

Well now, this man who dared to think, he loved his ancient, wrinkled, battered, white-haired friend no less than e'er a son had e'er a father loved, and yet he knew that sons eventually should try the world and suffer to the end for finding wisdom of their own, that youth should aptly learn from age and its experience, but with ambition seek a better lot than those who've lived before. He gently kissed his aged friend and offered thanks for such advice, departing with these words:

> *"Imagination is the hope for man...*
> *What Wisdom can't, Imagination can."*

And with those words, the man who dared to think went out into the world, when walking thoughtfully along a road all lined with trees for several thousand miles, he saw a group of men within the trees who cursed aloud and seemed to be unhappy with their lots in life. Approaching carefully, he spoke like this:

"For all your sufferings, I love you well, but come down to the earth and tell me who you are."

In answer, one bold man climbed from the tree and gave response like this:

"We're working men and we hate work, yet we are forced to climb these trees and pick this poison fruit. We do it every day of every year, and we will do it till we die. Our fathers did the same as did their fathers before them. And when we die our children who live after us are doomed to pick this poison fruit."

"If it is poison fruit," so said the man who dared to think, "of what good use is it to anyone? Why do you pick it off the trees?"

Another worker answered, saying this:

"An idiot you are! For it is obvious that poison fruit is bad to eat! We cannot leave it on the trees lest it be picked illegally and sold or taken home and used as food. Already in the world a multitude has died for eating it while it has made ten thousand thousand others sick. For that is why we're doomed to such a pointless life of picking poison fruit!"

"The sun is cruelly hot!" said one. "The days are long and nights too short!" another said. "They do not pay us much!" complained a third, and finally the man who dared to think, he sat for days and thought a while, and after many weeks of sitting watching all that passed before his eyes, he stood and jub'lantly proclaimed:

"My friends and brothers here, a good solution I have found for all your woes, but you must with me to the King at once, for with his help I'll make you happy men and free from such a lot in life!"

Well now, at once the men climbed from their trees to follow then the thinking man when, as they walked, they came across a group of men with giant barges on their backs.

"What are you men?" called loud the thinking man to which an answer came like this:

"We carry giant barges on our backs, these filled with poison fruit. We make our way to find the men who learned in school to burn the poison fruit, but O! Alas! Our backs are breaking under over-heavy loads. I am a man whose back was broken twice; my father broke his back a final mortal time, and still my son who is not yet a man will break his back one day for sure. Please let us go to find the men who learned in school to burn the poison fruit, for mark our trembling knees! O heavy are these giant barges full of poison fruit!"

"Wait but a while with me!" said thinking man, and, sitting once again for many weeks, he rubbed his head for thought and to the many thousand trembling men who struggled to support the heavy crates he said,

"Put down your heavy loads, you men who bear the poison fruit, and follow after me, and with the several thousand men who pick the poison fruit, we'll make entreaty to the King. I have solutions for your many ills, ideas to bring the best to man's society."

And so, at once the men who bore the giant barges full of poison fruit, they heaved a heavy sigh and with the men who picked the fruit, they followed close behind the man who dared to think.

Not after many hours walking up the road the thinking man and those who followed him, they chanced upon a certain group of several hundred men who clearly could be seen as men who learned in school to burn the poison fruit.

Their skin seemed black though rich and clean and smooth to touch, while on their heads it seemed the hair had curled, protecting heads and minds from worldly heat. To these skilled men did thinking man call out to say,

"The day is surely hot, but how is it with all you men who know the special method learned in school to burn the poison fruit?"

To this the master of these men came close to say,

"We're scorched by sun and by our ovens burned so that the very flesh is falling from our bones. Our lungs are ever filled with poison smoke that makes us cough great quantities of blood into our mouths, and yet, in spite of this, we want to burn more poison fruit as this is what we do. But stay a while and tell me, friend, why is it that so many follow after you?"

The opportunity then given him, the man who dared to think, he sat again, and finally though after many days, with joy he stood and called aloud,

"Burn poison fruit no more! For I have found a way to cure your every ill! Come follow after me to see the King!"

Then with great haste, these men did bathe themselves and gladly followed after O so large a hopeful crowd.

They travelled many years through tortuous path and painful circumstance until at last they came upon the gate and went into the city of the King, when all along the walls around the city of the seeming stately magistrate were peasants suff'ring lying there.

For look! A multitude that was ten thousand thousand writhed and groaned and covered thick palatial ground for many miles as far as eyes could see. The man who dared to think at once called out aloud for all those suff'ring on the ground to hear,

"Your suffering is surely obvious to me and all the men who follow after me, but speak you plain to tell me why you suffer here."

Well now, unknown to many gathered suff'ring there, within their midst were some who falsely groaned, were some whose suff'ring was a fabrication used to further darker purposes. In answer to the man who dared to think, these treach'rous politicians seized an opportunity to stir the crowds to frenzied fits of anger speaking words whose purpose was to undermine the King, so one imposter offered this,

"The King's to blame! Because he's made us poor and miserable, we're forced to steal and eat the poison fruit. If we could only end the fruitless suffering that we endure, we'd organize ourselves and seek election of another king, for though we're paid by government to languish as we do, it does not end our suffering, and while the King has hired many skilled physicians who have never slept since first they came, the air is full of suffering and pain and death. What problems that there are in man's society!"

Well now, the man who dared to think looked out and, seeing then an hundred thousand thousand who were sick and weak who had not strength or even confidence to raise their humble heads, he sat and wept an hundred forty days until physicians crowded 'round to diagnose his misery.

"I am not ill," so said the thinking man. "I look around and weep for all this pain and agony."

"Then weep for us!" the leader of physicians said. "For since we came, 'tis known that we have never slept. Because our special skill is needed here, we've had to leave our loving families. Our wives have made us cuckolds, while our children know not who we are. Of all the lots in life, ours surely is the worst!"

All stories being told, the man who dared to think decided then to take solutions and ideas before the King, but even when he went into the royal court, no king sat on the throne. The thinking man next called in princely speech to King who answered from a hidden place.

"How may I speak with you, O royal Majesty? I know not where you are!" said thinking man to King.

"I'm right before you here!" said unseen magistrate. "I am a king who hides behind the throne. Why have you come to speak with me?"

"To give solution for the problems in society," said thinking man.

"And have you one for me?" said hidden King. "For mine is sure a place of imbecility, for only I, a fool, have wanted to be King—to have a sword by thread forever hanging dang'rously above my head! To share my bread and even marriage bed with enemies! To hide behind the throne to save my face, for when I've made some dreadful error causing some disaster monstrous in proportion in the scope of man's society, the blame is placed upon the throne, and I, in hiding place, am thus absolved from any guilt or wrong, but foolish King I am, to live a shameful life of hiding here behind this throne. You are a man who dares to think I've heard in secret whispering about my court, so tell me what solution you have found for this so banal king!"

Well now, the thinking man remembered that within this very, very modern world a king or judge possessed no special wisdom as did kings in times before, for kings within this very, very modern world were kings elected by the ignorant and meant to do the will of wealthy men. No power rested in the throne but was by wealthy men usurped and cleverly disguised by politicians working for these wealthy few.

So finally, though after spying into all the matters of the royal court and in the world itself, the man who dared to think called all the men in man's society together that he might at last propound upon and give but one solution for the many ills in such society.

The men who picked the poison fruit stood 'round, as did the men who carried giant barges on their backs, and listening with careful ears were men who learned in school to burn the poison fruit. The hundred thousand thousand who had eaten poison fruit and suffered listened there and stood beside physicians who had never slept. The hidden King gave ear behind the golden throne awaiting some solution grand.

The politicians working for the wealthy few who grew the poison fruit were nervous then, for in society a man who dared to think was sure a dang'rous thing and could not be allowed to freely speak or lead the ign'rant crowds. The few who grew the poison fruit were called at once and they together with the politicians quick conspired to confuse the thinking man's solutions offered to society.

So as the man who dared to think stood up before the court, society of man was quiet then, for deep within their hearts the world that gathered hoped to hear some marvelous solution given in some lengthy speech with flourishes of phrase and adjectives profound, and yet to their dismay, the man who dared to think did speak a simple line and he was done. To man's society he said,

CHOP DOWN AT ONCE
THE TREES THAT BEAR THE POISON FRUIT!

And that was all that he did speak.

Well now, at first there was a lengthy pause and then a sigh and finally the crowds were marv'ling with imagination and with joy, for with a simple phrase, the man who dared to think did give solution solving every evil in society.

"We'll suffer picking poison fruit no more! Our seeming chains are gone!" said men whose blistered hands had plucked the poison fruit from trees.

A man with broken back proclaimed,

"Our children will not carry giant barges full of poison fruit! We'll send them off to school!"

"Instead of burning poison fruit," said those with blackened skin, "we'll burn our sacrifices to our God!"

Then all those sick from stealing and from eating poison fruit called out with one loud voice,

"We'll not eat poison as we did before! We'll fill our souls with honour and imagination!"

Physicians who were standing there went to their families and closed their eyes to sleep, and finally at last, the hidden King appeared from gathered veil and sat upon the throne.

In spite of all the machinations of the politicians working for the wealthy growers of the fruit, the problems of society were solved. All seemed to be in order, yet the politicians were determined to undo this peace, for politicians thrived on evil in society, and thus, preserving evil meant preserving politics.

And so conjunct with wealthy men who raped and plundered man's society, the same who owned the land and grew the trees that bore the poison fruit, these politicians then devised a way to turn society against the man who brought the peace, the very same who dared to think.

It was agreed the youth, who were ideal and never knew the evils in society, should bring about destruction of this man. So after waiting for these youth to reach a proper age, the politicians did seek selfishness within the sons of men.

As seeming friends of peace, these politicians went into society and to the sons of men they said,

"Why have you idle hands and empty minds? Why have mere peasants more to eat and to enjoy than you? 'Twas written long ago: *For he who does not work, then neither let him eat!* This peace your fathers have is truly good, but it has made you even poor! They had the opportunity to earn their wealth, but you are destined to great want. Was for your fathers plucking, barging, burning, eating, healing those who stole and ate the fruit so bad? When they received good wages for their honest work? When they could buy imported silk and brass and wine from worlds away? What have you their sons but peace that can't be worn or drank or used to satisfy your flesh?

"Remember if you will, recall the stories that your fathers told, and you shall mark that men were better off before, when men knew where they fit into society, when men found purpose in their lives. If you want more from life, you must not listen to your fathers who have been misled, and by a man who dares to think, deceived. Take for yourselves the luxuries that they have cast away! What riches you will make! What fleshly pleasures you will surely have! You'll bolster this depressed economy and help society besides, for never has there been a greater harvest yielded to this date. We secretly have planted other trees with poison fruit to stand for those chopped down according to the misconstruction of the man who dares to think. The world is ripe with poison fruit! Come pluck and barge and burn and steal and suffer to be healed by men who never sleep! Why stand you there? The world awaits!"

Still standing there, the sons of men to politicians said,

"We surely wish to pluck and barge and burn and heal the foolish ones who wish to steal and eat the poison fruit, but still there is a man alive who dares to think. As long as there is room for thought in our society, there is no place for industry. The man who thinks must be destroyed. As you are politicians skilled at making good seem bad and bad seem virtuous, then you must tell us how to go about destroying such a dang'rous man, this man who dares to think!"

The politicians had anticipated such a question from the youth, and so what followed were the careful words the smiling politicians had rehearsed in many years before:

"Go to the King, who with the help of thinking man has learned to sit upon the throne, and you must say to him, 'Why are you sitting on that throne when you are hated by society and in the world despised by multitudes? You'll save your head by hiding once again behind the throne.' "

That being said, the politicians further offered this:

"For know you sons of men, the King who's learned to love his place upon the throne will surely seek to draw from you what policy will find him favour in your eyes and in the ign'rant minds of your society. Then you must tell him and he will at once destroy the thinking man."

Well now, these sons of men, they did exactly as the politicians had instructed and prescribed, and when the nervous King upon the throne implored to know what he should do, the youth demanded then the hated head belonging to the man who dared to think.

"What crime should he be executed for?" said frightened King. "Who of you sons of men can tell me how such murder would be justified?"

Well then, within the sons of men were politicians so disguised in order to reply to such a question from the careful King.

"The crime for which he should be killed is THOUGHT! A man who dares to think will ruin sons of men and politics and enterprise and even yet a King who presently is brave enough to sit upon an unsubstantial throne, for thinking truly is the greatest evil in society. The King himself must kill the man who dares to think!"

The hidden politicians next aroused the sons of men to call the King to kill this thinking man so that ten thousand thousand voices spoke a single phrase:

THE KING HIMSELF MUST KILL
THE MAN WHO DARES TO THINK!

And as the crowds grew more aroused, the frightened King, he quickly found his hiding place behind the throne again and called his counsellors to hear what he should do, for in society, a counsellor was capable of minor thought acceptable to man and could predict and play upon the ign'rance of the multitude.

"You must not kill the man who dares to think," said counsellors to King, "and yet he must be surely killed. The sons of man demand his life, so give him over to society, that once again 'tis proven true that those who dare to think should wisely inactivity pursue and never should they fix it in their hearts and minds to change the course of man, for man will surely change, yet he will always be the same."

Well then, the apprehensive King considered carefully their words and he, with great regret and slowly wagging head, pronounced this speech:

"Bring out the man who dares to think, and as I close mine eyes, so let society do to the thinking man all that society must do. I'm but a king within a very, very modern, wicked world."

Then after saying this, the King into his ownself bosom drew a knife, and after cutting deep into his flesh, he plucked his poisoned heart from there, and with a final breath, he gasped aloud these words,

"The irony of thinking men and kings makes surely tragic art:

That e'er a thinking man was born with tongue or king was born with heart!"

No one could see the hidden king as dead he fell behind the throne. Well now, society closed in around the guiltless man who dared to think, and yet before he fell into the hands of sons of men, he thought of *Wisdom* then, that in society a man who dares to think should hold his tongue and should no seeming useful action take, for sons of men despise imagination in a living man yet praise it greatly when he's gone.

"How long will man continue to indulge in works so vain? Go to your fathers, please, you sons of men, and see how I have worked to bring the best to man's society! Yet realize this truth: Imagination comes from God! Go even to your holy men, for surely holy men must take a place before you to commend my works!"

"His works are from the *Wicked One!*" said politicians once again disguised this time within the forms of holy men.

"Imagination has no place in man's society nor in established practice of religious men. Man was not meant to think, but meant to listen and obey. Yet man was meant to sin that holy men might arbitrate and judge man for that sin. If man did ever think to go or pray directly to his God, there'd be no need for holy men. Because this man has sought to do away with holy men, his works are from the *Wicked One* and thus this man deserves to die!"

Because these politicians in the forms of holy men believed he was a dang'rous man, they left him to the sons of men, the ign'rant multitude of minds that could not think, who after beating him, they tortured him and nailed him to an ancient, twisted tree among the pods of poison fruit. To those who ever followed him, he with compassion spoke these words to give them hope:

"I die today, and yet tomorrow if you follow after me, I'll take your case before the greatest king in all the universe, who rules and judges with compassion and with love, and has no fear of man and man's society!"

Upon that tree this man who dared to think expired, calling for his father and his friend, who was in truth not far away. Then after many hours hanging there in death, the weeping, mourning, white-haired *Wisdom* came along and plucked him from among the pods of poison fruit and hid Imagination in the bosom of the Earth away from undeserving man, and ever after Wisdom hid himself away from sons of men so that the world remains a place of great stupidity.

For ever since that day, a man who dares to think will wisely hold his tongue and live, for those who've dared to think have learned by this to hold themselves away from dang'rous man.

Well now, the matter being settled then, the white-haired *Wisdom* made memorial for the man who dared to think, who seemed most like his son, and in the mind of every man within the world who's brave enough to think, he carved a simple phrase of thought which argued much like this:

> *To better man is vain, as time has shown—*
> *'Tis learned that man is better left alone.*

THE LOVE TRAGEDIES
STORY SEVEN

A cynic king once to his son this tragic story told:

The Tiny Crab Who Ruled a Patch of Mud

For once upon a time within a very, very ancient world, there stood a handsome little crab with bluish shell, who after drifting all his life within the sloshing seas, had landed on a tiny patch of mud along with many other little crabs who drifted landing there, and once upon this tiny patch the little crab proclaimed himself a king who even owned that tiny patch of muddy earth.

Yet much to his dismay, an older crab contested him and quick proclaimed as loud with clipping pincers stirring high above his head that he was ruler of the muddy patch, had ruled for several days, would never tolerate the challenge of another little crab.

Alack, the little handsome crab was strong enough and young, and after wrestling long and violently upon the muddy beach, the little crab pinched off the arms and eyes belonging to the older crab and drove him back into the sea, where he was quickly gobbled up by predators who waited there.

His rival thus defeated, he, the little crab, began the task of every little crab: He thought that he might rule and slowly swallow up the Earth, that by his eating he might own more land, for that is why until this day a crab will spend a lifetime eating mud to slowly swallow up the Earth.

With tiny, straining eyes on stalks that barely rose above his bluish shell, the little crab could see no farther than the distance he could reach and thus could see no other crab upon the crowded beach. He truly did believe he was alone a king who ruled the Earth.

One day a smaller, seeming soldier crab did come along who seemed to have a tiny periwinkle helmet on his head and added armor on his back. Well now, the little crab who ruled the tiny patch of mud believed this smaller, seeming soldier crab to be a servant in the service of the muddy kingdom there.

"Why do you come, my slave? What favour do you seek of me, the king of Earth?" said little crab, to which the smaller soldier nervously replied,

"I wish to travel in the world and see from differing perspectives mountains vast and shimm'ring deserts glist'ning in the brilliant sun, then worlds of ice where it is said the sun has never set, is always present in the skies. And in this world I seek to learn the truth and tragedie of life, the wisdom and serenity of death, and hopefully, I seek to know the greatest truth existing in the universe."

"Well then, young crab. As I am king of all the Earth you seek to know a world I rule," said little crab who wondered secretly about the world and truths therein, for deep within his heart he knew he dragged his belly on the ground and thus could be confused with ign'rant lowly creatures crawling close to Earth. He sought against the best he knew to know the mysteries of the world he ruled. Perhaps his slave would bring him answers then.

"Go forth young crab, find out about the world I rule, for I, the king of Earth, commission you to be my loyal royal spy, commission you to learn and plainly tell to me about the world you go to see and know."

To this the smaller soldier raised his periwinkle helmet and replied like this,

"Most noble royal little crab who rules this splendid patch of mud and sand, I live to serve your every pleasure and command. For you, I'll go into the world and bring you knowledge of the things beyond your scope, that you alone who rule this glorious land may be the wisest crab that ever lived!"

And after saying this, the tiny soldier, armor gleaming in the brilliant sun, he bowed and thanked his king and went his way into the world.

Well then, the little crab who ruled the tiny patch of mud and sand, the same who thought he ruled the very Earth in its entirety, he sat and he defended his great land for many days until the smaller soldier crab with periwinkle helmet did return.

"So tell me, slave," so said the royal little crab who ruled the tiny patch of mud and sand, "what have you seen and come to know about the wondrous world I rule?"

At that, the smaller crab bowed low to earth with periwinkle helmet in an humble claw, and in a careful quiv'ring voice responded much like this,

"Although your slave did not go far, my lord, I learned that you are but a little crab of many crabs in all the world, and even on this little beach, for after going out from you, and as I climbed a giant tree of knowledge reaching high into the very sky, I saw the beach is covered full with crabs like you who each can see no farther than his little claws can reach, and thus upon the beach are many foolish little crabs whose eyes are low and almost blind and thus each crab believes he rules the Earth. I've learned you are a foolish little crab and not a king, for in the world a king must be a man."

Then after hearing plain the soldier's words, the little bluish crab sat on a clam and thought awhile, and in a little time, he said,

"What is this creature 'man' that I might understand how I might be a king?"

Well then, the smaller soldier looked into his tiny crabby mind and then remembered what he saw upon the Earth and answered in this way,

"As I sat high within the branches of that giant tree, in man I saw a creature not unlike the many foolish little crabs a-crawling on the beach, but he was even more a fool. Like you, he fought and killed and worked himself to death for tiny plots of mud and sand, but this your common vulgar soldier knows:

There is no ownership for mortal, transitory, ever-fading creatures of the Earth like crabs and man. Yet worse for foolish man, he dares to even love with all his heart a creature in the world, thus here is where a crab is wiser than a man: Crabs do not love, yet man will love this creature 'woman' though she surely will destroy his flesh and soul."

Still sitting on the clam, the little crab with bluish shell unearthed a shiny ring of solid gold, and as it gleamed there in the brilliant shining sun, the handsome little crab deduced this truth:

"For this is what it is to be a man: to love this horrid creature woman crawling on the Earth, this wicked beast who feeds upon the flesh of hapless victims blinded by a foolish manly quality called love. But unlike man, have I not armor on?" so said the little bluish crab. "For though this creature woman be a brute at heart, my handsome cyan armor will protect my flesh. I'll love this woman creature to become a man, and then, since only men are kings, I'll quick subdue the Earth and be a mighty king who wisely rules a world of crabs and foolish men who cannot rule themselves, this from atop my lofty mound of mud and sand!"

At this the smaller soldier was convinced again the bluish crab would rule the Earth. He quickly clamped his periwinkle helmet on his head and urged his master to pursue the world at once. Thus to the little bluish crab he said,

"Until this time I've never seen the ugly, beastly woman creature crawling on the Earth, and yet I've heard the greedy creature can be lured with gold and other shiny instruments and pretty things, for woman's mind is full of lust and avarice for things and touched by vanity profound in all the world. Take up that golden ring you found, and let us set it out so that eventually we'll catch this greedy woman creature crawling close to earth!"

Well now, the plan seemed good and so the handsome little bluish crab, he placed the shiny solid golden ring upon a blackish coral flower rare in all the world and set it in a place where it was said the woman creature passed. Then after waiting hours there, a giant creature came with hungry eyes that seemed to swallow instantly the gold so that at once the creature took the ring and thought to put it on.

"Give back my ring!" clipped little bluish crab. "'Tis not for you, but meant to trap an ugly, brutish, savage beast called woman crawling on the Earth!"

"Dear little crab," the creature softly, sweetly said, "this shiny solid golden ring is meant for me, for I that very creature 'woman' am."

Well now, the little bluish crab was ever so surprised by what he saw that he forgot the reason why a crab was wiser than a man, for as he looked on woman there, he saw such beauty as a crab had never seen before. In woman was potential opportunity for fleshly joy and lasting earthly complement and happiness. Her voice was music ever sweetly played and still her manner caused such wanting in his little crabby heart that for a first and only time, he understood the manly quality of love.

"Do not be fooled, my falling king! Her outward beauty hides the inward savage beast she is within!" so said the smaller soldier crab with shiv'ring periwinkle helmet on his head. "You must not dare to love this creature woman crawling on the Earth! For there's no profit even though you gain the world if you must lose your very life! Do not become ambition's casualty! Why should my master seek to be a man, to be a creature you were never born to be. You're better off to be a foolish little crab who rules a tiny patch of mud and sand, for in a certain worldly sense, in ruling your domain however small you truly rule the world!"

But even as the soldier spoke, the deadly woman creature smiled and seemed to woo the handsome little crab, this while she gently stroked his pretty bluish shell.

"I must become a man to rule the Earth!" said little longing loving crab. "And thus as proof of my great love, I give this solid golden shining ring to woman that she may accept such offer of my heart and claw."

At that the woman smiled and took again the shiny golden ring and put it on.

"I gladly do accept your ring and such an eloquently-stated offer of your all-consuming love," the woman creature said, "for you are such a pretty bluish little crab! And now, I'd like to take you home with me, that we may live as crab-like man and woman wife, but I must say I do not like the smaller, seeming soldier here with periwinkle helmet serving you. See how he loves abusing me! He's very ugly and he must not come with us!"

And with those words the woman creature stepped down violently with heavy foot and all her might upon the smaller soldier crab and crushed him and the tiny periwinkle helmet on his head to powder on the Earth. Then as she raised her foot, the loyal soldier, body cracked and smeared into the ground, he spoke a final warning to his king:

"Fear most the creature woman when she smiles,
Whom she destroys, her prettiness beguiles."

The woman creature quick kicked sand upon the smaller soldier lying there and stepped down once again so that this soldier, covered all with bloody sand, was just an ugly blotch upon the Earth.

"Now I have deigned to woo a lowly crab," the woman creature said. "I let you love me though you are a simple crab who crawls upon the Earth, so you in gratitude must sacrifice your friends and dreams and still the life you had before upon the beach, a life of ruling tiny insubstantial plots of mud and sand. In gratitude you must forget yourself and all the things you love and follow after me, for it was you who chose to offer such ambitious love."

Now then, the little bluish crab remembered why at first he ever thought to love the woman creature crawling on the Earth: He sought her to become a man to rule the Earth. Yet as she urged him on, he looked back toward the beach and then upon the ugly blotch of bloody sand that was his slave and loyal friend.

"To leave this beach?" he said. "My kingdom's here!"

"There is no kingdom here!" said she. "This beach is full of sand and mud and foolish little crabs who cannot see how small and pitiful they are. You must forget your foolish little world and travel home with me into the realm of man."

"You are my wife!" said little crab. "And as I love you, I am man and master over you. You may not go back to your world, the realm of man, but stay right where you are and you must be my wife and queen to rule this place. Do not forget you're honoured to be loved by me, the man who rules the Earth, for am I not a very pretty crab-like man?"

The woman creature looked down on the love-ambitious crab in disbelief and, after scheming something in her head, she smiled a seeming subdued smile with seeming longing in her eyes and so she spoke all while she stroked his handsome cyan shell and said,

"You love me very much and with an all-consuming love, so I must stay with you, but I must say 'farewell' to friends and family I knew before I married you. Allow me please, my lord and manly king, a chance to see them one last time."

Within his quickly pacing heart the little crab did truly think he loved his wife, and so he could deny no craving she might have.

"Well, very well, go bid good-bye to all," said little crab.

"But you must come with me, my manly lord," the softly, sweetly, gently smiling woman said, "that you might meet and come to know and love my friends and family."

Well then, the little bluish crab, he did not wish to leave the safety of the beach, and so he offered many reasons why he had to stay, but then the creature woman smiled a certain lustful smile and he decided thus that he would go with her.

They traveled to the realm of man and in that world were foolish men who lived and died for tiny plots of mud and sand; were men important only to themselves; were men deceived, abused and finally destroyed by women offered their ambitious loves; were men whose eyes could see no farther than their tiny arms could reach.

For men were like all other lowly creatures in the world: They crawled along and dragged their bellies on the Earth. Man was no better or no worse than any beast that crawled along the muddy ground and more a fool to love this woman in the Earth.

The little crab at once decided he was better where he was upon the beach, but he had come to love the woman very much, though he was deeply discontent. For truly, he was only partially a man, a man at heart.

At night when he would crawl into her bed, when he would think to lie with her, to even hold her in his claws and love her in the night as man did woman in those days, he could not satisfy her as a woman should be satisfied. It seemed she longed for something more, and something he could never give.

All while he slept, he dreamed of beaches full of sand and mud, his bloody battles and the glorious victories, the kingdom he had left, the happy crab he was before he was a man. He even thought of his devoted soldier crab with tiny periwinkle helmet on his head. O what a kingdom he had given up! For then he learned what every slave to an ambitious love must learn: *First love yourself for who and what you are before you seek to love another in the world.*

Yet still, as plain as he could see just where his problem lay, because ambition made him leave the world he loved, he never could return. Because he ventured far into the realm of man, there was no way back to the beach. O how he longed to be a simple crab again! O what a waste was life to be a man! Again he tried to love the woman creature in her bed, but she could not be reached.

When morning came, his wife awoke and gently kissed his shell. Then next she said that she was hungry for an early meal and urged her husband to go out and bring it in. Well now, the little crab knew how to function on the beach, but in the realm of man, he could not find a meal. So sadly he returned with seeming empty claws back to his wife, who then pretended she was deathly sick because she had not ate.

"Give me your arm!" the woman creature told her husband then. "I know I will be better if you let me only eat your arm! I'll die if I do not!" and after that she smiled a loving smile. Unable to resist her charms, the little crab reluctantly tore off his arm and gave it to his wife. Then after she had sucked the flesh from there she found it tasted good and so she said,

"I do not mean to cause you any pain, my love, but that was not enough. I need to eat your other arm!" and quick before the little bluish crab could back away, she snatched his other arm and sucked the flesh from there. Then after she had gained more strength, she plucked his legs and ate them one by one till finally the little crab looked more like clam with mouth and nervous eyes than crab. The creature woman gently belched and smiled and kissed her armless, legless husband then and thanked him for providing such a tasty meal.

And yet, as days went by, her hunger grew profound again, and she called to her incapacitated husband saying this,

"You are my husband there who loves me more than life itself. Thus you are duty bound: Go out and find me food to eat!"

But there the less-than-handsome little bluish crab, he had no arms or legs and so he could not walk. He sat and thought for many days and hoped to find a way to feed his wife, but he was helpless, limbless in the realm of man, a world he wished he'd never ventured to. As tears swelled on his stalk-raised eyes, he answered her to say,

"I want to feed you, but there's nothing I can do!"

"What kind of man are you?" the woman said. "Will you refuse to feed your wife? Go out and bring me food!"

"I gave to you my arms and legs to eat," said he, "my only means to get around within the world, my only means to work and to provide for you! I gave to you my very arms and legs to eat!"

"And did you think that I would never need to eat again?" said she. "Have you no sense, you good-for-nothing man? You are yourself to blame for being such a fool!"

Well now, the little clam-like man-like crab looked toward his woman wife and said,

"My love, you must remember that I was a fool for you! For only you!"

"I have no use for fools but one!" she said. "For this is what is done to fools!"

With that she took a heavy rock and cracked the little bluish crab apart, and with a seeming sense of greed, she sucked and swallowed down his unprotected flesh and left an empty, lifeless shell.

For this is what is done to victims of a senseless and ambitious love. The woman, for her part, did hungry go into the world again to seek another foolish little crab to eat.

FINIS

And after telling to his son the story of the crab who ruled a tiny patch of mud, the King gave this advice: I told this story not to make you fear what woman is, but you must fear yourself, for soon, my son, you must decide if you are brave enough to love yourself and brave enough to rule your tiny patch of mud and sand, however small, or be the victim of an all-consuming love.

Time Out

My greatest ambition is to become an artist. A writer, yes, but an artist at writing first—an artist in a world where the idea of art has died a painful death of triviality. I mourn the loss and cringe as I realize I live in a world where everyone claims to be a so-called "artist." At risk of sounding elitist, I've never been able to accept those claims.

I grew up believing that art was "skill acquired by experience, study or observation," that art involved some manner of mastery in a particular discipline. Thus I studied the forms, ancient and modern; I struggled through the exercise of practice and emulation; I sacrificed time, loves and years of life because I sought the unique immortality that only an artist might attain. I earnestly studied poetry, history, religion, music, language, psychology, philosophy and politics with the hope that I could bring them all together in a form that could be esteemed as art.

It was one of my primary objectives in the synthesis of *Synchronicity*, and yet once again I believe I have fallen short of creating real art. I am thankful, however, I have the balance of the life God grants me to grow and learn, and I will continue to seek what humans have sought since the beginning of our existence: immortality.

Synchronicity contains nine stories, which can be divided as follows: The Early Stories—*Mister Peacock, Till Death Do Us Part* and *Anthropophagi*; The Main Text—*Synchronicity, Estéban* and *The Club*; and The Fables—*The Man Who Wore a Splendid Coat of Black, The Tragedie of Those Who Dare to Think* and *The Crab Who Ruled a Tiny Patch of Mud*.

I wrote The Early Stories at a time when I had left poetic plots and had just begun to write stories in prose. Although I had written several plays in college, I was apprehensive about dialogue in text, and this is reflected in

Mister Peacock and *Till Death Do Us Part*, where there is no dialogue. *Anthropophagi* contains dialogue and a message of love, which may not be readily apparent unless one considers all the possibilities "JC" might represent.

By the time I wrote *Synchronicity*, I had written two more plays, so I was much more comfortable with allowing my characters to assist at storytelling. Of the many quirkish personalities presented in this book, Ethel in *Synchronicity* and Tyler in *The Club* are my favorites.

I love wine and the romance associated with it, from production to consumption. Because I live in Northern California, I have frequently traveled to the Napa Valley in search of new knowledge. On one trip there, I met a memorable group of vineyard workers. On several occasions after, I found them and visited with them for hours. I listened to them; they provided me with a brief glimpse of the lives they lived. Since that time, whenever I raise a glass of California wine heavenward, I think of those workers, who were my friends. I wrote *Estéban* as a tribute to a family—a man and son—I met during that time. I don't know what became of them, but I hope someday Carlito will read the story.

Of all the stories in the book, *The Club* was the most personal to me. It was written during a painful time in my life and reflects the struggle associated with making choices and the inescapable consequences that follow. In the end, it offers the hope that we *can* get to the truly important things in life.

I wrote The Fables, or *The Love Tragedies* for my children at a time before I had any children. I wanted the tragedies to be stories that would evolve as my children evolved, providing separate instruction all along the way, according to their ages and maturity levels. To infuse the stories with art, I wrote them in iambic meter—this basically means that every other syllable is accented, producing a natural rhythm in the language of the work. Thus the stories can be appreciated best if they are read aloud.

Thank you for reading this book. I hope you have enjoyed my attempt at art, and I hope you will continue to read my work as I evolve into an artist.

My next work, a full-length novel called *The Last Year*, is less artful, though upon close inspection, the art will definitely be there.

Until next time—I'll see you between the sheets!

Marcus McGee